THE INVISIBLE MAN

H. G. WELLS (1866–1946) was born to lower middle-class parents in straitened circumstances in the Kentish market town of Bromley. He was apprenticed to a draper, a position he loathed, but won a scholarship to the Normal School of Science in Kensington, which had been recently established under the leadership of the eminent biologist T. H. Huxley. There he was trained to be amongst the first generation of school science teachers. He did not complete his degree, but did begin to write and edit a student journal. His brief career as a teacher was ended by illness, and he turned to science journalism and reviewing professionally. He finally published *The Time Machine* as his first book in 1895. This 'scientific romance' was enthusiastically received by leading critics and editors and Wells began a whirlwind writing career, often writing several books a year. By 1901 he had completed several of his most famous scientific romances, including *The Island of Dr Moreau* (1896), *The Invisible Man* (1897), *The War of the Worlds* (1898), and *The First Men in the Moon* (1901).

After his non-fiction speculations on the year 2000, *Anticipations* (1901), Wells became a leading social and political commentator. He wrote utopias, comic novels of lower middle-class life, and 'problem novels', often on controversial subjects, such as sexual freedom for women in *Ann Veronica* (1909). He was associated with the liberal–left Fabian Society, although scandalized respectable society with a string of affairs. He also alienated many literary figures, quarrelling with Henry James over the purpose of fiction. Modernists like Virginia Woolf and E. M. Forster despised his work and often defined their new style against his. Yet with *An Outline of History* (1919), his epic and controversial history of the world, Wells became a truly global figure. After the Great War, he campaigned for world government and in the 1930s visited both American and Soviet leaders to press for peaceful solutions. He lived long enough to see the atomic bomb, something he accurately predicted in *The World Set Free* (1914), used on Japan. One of his last books was called *Mind at the End of Its Tether* (1945).

MATTHEW BEAUMONT is a Professor in English Literature at University College London. He is the author of *Nightwalking: A Nocturnal History of London, Chaucer to Dickens* (2015), and *The Spectre of Utopia: Utopian and Science Fictions at the Fin de Siècle* (2012). He has edited Edward Bellamy's *Looking Backward* and Walter Pater's *Studies in the History of the Renaissance* for Oxford World's Classics.

OXFORD WORLD'S CLASSICS

For over 100 years Oxford World's Classics have brought readers closer to the world's great literature. Now with over 700 titles—from the 4,000-year-old myths of Mesopotamia to the twentieth century's greatest novels—the series makes available lesser-known as well as celebrated writing.

The pocket-sized hardbacks of the early years contained introductions by Virginia Woolf, T. S. Eliot, Graham Greene, and other literary figures which enriched the experience of reading. Today the series is recognized for its fine scholarship and reliability in texts that span world literature, drama and poetry, religion, philosophy and politics. Each edition includes perceptive commentary and essential background information to meet the changing needs of readers.

OXFORD WORLD'S CLASSICS

H. G. WELLS

The Invisible Man

Edited with an Introduction and Notes by
MATTHEW BEAUMONT

OXFORD
UNIVERSITY PRESS

OXFORD
UNIVERSITY PRESS

Great Clarendon Street, Oxford, OX2 6DP
United Kingdom

Oxford University Press is a department of the University of Oxford.
It furthers the University's objective of excellence in research, scholarship,
and education by publishing worldwide. Oxford is a registered trade mark of
Oxford University Press in the UK and in certain other countries

Published in the United States of America by Oxford University Press
198 Madison Avenue, New York, NY 10016, United States of America

British Library Cataloguing in Publication Data

Data available

Library of Congress Control Number: 2016943470

ISBN 978-0-19-870267-2

Printed in Great Britain by
Clays Ltd, St Ives plc

CONTENTS

INTRODUCTION

Readers who are unfamiliar with the plot may prefer to treat the Introduction as an Afterword.

'THE man's become inhuman, I tell you,' comments one character as the forces of justice close in on the fugitive known as the Invisible Man; 'He has cut himself off from his kind' (p. 114). H. G. Wells's fourth novel is a gripping tragicomedy that describes the apparently inexorable process whereby its eponymous hero, or anti-hero, a bitter but brilliant scientist called Griffin, who has invented an ingenious means of becoming invisible, aspires initially to superhuman status, but collapses finally into an abject, subhuman state.

A physicist and former chemist, Griffin is no more than 'a shabby, poverty-struck, hemmed-in demonstrator, teaching fools in a provincial college' (p. 83) when he first apprehends that it might be possible to make the 'whole fabric' of his body (p. 82), including in the end his blood, completely colourless and transparent. As he himself points out, he is 'almost an albino', 'with a pink and white face and red eyes', and this lack of skin pigmentation makes it easier for him to decolourize his tissues (p. 71): '". . . I could be Invisible," I said, suddenly realising what it meant to be an albino with such knowledge' (p. 82). In addition, his albinism reinforces his embattled sense of being a social outsider. In the nineteenth century, after all, albinos were exhibited at carnivals and fairs, and classed among degenerates. Because of his albinism the Invisible Man is already cut off from his kind.

Sick of confronting a sense of personal, professional, and social impotence, Griffin is driven, in his dream of making himself invisible, by what Friedrich Nietzsche, exactly a decade before the publication of *The Invisible Man*, identified as *ressentiment*—the vindictively resentful attitude fostered in the individual as a result of the negation of the self that, as opposed to the 'noble morality' of 'the masters', is characteristic of 'slave morality'.[1] In this respect, his psychological

---

[1] Friedrich Nietzsche, *The Genealogy of Morals: A Polemic*, ed. Douglas Smith (Oxford: Oxford World's Classics, 1998), 22. Nietzsche was first translated into English in 1896, but David S. Thatcher has noted that 'Nietzschean motifs appear in Wells's work long

condition anticipates that of the eponymous character of Wells's later novel _The History of Mr Polly_ (1910), who hates 'the whole scheme of life', which he regards as 'at once excessive and inadequate of him', and who consequently falls, each day, 'into a violent rage and hatred against the outer world'.[2] But Griffin is far more malicious than Mr Polly. He is sociopathic. At one point, in order to fund his research, he steals from his own father, who then kills himself because he is secretly in debt.

Frustrated in his ambitions, Griffin 'find[s] compensation in an imaginary revenge', to frame it in terms of Nietzsche's formulation—his dream of becoming an invisible Übermensch.[3] After discovering 'a general principle of pigments and refraction', Griffin devotes himself to his obsessive scientific labours in the laboratory he has surreptitiously set up in a cheap apartment in central London; and devises an elaborate method that makes it possible, 'without changing any other property of matter', as he puts it in his retrospective narrative, 'to lower the refractive index of a substance, solid or liquid, to that of air—so far as all practical purposes are concerned' (p. 80).[4] 'Wounded by the world', the Invisible Man thus sets out to dominate it through his command of experimental science, and so to make himself one of the 'masters of the world'.[5]

Once he has performed the painful metamorphosis that follows his secretive experiments, Griffin gives full expression to his contempt for 'the common conventions of humanity' and the 'common people' who embody them (p. 104). Inspired by his _ressentiment_, the Invisible Man's vengeful and destructive actions, which culminate in his

before Nietzsche was available in English—certainly before his ideas began to make themselves felt'—see _Nietzsche in England, 1890–1914: The Growth of a Reputation_ (Toronto: University of Toronto Press, 1970), 82. See too Paul A. Cantor, '_The Invisible Man_ and the Invisible Hand: H. G. Wells's Critique of Capitalism', _American Scholar_ 68/3 (1999), 99.

[2] H. G. Wells, _The History of Mr Polly_, ed. Simon J. James (Harmondsworth: Penguin, 2005), 8, 9.   [3] Nietzsche, _Genealogy of Morals_, 22.

[4] On the optical science behind Griffin's experiments, see Philip Ball, _Invisible: The Dangerous Allure of the Unseen_ (London: Bodley Head, 2014), 172–9. 'The invisibility of H. G. Wells,' Ball later concludes, 'in which light is not deviated by a substance because it has a refractive index equal to that of air, is possible in principle but not in practice, at least for an ordinary material' (257).

[5] These suggestive phrases are taken from Louis Althusser, _Philosophy and the Spontaneous Philosophy of the Scientists_, ed. Gregory Elliot (London: Verso, 1990), 250.

announcement that he will initiate a Reign of Terror, ensure that he quickly becomes universally feared. He announces 'the Epoch of the Invisible Man', and rumours of his terroristic campaign fan out across the nation (p. 119). The police, in response to the Invisible Man's attempt to implement this terroristic dream, instate 'a stringent state of siege' across an area of several hundred square miles surrounding the place in the countryside to which he has fled (p. 116). But this is too late for one man 'of inoffensive habits and appearance' whom Griffin beats to death, in 'a murderous frenzy', with an iron rod (p. 116): 'He stopped this quiet man, going quietly home to his midday meal, attacked him, beat down his feeble defences, broke his arm, felled him, and smashed his head to a jelly' (p. 116). This is not the 'judicious slaying' Griffin boasted of making when he insisted on establishing his Reign of Terror; it is a 'wanton killing' (p. 110). If he is sociopathic, he is almost psychopathic too. Even the insane moral code to which this monomaniac had hitherto adhered has collapsed.

Finally, in fulfilment of the function of an ancient scapegoat, the Invisible Man is hunted down and brutally killed in what amounts to a sacrificial ritual performed by the community. 'As if by irresistible gravitation towards the unpleasant,' explained one of Wells's most appreciative contemporaries, the campaigning journalist W. T. Stead, when he came to recapitulate its remorseless plot, 'the invisible man passes through a series of disastrous experiences, until finally he goes mad and is beaten to death as the only way of putting an end to a homicidal maniac with the abnormal gift of invisibility.'[6]

'A Grotesque Romance'

First printed in serial form in *Pearson's Weekly* from June to August 1897, then in book form in the autumn of the same year, *The Invisible Man* is at first sight little more than a novella. The front panel of Pearson's first English edition is illustrated with the playful, if not facetious, image of a plump but comically incorporeal dressing gown tipping back a tumbler of whisky as it complacently reclines in a wicker armchair. This illustration refers to a scene in which, seeking

---

[6] W. T. Stead, in Patrick Parrinder (ed.), *H. G. Wells: The Critical Heritage* (London: Routledge & Kegan Paul, 1972), 61.

asylum at the house of a former acquaintance from university—
a sober-minded professional scientist called Kemp, who will shortly
betray him to the police—Griffin borrows 'a robe of dingy scarlet'
(p. 72) and sits greedily eating and drinking as he appeals for protec-
tion: 'Kemp stared at the devouring dressing-gown' (p. 72). The
book's physical appearance is of 'light fiction' rather than 'literature',
to use a booksellers' distinction.

The spritely silhouette on the front panel of this edition recalls both
the cartoons that accompanied 'The Perils of Invisibility', a poem published by W. S. Gilbert in 1870, and its substantive content. Gilbert's
comic ballad is about a corpulent, henpecked husband who persuades
a fairy to render him invisible. This has an unforeseen and unfortu-
nate consequence: 'Old PETER vanished like a shot, | But then—*his
suit of clothes did not*!'[7] Instead of liberating him both from his wife
and his physical needs, as he had hoped, it enslaves him to them all
the more forcefully. Significantly, Wells pointed to 'The Perils of
Invisibility' as a precedent; but he failed to concede the prior existence of other, more troubling portrayals of invisible beings published
in the later nineteenth century, including Fitz-James O'Brien's 'What
Was It?' (1859), Guy de Maupassant's 'The Horla' (1887), George
Du Maurier's *Peter Ibbetson* (1891), and C. H. Hinton's *Stella* (1895).[8]

It seems probable, then, that the casual reader's first impression of
The Invisible Man, on its publication, was that it is simply a mischievous *jeux d'esprit*. In the subtitle of its first edition, Wells playfully but
also rather dismissively identified *The Invisible Man* as 'A Grotesque
Romance'. It is a slightly disconcerting generic ascription, because it
stages a sort of collision between benign and potentially malign associations. But it seems to promise nonetheless that the novel is finally
a harmless fantasia. No doubt this was his British publisher C. Arthur
Pearson's hope. One recent critic has contended that, 'following the

---

[7] W. S. Gilbert, 'The Perils of Invisibility', in *More Bab Ballads* (London: Macmillan,
1925), 150, 153.

[8] The anonymous reviewer for *The Spectator* on 25 September 1897 confirmed that
'the central notion of Mr H. G. Wells's grotesque romance, as he has frankly admitted,
has been utilized by Mr Gilbert in one of his *Bab Ballads*'—see H. G. Wells, *The Invisible
Man: A Grotesque Romance, A Critical Text of the 1897 New York First Edition, with an
Introduction and Appendices*, ed. Leon Stover (Jefferson, NC: McFarland, 1998), 206. For
an excellent brief overview of the Victorian short stories and novels that make use of the
invisibility motif, see John Sutherland, 'Introduction', in H. G. Wells, *The Invisible Man*,
ed. David Lake (New York: Oxford University Press, 1996), p. xvii.

barrage of criticism he received upon the publication of *The Island of Doctor Moreau*, Wells might well have been motivated to use comedy as a means of making his third scientific romance less intense than his evolutionary fables'.[9] The literary journalist Clement Shorter appeared to confirm the efficacy of this tactic when he concluded his contemporaneous review of the novel with the claim that it 'is bound to be popular, has not a suspicion of preaching about it, and in a quite unpretentious way will help to pass an amusing hour or so'.[10]

Certainly, after *The Island of Doctor Moreau* (1896)—a book that Wells feared was a 'festival of ʼorrors'—*The Invisible Man* seems at first disarmingly innocent.[11] Its opening chapters are set in Iping, the charmingly unsophisticated village in Sussex, south-east England, to which Griffin escapes, after realizing the appalling physical and psychological cost of his condition, in his desperate and ultimately doomed attempt to restore himself to visibility. The plot is propelled by pratfalls and other farcical incidents; and peopled with Dickensian caricatures that speak in a comically clumsy rural dialect. 'And what's ʼe doin' ʼith-out ʼis close, than?' asks the meddlesome landlady of the pub in which the Invisible Man is holed up, "Tas a most curius basness' (p. 28). Moments later, she is forced to flee from her mysterious guest's room when bedclothes, clothes, and pieces of furniture are flung at her as if by a malicious poltergeist. The narrative is indeed unpretentiously diverting at this point, as Shorter's assessment implied. It appears to constitute little more than an affectionate caricature of the idiocy of rural life.

In later chapters set in Iping, the novelist's recourse to slapstick evokes even more explicitly the harmless comic conventions of the late Victorian music hall. In 'The Invisible Man Loses His Temper', for example, the community's labourers tumble out of the pub in pursuit of their almost imperceptible protagonist, but are soon sent sprawling about the lane, suddenly conscious that they are 'involved not in a capture but in a rout' (p. 53). Griffin has stripped himself naked in order to escape detection, but he has taken the precaution of

[9] Steven McLean, *The Early Fiction of H. G. Wells: Fantasies of Science* (Basingstoke: Palgrave Macmillan, 2009), 70.

[10] Clement Shorter, in Parrinder (ed.), *H. G. Wells: The Critical Heritage*, 59–60.

[11] See H. G. Wells, *The Correspondence of H. G. Wells*, i. *1880–1903*, ed. David C. Smith (London: Pickering & Chatto, 1998), 261.

stealing his neighbours' clothes and giving a bundle of them to his extremely reluctant accomplice, Mr Marvel, a hapless tramp whose name is itself patently taken from the music-hall tradition. 'The face of Mr Cuss was angry and resolute,' remarks the narrator in reference to the local doctor, whose surname also indicates that he is a comic stereotype; 'but his costume was defective—a sort of limp, white kilt that could only have passed muster in Greece' (p. 52). Then the narrator delivers the punchline: ' "Hold him!" [Cuss] bawled. "He's got my trousers!—and every stitch of the vicar's clothes!" ' (p. 52). At this point the reader can almost hear the roar of ribald laughter erupting from a music-hall audience.

As scenes like these insinuate, Wells's novel also comprises a spryly witty satire of the contemporary fashion for spiritualism. In his disconcerting effects on the susceptible inhabitants of Iping, the Invisible Man resembles a peculiarly anarchic emissary of the spirit-world that acolytes of Madame Blavatsky, the charismatic founder of the Theosophical Society, along with other spiritualist adepts, cultivated during the seances conducted in the late nineteenth century. The 1880s and 1890s, the decades when the Society for Psychical Research was busy applying the principles of positivistic science to the conditions of the seance, were a golden age for ghosts. And for invisible forces more generally. Blavatsky's *Isis Unveiled* (1877), the bible of the theosophical movement, had been littered with references to the invisible: invisible worlds, invisible spirits, invisible spheres, invisible powers, invisible intelligences, and invisible bodies. Invisible forces were fashionable at the *fin de siècle*.

Wells directly addressed the theme of spiritualism in two distinct contexts in the mid-1890s: first, his sceptical and highly critical review of *Apparitions and Thought Transference* (1894), a 'popular exposition of telepathy' by Frank Podmore, which appeared in *Nature*;[12] second, his haunting short story 'Under the Knife' (1896), where with a certain seriousness he probed the idea that on the threshold of death an individual might have an out-of-body experience. Subsequently, Wells returned to the theme of spiritualism in *Love and Mr Lewisham* (1900), but this time in a slightly more satirical mood once again. The eponymous hero of this novel, to his exasperation, is in love with

[12] H. G. Wells, 'Peculiarities of Psychical Research', *Nature* 51 (6 December 1894), 121–2.

a woman whose 'mother is a spiritualist' and whose 'stepfather is a professional Medium'.[13]

It is in Chapters V and VI of *The Invisible Man* that Wells refers most explicitly to the table-rapping antics of the time. In the former, which reports on a crime committed by the increasingly desperate Griffin, Wells slyly observes that 'the facts of the burglary at the Vicarage came to us chiefly through the medium of the vicar and his wife' (p. 25). As this pun indicates, Wells relished the thought of these parochial, practical-minded Anglicans ironically acting as mediums. In the second of these chapters, 'The Furniture that Went Mad', the one in which the Invisible Man evicts his landlady from his room by hurling objects at her, she comments in almost self-satisfied tones, as if it confirms her deepest suspicions, 'I know 'tas sperits. I've read in papers of en. Tables and chairs leaping and dancing . . .' (p. 28). It seems possible that Wells is here conscious of Karl Marx's discussion of the 'mystical character of the commodity' in the first volume of *Capital* (1867), probably at second-hand. For in a satirical allusion to the spiritualism of the late 1840s Marx had there explained that, once it is defined by 'exchange-value' as opposed to 'use-value', a table 'evolves out of its wooden brain grotesque ideas, far more wonderful than if it were to begin dancing of its own free will'. This he called 'commodity fetishism'.[14]

Wells had a profound disgust for Marx, whom he castigated in his *Experiment in Autobiography* (1934) as 'that stuffy, ego-centred and malicious theorist'. But he did testify to coming 'full face on Marxism' as a student in London in the mid-1880s, at a time when his political convictions were by contrast 'built on the "primitives" of socialism'; and he cannot have remained entirely immune to its ideas and their most recent iterations. He later admitted, in fact, that he had admired Marx for being the first thinker to identify capitalism 'as a changing and self-destroying order'.[15] Although *Capital* did not appear in English translation until 1887, British socialists had been circulating its ideas, under the guidance of Friedrich Engels, for several years.

[13] H. G. Wells, *Love and Mr Lewisham*, ed. Simon J. James (Harmondsworth: Penguin, 2005), 78.
[14] Karl Marx, *Capital: A Critique of Political Economy*, i, trans. Ben Fowkes (Harmondsworth: Penguin, 1976), 163–4.
[15] H. G. Wells, *Experiment in Autobiography: Discoveries and Conclusions of a Very Ordinary Brain (Since 1866)* (London: Victor Gollancz, 1934), i. 180, 247.

William Morris, for example, who presided over socialist meetings to which Wells came, read it in the French translation in 1880. Certainly, Wells's satire of spiritualism in *The Invisible Man* is at its sharpest when it seems most conscious of Marx's critique of commodity fetishism, as when the narrator reports the rumour spreading throughout south-east England of 'a "fist full of money" (no less) travelling without visible agency' (p. 61). This simultaneously satirizes both the spiritualization of commodities and the commoditization of spirits at the *fin de siècle*.

Wells's mischievous interest in spirits and spiritualism, more or less inflected by his socialist politics, persists throughout the novel. In Chapter XVII, 'Dr Kemp's Visitor', when the Invisible Man steals into his former acquaintance's house after escaping from Iping, he leaves behind him the kind of material traces that were eminently familiar to late nineteenth-century readers of the ghost story, one of the most popular genres of the period. Kemp first notices the intrusion of an alien presence in his home when, having conducted his highly respectable scientific pursuits till deep into the night, he crosses the ground floor and perceives 'a dark spot on the linoleum near the mat at the foot of the stairs' (p. 69). 'Apparently some subconscious element was at work', the narrator comments enigmatically, implicitly ventriloquizing Kemp's thoughts. On investigating the unsightly spot, Kemp discovers that it has 'the stickiness and colour of drying blood' (p. 69). Some of the details of this scene evoke Oscar Wilde's comic short story 'The Canterville Ghost' (1887), in which an exasperated English spectre from a long line of aristocrats tries to use bloodstains, among other stereotypical ghostly devices, to scare off the American bourgeois family that, resolutely unsentimental and unsuperstitious, has snapped up his ancestral mansion.

Once upstairs, Kemp apprehends that the door handle to his bedroom is bloodstained. And that his bed is wildly disordered: 'On the counterpane was a mess of blood, and the sheet had been torn' (p. 69). The atmosphere increasingly recalls contemporary supernatural stories rather more minatory than Wilde's touching satire, and in this respect Wells's novel seems closer to 'Lord Arthur Savile's Crime' (1887) or even *The Picture of Dorian Gray* (1891). The light mood has darkened; the romance has become more grotesque. Even more disturbingly, Kemp then suddenly glimpses 'a coiled and bloodstained bandage of linen rag hanging in mid-air, between him and the washhand-stand' (p. 69). This obscene, animate thing is like one of those stringy ropes of ectoplasm produced alongside the spirits themselves at an especially productive seance. It is also, more ominously still, like some domestic variant of the unearthly and almost unrepresentable entities that appear in Wells's contemporaneous science fictions: the 'moving thing' with tentacles trailing from it that the Time Traveller encounters at the limits of his journey into the future in *The Time Machine* (1895); or the Martians in *The War of the Worlds* (1898), shapeless masses of matter with 'Gorgon groups of tentacles' that 'heaved and pulsated convulsively'.[16]

Chapter XVII also evokes those late Victorian variants of the Gothic form that can conveniently be classified as horror stories, such as Bram Stoker's *Dracula* (1897) and Richard Marsh's *The Beetle* (1897), both published in the same year as *The Invisible Man*. In Marsh's novel, Robert Holt narrates how, as an unemployed vagrant, he entered an uninhabited villa in Hammersmith at night in order to sleep in an empty, unlit room he sees from the road, only to apprehend that 'something strange, something evil' is invisibly present: 'I had a horrible persuasion that, though unseeing, I was seen.'[17] In Stoker's novel, according to Keith Williams, as in Wells's, there are signs 'of a growing culture of eerily "disembodied" speech, what Lucy Westenra, hearing the call of the vampire, calls "distant voices which seemed close to me"'.[18] The rise of invisible technologies such as the telephone, along with the fashion for paranormal modes of communication like telepathy, created a widespread sense, at the end of the nineteenth century, of the uncanny power of the unseen as a force combining ancient magic and modern science.[19]

Finally, in its use of the material traces of an unseen antagonist as clues, 'Dr Kemp's Visitor' leans too on the mechanics of late nineteenth-century crime fiction, as exemplified above all, of course, in Arthur Conan Doyle's Sherlock Holmes stories, which appeared from 1887.

---

[16] H. G. Wells, *The Time Machine*, ed. Roger Luckhurst (Oxford: Oxford World's Classics, 2017), 79; and *The War of the Worlds*, ed. Darryl Jones (Oxford: Oxford World's Classics, 2017).

[17] Richard Marsh, *The Beetle*, ed. Julian Wolfreys (Toronto: Broadview Press, 2004), 49.

[18] Keith Williams, *H. G. Wells, Modernity and the Movies* (Liverpool: Liverpool University Press, 2007), 55.

[19] For the broader context, see Roger Luckhurst, *The Invention of Telepathy, 1870–1901* (Oxford: Oxford University Press, 2002).

And it looks forward, moreover, to early twentieth-century detective fiction—including G. K. Chesterton's short story entitled 'The Invisible Man' (1911), in which Father Brown investigates the predicament of a client who is 'perpetually being haunted and threatened by an invisible enemy', an enemy who assumes the form not of a literally but of 'a mentally invisible man'.[20] As this chapter illustrates, Wells's grotesque romance offers a kind of compendium of populist forms of fiction that are in the ascendance at the *fin de siècle*.

Alienation and Identity

Like the pioneering science fictions that Wells published shortly before and after it, *The Invisible Man* exploited topical scientific debate as the basis for an enduring myth about the moral and social consequences of those Promethean aspirations that, at both an individual and collective level, were shaping and reshaping industrial capitalist society. In his review in *The Bookman*, Shorter recognized this when he pointed to the grim 'pessimism' permeating its moral claim that, as he put it in deliberately understated tones, 'scientific experiment never makes the world any better or happier'.[21]

In addition to a critique of spiritualism, then, *The Invisible Man* is a critique of scientism (as the late nineteenth-century conviction that scientific method is the secret to understanding the universe later came to be called). It built in particular on contemporary scientific debates about the invisible inspired by the German physicist Wilhelm Röntgen, who accidentally discovered X-rays, sometimes known at this time as the 'photography of the invisible', in 1895.[22] In *The Invisible Man*, as one critic has underlined, Griffin 'acts out the nightmare that X-rays created in the Victorian imagination', applying it for purely individualistic purposes that quickly become collectively destructive.[23] To appropriate Marx's allegorical image of the bourgeois class itself in the

---

[20] G. K. Chesterton, 'The Invisible Man', in *The Complete Father Brown* (Harmondsworth: Penguin, 1981), 73, 76.

[21] Shorter, in Parrinder (ed.), *H. G. Wells: The Critical Heritage*, 59.

[22] For further details, see Ball, *Invisible*, 92–3, 124–7. As Ball observes, *Pearson's Weekly* printed an interview with Röntgen in April 1896, fourteen months before the same periodical began its serial publication of *The Invisible Man*.

[23] See Allen W. Grove, 'Röntgen's Ghosts: Photography, X-Rays, and the Victorian Imagination', *Literature and Medicine* 16/2 (1997), 169.

nineteenth century, he is like 'the sorcerer, who is no longer able to control the powers of the nether world which he has called up by his spells'.[24] A descendant of the scientist at the centre of Mary Shelley's *Frankenstein* (1818), then, and a close cousin of both the Time Traveller and Dr Moreau, Wells's anti-hero is a distinctly 'Modern Prometheus'.[25]

At the moment the Invisible Man first grasps a scientific means of altering the refractive index of his body's fabric in order to make it completely transparent, he glimpses 'a magnificent vision of all that Invisibility might mean to a man. The mystery, the power, the freedom' (p. 83). The Invisible Man's dream of escaping both the social and technical constraints of his time and the limits of the human form itself, in pursuit of an impossible power and freedom, is of course an ancient one. John Sutherland, who has pointed to the plentiful presence of 'the invisibility motif' in popular literature of the nineteenth century, notes that the 'primeval origins' of the Invisible Man plot 'are buried deep in pre-literate myth and infantile fantasies of omnipotence'.[26] It is for example a staple feature of fairy tales, such as *Jack the Giant Killer*, and of Greek legends, including the story of Perseus.

But as a means of anatomizing power—both its dynamics and its ethics—the invisibility motif also has an ancient literary and philosophical provenance. In composing *The Invisible Man*, Wells indubitably recalled an important episode in Plato's *Republic*, a philosophical work he characterized in retrospect as having acted, when he first encountered it as an adolescent in the early 1880s, as 'a very releasing book indeed for my mind'.[27] In Book 2 of the *Republic*, Glaucon recounts the legend of Gyges, a shepherd who discovers a magic ring, in order to argue that, if an individual is suddenly given the gift of invisibility, and is therefore in effect rendered free to act with impunity, he will be unable to resist the temptation to 'go about among men with the powers of a god'.[28] Here, more explicitly than in other

[24] Karl Marx and Friedrich Engels, *The Manifesto of the Communist Party*, in *Karl Marx: Selected Writings*, ed. David McLellan (Oxford: Oxford University Press, 1977), 226.

[25] See Mary Shelley, *Frankenstein, or, The Modern Prometheus*, ed. Marilyn Butler (Oxford: Oxford World's Classics, 1998).

[26] Sutherland, 'Introduction', in Wells, *The Invisible Man*, ed. Lake, p. xvii.

[27] Wells, *Experiment in Autobiography*, i. 138.

[28] Plato, *The Republic of Plato*, trans. and ed. Francis Macdonald Cornford (Oxford: Oxford University Press, 1941), 45. See also Philip Holt, 'H. G. Wells and the Ring of Gyges', *Science Fiction Studies* 57 (July 1992), 236–47.

ancient versions of the legend, but as in Marlowe's *Dr Faustus*, the
metaphorical value of invisibility pivots on the moral implications of
using and abusing power. 'An Invisible Man is a man of power,' Griffin
states at one point (p. 43).

But Wells deliberately embedded this Faustian dream of freedom
and divine potency in the specific conditions of industrial and metropolitan capitalist society at the end of the nineteenth century. For in
attempting to emancipate himself from his physical form, Griffin
presses to an apparently utopian extreme the social or spiritual condition that the contemporary German sociologist Georg Simmel, identifying the individual's attempt to preserve their autonomy 'in the
face of overwhelming social forces' as the central challenge of 'modern
life', classified in terms of the 'intellectualistic' mentality characteristic of the metropolis.[29] Wells had himself faced precisely such an existential challenge when, impoverished and unemployed, he moved to
London in 1888 and discovered that his brain was 'so occupied with
the immediate struggle for life, so near to hunger and exposure and so
driven by material needs' that it seemed not to be developing at all.[30] In
Simmel's terms, Wells was overwhelmed by social forces and therefore almost forfeited his autonomy. The 'intellectualistic' mentality
he fostered in response provided both a refuge from this fraught situation and a retreat further into it.

Later, Wells openly explored the embattled relationship of the metropolis and mental life in *Tono-Bungay* (1909), whose narrator finds that
the most corrosive everyday condition of his alienation is a sense of
being universally unnoticed and unseen. For his part, Griffin trans-
mutes the lonely condition of anonymity and invisibility in the streets
of the metropolis, as he struggles to maintain his sense of intellectual
potential, into something positive, glorifying his nonentity. Almost
homeopathically, he transforms his social invisibility into physical
invisibility. His powerlessness becomes the source of his power. But
if, after successfully conducting his experiment on himself, Griffin
briefly experiences a sense of evolutionary superiority over the rest
of his species, because he appears almost to have transcended the
limitations of his bodily existence, his body promptly takes revenge

---

[29] Georg Simmel, 'The Metropolis and Mental Life', in *Simmel on Culture: Selected
Writings*, ed. David Frisby and Mike Featherstone (London: Sage, 1997), 174–5, 177.
[30] Wells, *Experiment in Autobiography*, i. 311–17.

on him for this attempt to escape its limits. To put it in terms of *The Time Machine*, the primitive Morlock in him takes revenge on the over-civilized Eloi. Dystopian realities irrupt into his utopian dreams.

On first leaving the apartment where he has conducted his experiment, Griffin momentarily feels 'as a seeing man might do, with padded feet and noiseless clothes, in a city of the blind'. Seconds later, though, he realizes that—naked as he is in order not to betray his existence—it might not be so easy to 'revel in [his] extraordinary advantage' (p. 92). On the busy streets of central London, his back is jabbed by a heavy basket, his ear grasped by a cabman, and his shoulder blade bruised by the shaft of a hansom cab; finally, his feet are trodden upon by a stream of pedestrians. In the wintry conditions of the capital, he then contracts the first of several persistent colds, which as well as proving debilitating are inconvenient because they reveal his hidden presence to passers-by or, more fatally, those pursuing him. Thereafter, as Simon James points out, Griffin's 'dreams of a bodiless existence as pure mental abstraction' founder on his need for food; and his 'megalomaniacal plans of world domination are compromised by his simple needs to eat, sleep, and protect himself from the British climate'.[31]

In *The Invisible Man*, Griffin reanimates and personifies a Platonic dream of becoming pure intellect. Wells's novel therefore dramatizes in tragicomic form its protagonist's doomed desire to deny that his corporeal frame fatally impedes his intellectual and spiritual ambitions. In striving to escape his body, the Invisible Man imprisons himself in it. On the polluted London streets, he accumulates 'dirt about [his] ankles, floating smuts and dust upon [his] skin'. Rain and fog, he realizes, will not obscure him as they obscure ordinary people. Rain will make him 'a watery outline, a glistening surface of a man—a bubble'. More devastatingly still, he intuits that 'I should be like a fainter bubble in a fog, a surface, a greasy glimmer of humanity' (p. 101). He is a mere silhouette of a man; as empty, insubstantial, and vulnerable as an oily bubble of air.

The Invisible Man is therefore a cautionary tale about the fatal dialectic of, on the one hand, intellectual and spiritual aspiration, and,

---

[31] Simon J. James, *Maps of Utopia: H. G. Wells, Modernity, and the End of Culture* (Oxford: Oxford University Press, 2012), 72.

on the other, social and psychological alienation, that makes and unmakes modern human identity. In this sense, the short fictions that it most closely resembles are not so much Wells's recent scientific romances as the celebrated, near-mythical accounts of the crisis or collapse of the bourgeois ego published at the *fin de siècle* by Robert Louis Stevenson and Joseph Conrad—respectively *Strange Case of Dr Jekyll and Mr Hyde* (1886) and *Heart of Darkness* (1899). For the metaphor of an Invisible Man proves an extremely potent one for reconstructing the acutely alienated, overdeveloped states of consciousness that interested Wells's contemporaries.

In Stevenson's novel, for example, it is Dr Jekyll's excessive faith in 'the trembling immateriality, the mist-like transience of this seemingly so solid body in which we walk attired' that, in a tragic irony, ends up affirming, in the form of Mr Hyde, the beastly materiality of his body. A decade later, it is as a result of this same antinomy that Griffin dramatically 'cut[s] himself off from his kind' (p. 114). Wells, indeed, appears deliberately to allude to *Dr Jekyll and Mr Hyde* in *The Invisible Man*. The scene in the latter where 'a little child playing near Kemp's gateway [is] violently caught up and thrown aside, so that its ankle [is] broken' (p. 115), irresistibly recalls the one in the former where Hyde, who is stumping along a street, callously collides with 'a girl of maybe eight or ten' and tramples calmly over her body: 'It wasn't like a man.'[32] There is no more indisputable proof of the inhumanity of either of these monstrous men than their vindictively violent treatment of these anonymous children. *The Invisible Man* brilliantly captures the experience of becoming-inhuman, as it might be called, which is a consequence, as in the case of Dr Jekyll, of simultaneously aspiring to a condition that is more than human and lapsing into one that is less than human.

If Griffin hopes that by becoming invisible he will transform himself from a nobody into a somebody, he ultimately realizes that he has merely transformed himself into a 'nothingness' (p. 33). As both his correspondence and his fiction indicates, Wells's friend Conrad instinctively grasped that *The Invisible Man* was about the competing impulses that, in both reaching beyond the body and relentlessly relapsing into it, tear apart the subject at the turn of the twentieth

---

[32] Robert Louis Stevenson, *The Strange Case of Dr Jekyll and Mr Hyde and Other Tales*, ed. Roger Luckhurst (Oxford: Oxford World's Classics, 2006), 52, 7.

century. Two of his most terrifying creations are genetically related to Griffin: the terroristic Professor in *The Secret Agent* (1907)—a novel he dedicated to Wells—who was probably based on Griffin; and Kurtz. The horrifying character at the centre of *Heart of Darkness* is, according to Marlow, one of those rare, remarkable men who, 'hollow at the core', have stepped over 'the threshold of the invisible'.[33] In spite of *The Invisible Man*'s initially light, playful tone, its narrative too finally derives its force from an apprehension of the emptiness and horror at the heart of the individual subject's sense of self. Paradoxically, it is precisely in its refusal to reproduce the intricate operations of consciousness, in contrast to contemporaneous novels by Henry James and others, that it mimes so effectively the crisis of interiority that was such a significant feature of the *fin de siècle*.

From the perspective afforded by the late nineteenth- and early twentieth-century novel's forensic concerns with what might be characterized as the case of the disappearing subject, the Invisible Man is one of those whom T. S. Eliot subsequently characterized as Hollow Men.[34] In Eliot's poem of that name—which takes the first of its epigraphs, '*Mistah Kurtz—he dead*', from *Heart of Darkness*—he delineates this condition of desolation in these despairing tones: 'Shape without form, shade without colour | Paralysed force, gesture without motion.'[35] The Hollow Man, Eliot's archetype of emptiness, has in existential terms lowered his refractive index to the zero degree.

Terror and Tragedy

There is an irreversible darkening of the mood of *The Invisible Man* about two-thirds of the way through the narrative, at the precise point

---

[33] Joseph Conrad, *Heart of Darkness and Other Tales*, ed. Cedric Watts (Oxford: Oxford World's Classics, 1998), 221, 241. Linda Dryden notes that other descriptions of Kurtz—as 'very little more than a voice', for example, and 'indistinct like a vapour exhaled by the earth'—are also 'suggestive of Griffin's insubstantiality'—see 'H. G. Wells and Joseph Conrad: A Literary Friendship', in John S. Partington (ed.), *H. G. Wells's Fin de Siècle: Twenty-First Century Reflections on the Early H. G. Wells* (Frankfurt: Peter Lang, 2007), 103–4.

[34] See Patrick A. McCarthy, '*Heart of Darkness* and the Early Novels of H. G. Wells: Evolution, Anarchy, Entropy', *Journal of Modern Literature* 13/1 (1986), 49.

[35] T. S. Eliot, 'The Hollow Men', in *Collected Poems, 1909–1962* (London: Faber & Faber, 1963), 89.

at which Griffin, in his doomed attempt to solicit assistance from Kemp, commences in his own voice retrospectively to recount the events that have led to the present, catastrophic situation. From this moment on, when the action shifts for a time from Sussex to central London, its protagonist comes to seem increasingly tragic. When the plot reverts again to the present, and to the increasingly frenzied efforts of the Invisible Man to escape the forces of justice that are closing in on him throughout the countryside, the sense of tragedy deepens. No longer a 'tragic farce', as Bernard Bergonzi called it, it is finally a grimly farcical tragedy.[36]

There are hints of this tragedy, though, which hinges on Griffin's horrifying nihilistic condition, long before this. It is intermittent in the more or less comic scenes set in and around the rural communities of south-east England in the first eighteen chapters of *The Invisible Man*. From the instant Griffin falls 'out of infinity into Iping village' a sense of the void, of non-being, intrudes on the ordinary and everyday (p. 14). The appearance of the stranger, whose head is wrapped in white bandages, whose eyes are screened by 'inscrutable blank glasses', and whose mouth and jaws are covered by a white cloth, is from the start unsettling as well as ridiculous (p. 7). He is a 'strange man', as the title of the opening chapter indicates, as well as a stranger; 'an unusually strange sort of stranger' (p. 13). An alien. The local clock-mender, Mr Henfrey, encountering him in the parlour of the pub soon after his appearance in Iping, comments that he is 'like a lobster' (p. 10). Mrs Hall, Griffin's landlady, insists that he looks 'more like a divin' 'elmet than a human man!' (p. 8). That night, moreover, she has a nightmare about 'huge, white heads like turnips, that came *trailing* after her, at the end of interminable necks, and with vast black eyes' (p. 13). It is the Invisible Man's grotesque physical appearance, however absurd in its associations, that conducts the creeping horror that overtakes the book.

And it is above all the intimations of empty space beneath the Invisible Man's peculiar surface appearance that prove horrifying. When Mrs Hall delivers a tray of food to Griffin's bedroom, where he has ensconced himself with his scientific equipment the day after his arrival, she suddenly notices he has absent-mindedly removed his

[36] Bernard Bergonzi, *The Early H. G. Wells: A Study of the Scientific Romances* (Manchester: Manchester University Press, 1961), 119.

spectacles: 'they were beside him on the table, and it seemed to her that his eye sockets were extraordinarily hollow' (p. 16). Later that afternoon, the carter Mr Fearenside reports that, when his suspicious dog bit Griffin, for a second he 'seed through the tear of his trousers and the tear of his glove'. Instead of the pale pink flesh he expected to see, he explains, there was nothing: 'Just blackness.' This is a glimpse into Infinity in Iping. Fearenside rationalizes this experience by deciding that, far from being an albino, Griffin is in fact a black man— 'I tell you he's as black as my hat.' Or, on further reflection, that he is 'a piebald' or 'a kind of half-breed' (p. 18). He does not understand, of course, that the blackness beneath the stranger's clothing is simply that of blank space (the association of blackness and blankness is subsequently underlined when the narrator describes the Invisible Man as 'staring more blackly and blankly than ever' (p. 29).

Henfrey had himself unconsciously mimed or replicated the emptiness of the Invisible Man's interior when, in Chapter II, he mended the clock in the parlour where Griffin, mysteriously muffled in his disguise, sat by the fire on taking refuge in the pub. Henfrey, the narrator reports, not only took off the hands and face of the clock, but 'removed the works' (p. 12). Is a clock without its face, hands, and works still a clock? Is a man whose face, hands, and body are invisible still a man? This is the metaphysical question that Wells implicitly poses. In the meantime, as Henfrey pretends to tinker with the clock, he looks up at Griffin and is promptly paralysed by the sight of 'the bandaged head and huge, dark lenses, staring fixedly' at him: 'It was so uncanny to Henfrey that for a minute they remained staring blankly at one another' (p. 12). In a double sense, the Invisible Man has a blank look.

It is in this chapter that Mrs Hall too first intuits, in addition to his strangeness, the stranger's monstrous blankness. On entering the parlour in order to warn her guest that the clock-mender is about to interrupt his privacy, she catches Griffin at a moment when, thinking himself alone, he has lowered the white cloth that covers his mouth and chin. The room is dark, her eyes are dazzled by the lamp that she has just lit, and he quickly screens himself again, 'But for a second it seemed to her that the man she looked at had an enormous mouth wide open, a vast and incredible mouth that swallowed the whole of the lower portion of his face' (p. 10). This terrifying, self-cannibalizing mouth is a fragment of infinity that instinctively takes a ravenous bite out of the everyday. Like the mouth in Edvard Munch's *The Scream*, first painted in 1893, it threatens to contort or warp the world of which it is part.

A couple of chapters later—in 'The Unveiling of the Stranger'—it becomes impossible for the inhabitants of Iping to suppress their glimpse into nothingness. There, exasperated by Mrs Hall's repeated complaints about his inexplicable activities, he resolves to shock both her and the other local people assembled in the public bar into silence: 'Then he put his open palm over his face and withdrew it. The centre of his face became a black cavity' (p. 33). He has removed his false nose. Performing a grotesque striptease, he takes off his disguise item by item—hat, spectacles, false hair, and bandages. 'They were prepared for scars, disfigurements, tangible horrors—but *nothing!*' The residents of Iping scramble to escape. 'For the man who stood there shouting some incoherent explanation was a solid, gesticulating figure up to the coat-collar of him, and then—nothingness, no visible thing at all!' (p. 33). His entire head is a black cavity.

It is probably in Chapter IX—when, after fleeing Iping, he recruits Marvel to assist him in his attempt physically to survive—that the reader of *The Invisible Man* starts to perceive Griffin as someone not simply to be feared but also to be pitied. The Invisible Man is still a brutal monomaniac, and he will become more and more homicidally violent in subsequent scenes—not least when he returns to the streets of Iping and, in the form of the 'raging unseen', 'set[s] to smiting and overthrowing for the mere satisfaction of hurting', like a vengeful Old Testament prophet (p. 53). But he is also a victim. Significantly, the author of the review of *The Invisible Man* in *The Spectator* was in no doubt that Griffin 'is really a tragic figure'.[37]

'I am just a human being—solid, needing food and drink, needing covering too,' he appeals to the tramp, who is sitting beside a road on the South Downs, '. . . But I'm invisible' (p. 42). If his motives for persuading Marvel to help him are in one sense cynically self-seeking, in another they are a matter of the most fundamental human survival. 'I was wandering, mad with rage, naked, impotent,' he announces (p. 42). Griffin on the Downs thus echoes Lear on the Heath. In King Lear's terms, the unaccommodated Invisible Man is 'the thing

[37] See Wells, *The Invisible Man*, ed. Stover, 206.

itself', 'a poor, bare, forked animal'.[38] He claims at least that the reason
he stopped to communicate with Marvel, when he could have murdered
him, is because he felt a sense of solidarity with his rootless condition:
' "Here," I said, "is an out-cast like myself" ' (p. 43). Both are fugitives
from society.

'He was certainly an intensely egotistical and unfeeling man,' the
narrator later remarks of the Invisible Man (p. 118). In Chapter XX,
it is Griffin's startling lack of sympathy, ironically, that secures the
reader's empathy. His apparently callous account of returning to his
former home, his father's house, in a 'place that had once been a village and was now patched and tinkered by the jerry builders into the
ugly likeness of a town', is oddly moving (p. 84). This is a man who,
profoundly alienated from the everyday conditions of industrial capitalist society to which he feels condemned, in part because of the
'frightful disadvantages' under which he must pursue his unorthodox
scientific research, is suffering from an acute state of anomie (p. 82).
'I remember myself as a gaunt, black figure, going along the slippery,
shiny side-walk, and the strange sense of detachment I felt from the
squalid respectability, the sordid commercialism of the place' (p. 84).
This cold-blooded 'black figure', whose albino features have been oblit-
erated by the gloom, transforms himself soon after the funeral into an
almost bloodless, transparent figure. Ingesting 'drugs that decolorise
blood', he undergoes a 'night of racking anguish' (p. 89). Finally, he
informs Kemp, 'I became insensible, and woke languid in the darkness'
(p. 89). It is an existential alchemy. Griffin's insensibility, it might be
said, is the basis of his invisibility.

Griffin's identity as an outcast, which his accommodation in an
unfurnished room in a slum on Great Portland Street confirms, is
dramatically reconfirmed as soon as he leaves this lodging once he
has successfully conducted his experiment on himself. Naked on the
muddy roads around Oxford Street, on a freezing cold January day,
he first assumes the form of the poor, bare, forked animal that will
later implore Marvel for assistance in the Sussex countryside. 'I was
now cruelly chilled,' he explains to Kemp, 'and the strangeness of my
situation so unnerved me that I whimpered as I ran' (p. 93). Leaving
the 'ghost of a foot' in the mud, he is chased through Bloomsbury,

[38] William Shakespeare, *The History of King Lear*, ed. Stanley Wells (Oxford: Oxford
World's Classics, 2001), 191.

feeling increasingly desperate, by a group of inquisitive boys, before concealing himself in a department store for the night (p. 96). In the metropolis, there is no one to whom he can appeal for help. 'I knew too clearly the terror and brutal cruelty my advances would evoke' (p. 96). So commences his life on the run, which he reconstructs for Kemp, who begs him not to be 'a lone wolf' (p. 111). But Griffin has announced his intention of implementing a Reign of Terror, a 'brutal dream of a terrorised world' (p. 115). When he realizes that, even though he has taken his former friend into his confidence, Kemp has betrayed him to the police, he is forced on the run again.

'He is mad,' Kemp declares, 'inhuman' (p. 113). It is Kemp who supervises the manhunt with which the narrative concludes. He directs the police to 'set a watch on trains and roads and shipping' (p. 113). And he issues a proclamation that presents the Invisible Man not simply as 'a legend' but also 'as a tangible antagonist, to be wounded, captured, or overcome' (p. 115). As the plot accelerates, mounted police enforce a curfew throughout the countryside. In a 20-mile circle around Port Burdock, where Griffin is assumed to be in hiding, groups of 'men armed with guns and bludgeons' set out with dogs 'to beat the roads and fields' (p. 116). The narrator refers to them as 'men-hunters'; and he concludes with some compassion that, though Griffin was soon 'active, powerful, angry and malignant' again, 'he was a hunted man' (p. 118). According to the philosopher Grégoire Chamayou, there are two kinds of manhunt, 'a hunt of pursuit and a hunt of expulsion', but these distinct operations have a complementary relationship: 'hunting human beings, tracking them down, often presupposes that they have been previously chased out, expelled, or excluded from a common order'.[39] The Invisible Man's identity as the object of a manhunt that seeks to capture or kill him is predicated on his prior social exclusion—as an albino, as a dissident scientist, and as a sort of man without content.

For a time, the Invisible Man manages to reverse the apparently implacable logic of the manhunt. He besieges Kemp's home in an attempt to take revenge on him, then chases him through the countryside on foot. In the end, however, it is Griffin who is entrapped by his pursuers, even though at this point he remains invisible. The final

---

[39] Grégoire Chamayou, *Manhunts: A Philosophical History*, trans. Steven Rendall (Princeton: Princeton University Press, 2012), 1–2.

chapter is entitled 'The Hunter Hunted'. At the climax of the narrative, a 'heap of struggling men' consisting of navvies, police con-
stables, and a tram conductor wrestle the invisible form of Griffin to
the ground. 'Kemp clung to him in front like a hound to a stag, and
a dozen hands clutched and tore at the unseen.' Savagely beaten, and
bleeding badly from a wound inflicted by a spade, the Invisible Man
emits 'a wild scream of "Mercy, mercy!"' that died down swiftly to
a sound like choking' (p. 130). At the culmination of this manhunt,
a mob encircles 'the thing unseen', which is held fast by its 'invisible
arms' and 'invisible ankles' (p. 130). Griffin's mouth, which Kemp feels
with his groping hands as he kneels beside him, is wet with blood: the
Invisible Man is dying.

Suddenly, an elderly woman screams and points. '[F]aint and transparent as though it was made of glass, so that veins and arteries, and
bones and nerves could be distinguished', the 'outline of a hand'
becomes visible to the assembled people. It becomes increasingly
'clouded and opaque' (p. 131). Then the rest of the Invisible Man's
body gradually materializes: 'First came the little white veins, a hazy
grey sketch of a limb, then the glassy bones and intricate arteries, then
the flesh and skin, first a faint fogginess and then growing rapidly
dense and opaque' (p. 131). It is an eerie metamorphosis; a coming-to-
life in death. The monstrous terrorist who has menaced the nation, as
a tyrant both superhuman and subhuman, can finally be seen in his
entirety, and in his humanity.

Griffin really is nothing more than the poor, bare, forked creature
he had claimed to be when he first encountered Marvel. 'When at last
the crowd made way for Kemp to stand erect, there lay, naked and
pitiful on the ground, the bruised and broken body of a young man
about thirty.' Once he has been covered with a sheet, he is lifted from
the street and carried into an adjacent pub. 'And there, on a shabby
bed in a tawdry, ill-lighted bedroom, ended the strange experiment of
the Invisible Man' (p. 131). In his sordidly commonplace experience
of dying, this homeless, hunted, battered man is absolutely emblem-
atic of the ordinary humanity he dreamed of transcending. It is to this
that Arnold Bennett referred in his review of Wells's novel in *Woman*
magazine when he remarked that 'the last few pages are deep tragedy,
grotesque but genuine'.[40]

[40] See Wells, *Invisible Man*, ed. Stover, 208.

The pathos of the painful process of becoming-human described in the final paragraphs of *The Invisible Man* is reinforced rather than undermined by his anomalous physical appearance: 'His hair and brow were white—not grey with age but white with the whiteness of albinism' (p. 131). His albino features signify his status as a social outsider, as they have done throughout the narrative, but at the Invisible Man's death they are also symbolic of a redemptive purity. Indeed, as his age and his 'broken body' indicate, Griffin is implicitly Christlike at the end. 'Cover his face!' a nameless man cries out after he has died, in a revealing addition Wells made to the first American and second British editions of *The Invisible Man*, both published in 1897. The man's exclamation is an attempt to shield the children present from the horrifying expression of 'anger and dismay' that contorts the dead man's appearance (p. 131); but it also echoes the scene in St Mark's Gospel when, after his arrest and shortly before his crucifixion, the high priest of the Sanhedrin pronounces Christ guilty and rends his clothes: 'And some began to spit on him, and to cover his face, and to buffet him' (Mark 14:65). Christ is here performing the ancient role of the scapegoat—the deformed, polluted creature that is sacrificed in order ritually to cleanse and purify the community from which it has been expelled.

Griffin too performs the tragic role of society's scapegoat. 'The whole point of the scapegoat', Terry Eagleton has insisted, 'is its anonymity, as a human being emptied of subjectivity and reduced to refuse or nothingness.'[41] The Invisible Man—who aspired to a state of nothingness, in the form of invisibility, and has been reduced to nothingness, as his shabby death indicates—is precisely this human being emptied of subjectivity. His social function at the end of the narrative is to constitute the non-being that symbolically secures the community's sense of belonging. In an atomized industrial society defined by what he had referred to as 'sordid commercialism', Griffin's identity as an alien is in the end the precondition for a renewed sense of social cohesion.

Like Dracula, then, and like Frankenstein's demon, the Invisible Man 'serves to displace the antagonisms and horrors evidenced *within* society *outside* society itself', in Franco Moretti's formulation. 'Professing to save the individual', Moretti continues, the society that

---

[41] Terry Eagleton, *Sweet Violence: The Idea of the Tragic* (Oxford: Blackwell, 2003), 278.

destroys the monster 'in fact annuls him'.[42] *The Invisible Man* repre-
sents a forensic attempt, in the specific conditions of the *fin de siècle*,
to investigate the meanings of this annulation, or annihilation, or
nihilation, of the individual subject.

Afterlives of The Invisible Man

Like a handful of other short fictions published after the demise
of the three-volume Victorian novel, including the novellas produced
by Stevenson and Conrad, *The Invisible Man* has had an impact on
the modern cultural imagination that far outstrips its fairly slight
appearance.

Probably the most popular testament to the impact of Wells's metaphor of invisibility is James Whale's fascinating film adaptation of
The Invisible Man (1933). Featuring Claude Rains as Griffin, in his
debut film, it is a black farce full of disconcerting scenes that seem at
the same time comic and horrific. The film was an immensely popular
as well as critical success; and, like the same director's *Frankenstein*
(1931), continued to inspire imitations and sequels throughout the
twentieth century. In a statement at once rueful and grateful, Wells
himself observed in his *Experiment in Autobiography* (1934), which
appeared in print shortly after the film's release, that 'to many young
people nowadays I am just the author of *The Invisible Man*'.[43]

'In both Wells's novella and Whale's film,' Keith Williams has
claimed, 'the most philosophically vertiginous conceit is that nothing
is being concealed at all except for vacancy itself'; that is, that the disguised protagonist is only 'an empty signifier of a being'.[44] Indirectly,
The Invisible Man surely influenced not only James Whale but also
Samuel Beckett and J. G. Ballard in this respect. More immediately, it
inspired D. H. Lawrence, Vladimir Nabokov, and, most explicitly,
Ralph Ellison.

Invisible Man (1952), Ellison's fascinating and troubling novel about
the experiences of race and racism in the United States in the first
half of the twentieth century, is a potent testament to the existential

[42] Franco Moretti, 'Dialectic of Fear', in *Signs Taken for Wonders: Essays in the Sociology of Literary Forms*, trans. Susan Fischer, David Forgacs, and David Miller (London: Verso, 1997), 84, 107.   [43] Wells, *Experiment in Autobiography*, ii. 561.
[44] Williams, *H. G. Wells, Modernity and the Movies*, 54.

implications of Wells's fable. Its first sentence—like its blunt, deliberately derivative title—is forthright about Ellison's debt to Wells:
'I am an invisible man,' the narrator announces. This novel, too, is to
some extent a study of *ressentiment*, albeit in a subtle and politically
complex form. In prose of dreamlike intensity, Ellison reconstructs
the experiences of an ambitious, charismatic individual who, purely
because his skin is black, is constantly and consistently not seen. 'I am
a man of substance, of flesh and bone, fibre and liquids,' he insists.
But this does not prevent him from effectively becoming invisible—
'simply because people refuse to see me'.[45] In reinventing the idea of
the invisible man in order to represent the experiences of an individual whose consciousness and identity is constituted by a ceaseless conflict with the conditions of everyday life in a racist society, Ellison's
novel implicitly proposed a perceptive reinterpretation of Wells's
ostensibly far simpler, far more superficial novella.

For *Invisible Man* hints that, though not notably interested in the
racial politics of identity, in spite of the fact that its central character
is an albino, *The Invisible Man* itself is nonetheless a book about
the existential condition of both being and not-being. It is about the
experience of feeling that, as a social outsider, one is something and
nothing at the same time. 'I was and yet I was unseen,' Ellison's narrator comments; 'It was frightening.'[46] From this perspective, in spite
of its apparent emphasis on plot as opposed to characterization, Wells's
novel is above all about what it feels like to be invisible. His protagonist is someone who only starts to matter, in the social sense, because
he discovers a scientific means of making himself into a form of non-
matter. But if this achievement brings him notoriety, and a sort of
sovereignty, it also induces in him a corrosive sense of futility. In
becoming physically immaterial he comes to feel existentially immaterial too. The former condition is indeed merely the embodiment, if
that is the right term, of the latter. And in this sense, as his kinship with
Dr Jekyll and Mr Kurtz underlines, he constitutes a characteristic *fin
de siècle* anti-hero.

The Invisible Man also shaped the attempts by several other writers
associated with the modernist movement and its aftermath to represent the blankness or nothingness they perceived at the core of

---

[45] Ralph Ellison, *Invisible Man* (Harmondsworth: Penguin, 1965), 7.
[46] Ellison, *Invisible Man*, 408.

contemporary subjectivity. In the penultimate chapter of *The Rainbow* (1915), for example, Lawrence describes Ursula's deepening sense that the people around her are empty ciphers. In trains and on trams she stares at other passengers and sees, 'beneath their pale, wooden pretence of composure and civic purposefulness, the dark stream that contained them all'. 'They were dressed-up creatures,' the narrator continues; 'She was reminded of the Invisible Man, who was a piece of darkness made visible only by his clothes.' These people deny that, at their core, they are 'dark, fertile beings that exist in the potential darkness', as Lawrence puts it in one of several echoes of *Heart of Darkness* in this chapter. Ursula does not. She is like the Invisible Man when he rips off his disguise and strips himself naked, for she refuses to falsify his 'primeval darkness' in the form of 'a social mechanism'.[47]

Vladimir Nabokov, too, testified explicitly to the influence of *The Invisible Man*. 'H. G. Wells,' he once announced, 'a great artist, was my favorite writer when I was a boy.' He remained especially fond of *The Invisible Man*. From *The Real Life of Sebastian Knight* (1941), his first novel in English, to *Ada* (1969), Nabokov's prose consistently evinces a fascination for 'transparent things', to cite the title of another of his late fictions. In the former, Wells's novel is one of the fifteen books listed in Sebastian Knight's library ('*Doctor Jekyll and Mr Hyde*' is another).[48] In the latter, the narrator directly alludes to 'the Invisible Man in Wells' delightful tale'. But it is in *Invitation to a Beheading* (1935) that Nabokov probably pays his most detailed tribute to *The Invisible Man*, even though he doesn't mention it by name. For the central character of this novel, who languishes in a mysterious jail, is a kind of anti-Invisible Man. Cincinnatus, as he is called, is an individual who is in some existential or even ontological sense opaque, and who creates an impression 'as of a lone dark obstacle in this world of souls transparent to one another'. He longs to be transparent,

---

[47] D. H. Lawrence, *The Rainbow*, ed. John Worthen (Harmondsworth: Penguin, 1989), 498–9. Invisibility is at the core of Lawrence's conception of the self. In *Aaron's Rod* (1922), elaborating this precept, Lawrence depicts Aaron himself, after reflecting on his conflict with his wife, as experiencing an epiphany that involves 'his idea of himself' shattering and leaving him 'maskless and invisible'. 'Like the Invisible Man,' the narrator concludes, 'we are only revealed through our clothes and masks.' See D. H. Lawrence, *Aaron's Rod*, ed. Mara Kalnins (Harmondsworth: Penguin, 1995), 163–4.

[48] Vladimir Nabokov, *The Real Life of Sebastian Knight* (Harmondsworth: Penguin, 2011), 33.

however, like everyone else in society; and has therefore learned 'to feign translucence, employing a complex system of optical illusions'.[49] At times, too, he seems to strip himself down to the state of nothingness that defines others.

One evening, for instance, after removing his clothes, 'he took off his head like a toupee, took off his collarbones like shoulder straps, took off his rib cage like a hauberk'. When he has completely finished, 'what was left of him gradually dissolved, hardly colouring the air'. Cincinnatus here closely mimes Griffin's movements during the scene in the inn when he removed his disguise. And, if he is an anti-Invisible Man because of his obdurate opacity, Cincinnatus nonetheless shares the Invisible Man's sense of isolation, precisely because he is impenetrable, 'impervious to the rays of others'. Moreover, he dreams of 'taking off layer after layer' of his self until, 'through the process of gradual divestment', he reaches 'the final, indivisible, firm, radiant point, and this point says: "I am!"'[50] In this sense, Cincinnatus reinscribes Griffin's ambition both of abstracting himself from his body and, like Lawrence's invisible men and women, of definitively identifying not an empty space but a concrete self at his core.

Like Nabokov, Jorge Luis Borges testified to the importance of Wells's romances and singled out *The Invisible Man* as especially significant. He seems to have valued above all its evocation of the individual's fundamental emptiness, futility, and isolation. He summarized it in these haunting terms: 'The harassed invisible man who has to sleep as though his eyes were wide open because his eyelids do not exclude light is our solitude and our terror.'[51] The condition of solitude and terror evoked by Borges—that of an individual compelled to stare into the void lodged like an irreducible fragment at the core of his being— is a long way from the 'perils of invisibility' innocuously imagined by W. S. Gilbert in his comic ballad. The perils of invisibility explored by Wells involve not simply physical vexation, or even social exclusion, but also spiritual annihilation.

In this respect, *The Invisible Man* enacts the state of being—or non-being—experienced the previous year by the narrator of 'Under

---

[49] Vladimir Nabokov, *Invitation to a Beheading* (Harmondsworth: Penguin, 2010), 11.

[50] Nabokov, *Invitation to a Beheading*, 19, 66.

[51] Jorge Luis Borges, 'The First Wells', in *Other Inquisitions, 1937–1952*, trans. Ruth L.C. Simms (Austin: University of Texas Press, 1964), 86–7.

the Knife'. After apparently experiencing his death, he speculates about his physical and metaphysical status in the moments immediately before he starts to return to life:

Were there other souls, invisible to me as I to them, about me in the blackness? or was I indeed, even as I felt, alone? Had I passed out of being into something that was neither being nor not-being? The covering of the body, the covering of matter, had been torn from me, and the hallucinations of companionship and security. Everything was black and silent. I had ceased to be. I was nothing. There was nothing, save only that infinitesimal dot of light that dwindled in the gulf. I strained myself to hear and see, and for a while there was naught but infinite silence, intolerable darkness, horror, and despair.[52]

Darkness, blackness, nothingness . . . This undead condition, which will haunt a succession of modernist anti-heroes, is the one that the Invisible Man, too, inhabits.

---

[52] H. G. Wells, 'Under the Knife', in *Selected Stories of H. G. Wells*, ed. Ursula K. Le Guin (New York: Modern Library, 2004), 61–2.

NOTE ON THE TEXT

THE composition and publication history of *The Invisible Man*—the manuscripts or typescripts for which have not survived—is relatively complicated. There are several printed versions, four of which appeared in 1897, and all of them are slightly different. The version reproduced for this Oxford World's Classics edition is the first English edition, published by C. Arthur Pearson in London in September 1897. Obvious errors have been silently corrected.

Wells seems to have worked on a first draft of the story in May and June 1896, and on 12 June 1896 he sent his literary agent James Brand Pinker a 20,000-word version entitled 'The Man at the Coach and Horses'. He did a good deal more writing in two additional periods, from July to August 1896 and from January to February 1897. Then, three weeks before the novel's publication in serial form, he decided that it was such a mess that he needed substantially to redraft it. He later testified to the sense of frustration he had felt at this stage of its composition in a letter, dated 2 October 1897, to the critic Edmund Gosse, who had praised *The Invisible Man*: 'I am delighted to find that you think well of my story & that you read my work of *The Invisible Man*. I've had the gravest doubts. I've scarcely any facility in story building and simple as the thing seems it cost me a vast deal of labour. After it was sold & within three weeks of its serial printing I discovered so much clumsiness that I had to take it all to pieces & reconstruct it. Since when I have funked reading it.'

The novel first appeared in *Pearson's Weekly* from 12 June to 7 August 1897, though it was both abridged and censored for this publication in periodical form—five chapters were removed, as were a number of substantial passages in other chapters, and potentially blasphemous words were systematically cut. The first English edition in book form, subtitled *A Grotesque Romance*, appeared in Pearson's imprint on approximately 25 September 1897. Like the serial publication that preceded it, it did not contain the Epilogue that Wells subsequently added, but it does make a considerable number of changes. Pearson then produced a second English edition in November 1897, which contains both a revised ending to the narrative and the Epilogue. In the same month, Edward Arnold published the first American edition, which also contains the Epilogue, albeit a slightly different version, and which also alters the ending of the narrative. In 1924, when Wells was preparing the Atlantic Edition of the novel, he elected to use Arnold's first American edition as his copy-text.

It seems to me that the ending of the first English edition—'And there, on a shabby bed in a tawdry, ill-lighted bedroom, ended the strange experiment of the Invisible Man'—is more immediate and more haunting than the endings of the New York and Atlantic editions. I don't think Wells improved the book when he introduced the Epilogue, which speculates about the fate of the Invisible Man's secret scientific notebooks, as a framing device. The unsettling tawdriness of the original is replaced by a certain folksiness in the revised versions. I have, however, elected to include two short appendices in this edition. The first reprints the Epilogue; the second contains the three variant endings to Chapter XXVIII published in 1897, namely *Pearson's Weekly*, Pearson's second English edition, and Arnold's first US edition. For a more detailed account of the publication history of *The Invisible Man*, readers might like to consult David Lake's 'Note on the Text', which is included in the World's Classics paperback, published in the United States, that he edited for Oxford University Press in 1996.

SELECT BIBLIOGRAPHY

Biography and Letters

Coren, Michael, *The Invisible Man: The Life and Liberties of H. G. Wells* (London: Bloomsbury, 1993).

Sherborne, Michael, *H. G. Wells: Another Kind of Life* (London: Peter Owen, 2010).

Smith, D. C., *H. G. Wells: Desperately Mortal: A Biography* (New Haven: Yale University Press, 1986).

Wells, H. G., *The Correspondence of H. G. Wells*, i. *1880–1903*, ed. David C. Smith (London: Pickering & Chatto, 1998).

Wells, H. G., *Experiment in Autobiography: Discoveries and Conclusions of a Very Ordinary Brain (Since 1866)*, 2 vols. (London: Victor Gollancz, 1934).

The Invisible Man *and Wells's Early Fiction*

Batchelor, John, *H. G. Wells* (Cambridge: Cambridge University Press, 1985).

Bergonzi, Bernard, *The Early H. G. Wells: A Study of the Scientific Romances* (Manchester: Manchester University Press, 1961).

Bloom, Harold (ed.), *H. G. Wells* (New York: Chelsea House, 2005).

Bowser, Rachel A., 'Visibility, Interiority, and Temporality in *The Invisible Man*', *Studies in the Novel* 45/1 (2013), 20–36.

Cantor, Paul A., '*The Invisible Man* and the Invisible Hand: H. G. Wells's Critique of Capitalism', *American Scholar* 68/3 (1999), 89–102.

Hammond, J. R., *H. G. Wells and the Modern Novel* (Basingstoke: Macmillan, 1988).

Haynes, Roslynn D., *H. G. Wells: Discoverer of the Future* (Basingstoke: Macmillan, 1979).

Holt, Philip, 'H. G. Wells and the Ring of Gyges', *Science Fiction Studies* 57 (July 1992), 236–47.

Huntington, John, *The Logic of Fantasy: H. G. Wells and Science Fiction* (New York: Columbia University Press, 1982).

James, Simon, *Maps of Utopia: H. G. Wells, Modernity and the End of Culture* (Oxford: Oxford University Press, 2012).

McCarthy, Patrick A., '*Heart of Darkness* and the Early Novels of H. G. Wells: Evolution, Anarchy, Entropy', *Journal of Modern Literature* 13/1 (1986), 37–60.

McConnell, Frank (ed.), *The Science Fiction of H. G. Wells* (Oxford: Oxford University Press, 1981).

McLean, Steven, *H. G. Wells: Interdisciplinary Essays* (Newcastle: Cambridge Scholars Publishing, 2008).

McLean, Steven, *The Early Fiction of H. G. Wells: Fantasies of Science* (Basingstoke: Palgrave Macmillan, 2009).

Parrinder, Patrick, *H. G. Wells* (Edinburgh: Oliver & Boyd, 1970).

Parrinder, Patrick (ed.), *H. G. Wells: The Critical Heritage* (London: Routledge & Kegan Paul, 1972).

Parrinder, Patrick, *Shadows of the Future: H. G. Wells, Science Fiction and Prophecy* (Liverpool: Liverpool University Press, 1995).

Partington, John S. (ed.), *H. G. Wells's Fin de Siècle: Twenty-First Century Reflections on the Early H. G. Wells* (Frankfurt: Peter Lang, 2007).

Philmus, Robert M., *Into the Unknown: The Evolution of Science Fiction from Francis Godwin to H.G. Wells* (Berkeley and Los Angeles: University of California Press, 1970).

Ray, Martin, 'Conrad's Invisible Professor', *The Conradian* 11/1 (May 1986), 35–41.

Wagar, W. Warren, *H. G. Wells: Traversing Time* (Middletown, Conn.: Wesleyan University Press, 2004).

Williams, Keith, *H. G. Wells, Modernity and the Movies* (Liverpool: Liverpool University Press, 2007).

Literary and Cultural Contexts

Ball, Philip, *Invisible: The Dangerous Allure of the Unseen* (London: Bodley Head, 2014).

Beaumont, Matthew, *The Spectre of Utopia: Utopian and Science Fiction at the Fin de Siècle* (Oxford: Peter Lang, 2012).

Daly, Nicholas, *Modernism, Romance, and the Fin de Siècle: Popular Fiction and British Culture, 1880–1914* (Cambridge: Cambridge University Press, 1999).

Donghaile, Deaglán Ó, *Blasted Literature: Victorian Political Fiction and the Shock of Modernism* (Edinburgh: Edinburgh University Press, 2011).

Dryden, Linda, *The Modern Gothic and Literary Doubles: Stevenson, Wilde and Wells* (Basingstoke: Palgrave Macmillan, 2003).

Faulk, Barry J., *Music Hall and Modernity: The Late Victorian Discovery of Popular Culture* (Athens: Ohio University Press, 2004).

Ferguson, Christine, *Language, Science, and Popular Fiction in the Victorian Fin de Siècle: The Brutal Tongue* (Aldershot: Ashgate, 2006).

Greenslade, William, *Degeneration, Culture, and the Novel, 1880–1940* (Cambridge: Cambridge University Press, 1994).

Grove, Allen W., 'Röntgen's Ghosts: Photography, X-Rays, and the Victorian Imagination', *Literature and Medicine* 16/2 (1997), 141–73.

Hurley, Kelly, *The Gothic Body: Sexuality, Materialism, and Degeneration at the Fin de Siècle* (Cambridge: Cambridge University Press, 1996).

Ledger, Sally, and McCracken, Scott (eds.), *Cultural Politics at the Fin de Siècle* (Cambridge: Cambridge University Press, 1995).

Luckhurst, Roger, *The Invention of Telepathy, 1870–1901* (Oxford: Oxford University Press, 2002).

Marshall, Gail (ed.), *The Cambridge Companion to the Fin de Siècle* (Cambridge: Cambridge University Press, 2007).

Stiles, Anne, *Popular Fiction and Brain Science in the Late Nineteenth Century* (Cambridge: Cambridge University Press, 2012).

Stokes, John (ed.), *Fin de Siècle / Fin du Globe: Fears and Fantasies of the Late Nineteenth Century* (Basingstoke: Macmillan, 1992).

Thatcher, David S., *Nietzsche in England, 1890–1914: The Growth of a Reputation* (Toronto: University of Toronto Press, 1970).

Further Reading in Oxford World's Classics

Conrad, Joseph, *Heart of Darkness and Other Tales*, ed. Cedric Watts.

Stevenson, Robert Louis, *Strange Case of Dr Jekyll and Mr Hyde and Other Tales*, ed. Roger Luckhurst.

Wells, H. G., *The First Men in the Moon*, ed. Simon James.

Wells, H. G., *The Island of Doctor Moreau*, ed. Darryl Jones.

Wells, H. G., *The Time Machine*, ed. Roger Luckhurst.

Wells, H. G., *The War of the Worlds*, ed. Darryl Jones.

A CHRONOLOGY OF H. G. WELLS

1866   (21 September) Herbert George Wells born in Bromley, Kent.

1869   Jules Verne, *Twenty Thousand Leagues Under the Sea*; Matthew Arnold, *Culture and Anarchy*.

1870   Elementary Education Act, providing compulsory education for all children 5–13 years old.

1871   Charles Darwin, *The Descent of Man*; Edward Bulwer-Lytton, *The Coming Race*. The Paris Commune: revolutionary period, ending in destruction and massacre.

1872   Samuel Butler, *Erewhon*.

1874–80 HGW pupil at Morley's Academy, Bromley.

1877   Injury to father leaves Wells family in sudden poverty.

1880   HGW apprenticed to Rodgers and Benyer, Drapers, for a month's trial after which he is dismissed; his mother takes position as resident housekeeper, Uppark. Ray Lankester's lecture *Degeneration: A Chapter in Darwinism* a big influence on HGW's biological thought.

1881   Attends Alfred Williams School, then Midhurst Grammar School; apprenticed to Hyde's Drapery Emporium in Southsea.

1882   Robert Louis Stevenson's *Treasure Island*.

1883   HGW's indentures cancelled.

1884   Wins scholarship to Normal School of Science in South Kensington, where T. H. Huxley is dean.

1885   Robert Louis Stevenson, *Strange Case of Dr Jekyll and Mr Hyde*; Richard Jefferies, *After London*.

1886   HGW matriculates. Attends socialist meetings at home of William Morris. Founds and edits *Science School Journal*. Charles Howard Hinton, *Scientific Romances*. Colonial and Indian Exhibition held opposite Normal School of Science.

1887   HGW's first published work in *Science Schools Journal*. Fails geology exam at Normal School, so loses scholarship; teaches at Holt Academy in Wales. Severely injured in accident during football match, resulting in lung haemorrhage which forces him to convalesce. Edward Bellamy, *Looking Backwards*, influential utopian fiction; Gaspar Enrique, *The Time Ship*, Spanish novel featuring time machine. (13 November) 'Bloody Sunday' riots in London, following police charge on marchers in Trafalgar Square.

1888 HGW returns to London; teaches at Henley House School. Publishes three parts of 'The Chronic Argonauts' in *Science Schools Journal*, which is the unfinished first version of *The Time Machine*.

1889 Mark Twain's time travel satire *A Connecticut Yankee in King Arthur's Court*; Elizabeth Corbett, *New Amazonia*, feminist utopia. London Dock Strike.

1890 HGW passes Bachelor of Science exams and is awarded University of London degree. Elected Fellow of the Zoological Society. William Morris, *News from Nowhere*, socialist utopia written as riposte to Bellamy; William Booth, *In Darkest England and the Way Out*.

1891 Tutor for University Tutorial College; publishes essay 'The Rediscovery of the Unique' in *Fortnightly Review*, his first major publication. Marries cousin Isabel Wells. Wilde, *The Picture of Dorian Gray*.

1892 Max Nordau, *Degeneration*.

1893 Recurrence of lung haemorrhage. Publishes *A Text Book of Biology*, his first book. Career as professional journalist begins. T. H. Huxley, *Evolution and Ethics*; Robert Blatchford's political vision *Merrie England*, hugely influential in popularizing socialist ideas; George Griffith's novel about futuristic war in London, *Angel of the Revolution*. Gilbert and Sullivan's satirical *Utopia, Limited* operetta opens.

1894 HGW elopes with Amy Catherine Robbins ('Jane'). Seven episodes of 'The Time Machine' published by W. E. Henley in *National Observer*. Writes as journalist for *Pall Mall Gazette*, and for the *Saturday Review* under Frank Harris's editorship. Publishes 'Popularising Science' in *Nature*. Camille Flammarion, *Omega: The Last Days of the World*.

1895 (January–May) *The Time Machine* serialized in *New Review*, again edited by Henley; HGW declared 'a man of genius' by leading journalist W. T. Stead. Meets G. B. Shaw on opening night of Henry James's play, *Guy Domville*. (May) *The Time Machine* issued. Also publishes *Select Conversations with an Uncle*; *The Wonderful Visit*; *The Stolen Bacillus*. (April–May) Arrest and prosecution of Oscar Wilde. Decadent movement in retreat. Max Nordau's *Degeneration*; Grant Allen's *The British Barbarians: A Hill-Top Novel*.

1896 *The Island of Doctor Moreau*; *The Wheels of Chance*. Meets novelist George Gissing.

1897 *The Invisible Man*; *The Plattner Story*; *Thirty Strange Stories*; *The Star*; *Certain Personal Matters*. Begins friendship with Arnold Bennett. Queen Victoria's Diamond Jubilee.

1898   *The War of the Worlds*. Suffers from lung damage again; recovering on south coast, meets Henry James and Joseph Conrad. Also travels to Italy, where stays with Gissing. Dislikes Rome intensely.

1899   *When the Sleeper Wakes*; *Tales of Space and Time*.

1900   House designed and built for HGW at Sandgate in Kent where he becomes near neighbour of Henry James. *Love and Mr Lewisham*.

1901   *Anticipations*, HGW's speculations on the year 2000. Rediscovers Mendel's theory of 'genetics'. *First Men in the Moon*, the last of his early scientific romances. Birth of first son.

1902   Lecture 'The Discovery of the Future' at Royal Institution.

1903   Joins Fabian Society. Birth of second son.

1904   *The Food of the Gods*.

1905   *Kipps*; *A Modern Utopia*. Einstein's Special Theory of Relativity.

1906   *In the Days of the Comet*; *The Future in America*. Affairs with Dorothy Richardson, Rosamund Bland, Amber Reeves.

1908   *First and Last Things*; *The War in the Air*; *New Worlds for Old*. Resigns from the Fabian Society after dispute with G. B. Shaw.

1909   *Tono-Bungay*; *Ann Veronica*, HGW's transparently autobiographical account of relationship with Amber Reeves, who gives birth to their daughter Anna-Jane at the end of the year. E. M. Forster publishes 'The Machine Stops', an anti-Wellsian dystopia.

1910   *The History of Mr Polly*. Affair with Elizabeth von Arnim.

1911   *The New Machiavelli*.

1912   *Marriage*. Essay 'The Contemporary Novel' for *Atlantic Monthly*.

1914   Birth of son Anthony, from affair with Rebecca West. Publishes *The World Set Free*, which predicts the invention of the atomic bomb (and became the inspiration for the physicist Leo Szilard). Henry James criticizes HGW in essay 'The Younger Generation'. Great War begins after assassination of Archduke Franz Ferdinand.

1915   *Boon* contains HGW's savage parody of Henry James, which ends their friendship.

1916   Visits western front; publishes *Mr Britling Sees It Through* and *What Is Coming?*

1917   HGW has brief Christian phase. Writes positive review for Joyce's *A Portrait of the Artist as a Young Man*. Russian Revolution.

1918   Joins Ministry of Information. Vote given to women over 30.

1919   Joins committee to set up League of Nations and contributes to *The Idea of a League of Nations*; advocates world government. Publishes his controversial but bestselling *Outline of History*.

1920 Visits Russia and meets Lenin, Trotsky, and Maxim Gorky.

1921 Affair with Margaret Sanger. Red Army victory in Russian Civil War.

1922 *A Short History of the World*. Mussolini in power in Italy.

1923 *Men Like Gods* and *The Dream*. Affair with Odette Keun. Virginia Woolf's essay 'Mr Bennett and Mrs Brown' famously attacks the novels of Bennett and Wells.

1924 The Atlantic Edition of his works published: substantially reworks *The Time Machine*. Zamyatin's Russian dystopia *We*, much influenced by Wells.

1926 Fritz Lang science fiction film *Metropolis*.

1928 *The Open Conspiracy*. Equal voting rights for men and women.

1929 HGW begins to broadcast on BBC. Wall Street Crash.

1930 *The Science of Life*, co-written with son G. P. Wells and Julian Huxley.

1932 *After Democracy*. Aldous Huxley's dystopia *Brave New World*, with one target: Wells's utopian technocracy.

1933 *The Shape of Things of Come*. Adolf Hitler elected as Chancellor of Germany.

1934 HGW interviews both Stalin and F. D. Roosevelt. Publishes *Experiment in Autobiography*.

1935 Alexander Korda's film of *The Shape of Things to Come*.

1938 Lecture tour of Australia.

1939 *The Holy Terror*. Beginning of Second World War.

1940 HGW stays in London during the Blitz.

1941 Last novel, *You Can't Be Too Careful*.

1942 *Science and the World Mind*.

1945 Last books: *The Mind at the End of Its Tether*; *The Happy Turning*. Allied victory in Europe. (January) liberation of Auschwitz; (April) British and American troops find Bergen-Belsen. (August) atomic bombs dropped on Hiroshima and Nagasaki. Election of Labour Government. HGW demonized as scientific technocrat in C. S. Lewis's novel, *That Hideous Strength*.

1946 (13 August) HGW dies in London.

1967 First publication of *H. G. Wells in Love*, the annexe of his autobiography about his sexual relationships.

THE INVISIBLE MAN

A Grotesque Romance

CONTENTS

I

THE stranger came early in February, one wintry day, through a bit-ing wind and a driving snow, the last snowfall of the year, over the down, walking from Bramblehurst* Railway Station, and carrying a little black portmanteau in his thickly-gloved hand. He was wrapped up from head to foot, and the brim of his soft felt hat hid every inch of his face save the shiny tip of his nose; the snow had piled itself against his shoulders and chest, and added a white crest to the burden he carried. He staggered into the 'Coach and Horses' more dead than alive, and flung his portmanteau down. 'A fire,' he cried, 'in the name of human charity! A room and a fire!' He stamped and shook the snow from off himself in the bar, and followed Mrs Hall into her guest par-lour to strike his bargain. And with that much introduction, that and a couple of sovereigns* flung upon the table, he took up his quarters in the inn.

Mrs Hall lit the fire and left him there while she went to prepare him a meal with her own hands. A guest to stop at Iping* in the winter time was an unheard-of piece of luck, let alone a guest who was no 'haggler,' and she was resolved to show herself worthy of her good fortune.

As soon as the bacon was well under way, and Millie, her lymphatic aid, had been brisked up a bit by a few deftly chosen expressions of contempt, she carried the cloth, plates, and glasses into the parlour, and began to lay them with the utmost *éclat*. Although the fire was burning up briskly, she was surprised to see that her visitor still wore his hat and coat, standing with his back to her and staring out of the window at the falling snow in the yard.

His gloved hands were clasped behind him, and he seemed to be lost in thought. She noticed that the melted snow that still sprinkled his shoulders dropped upon her carpet.

'Can I take your hat and coat, sir,' she said, 'and give them a good dry in the kitchen?'

'No,' he said without turning.

She was not sure she had heard him, and was about to repeat her question.

He turned his head and looked at her over his shoulder. 'I prefer to keep them on,' he said with emphasis; and she noticed that he wore big blue spectacles* with side-lights, and had a bushy side whisker over his coat collar that completely hid his cheeks and face.

'Very well, sir,' she said. '*As* you like. In a bit the room will be warmer.'

He made no answer, and had turned his face away from her again, and Mrs Hall, feeling that her conversational advances were ill-timed, laid the rest of the table things in a quick staccato manner, and whisked out of the room. When she returned he was still standing there, like a man of stone, his back hunched, his collar turned up, his dripping hat-brim turned down, hiding his face and ears completely. She put down the eggs and bacon with considerable emphasis, and called rather than said to him:

'Your lunch is served, sir.'

'Thank you,' he said at the same time, and did not stir until she was closing the door. Then he swung round and approached the table with a certain eagerness.

As she went behind the bar to the kitchen she heard a sound repeated at regular intervals. Chirk, chirk, chirk, it went, the sound of a spoon being whisked rapidly round a basin. 'That girl!' she said. 'There! I clean forgot it. It's her being so long!' And while she herself finished mixing the mustard, she gave Millie a few verbal stabs for her excessive slowness. She had cooked the ham and eggs, laid the table, and done everything, while Millie (help, indeed!) had only succeeded in delaying the mustard. And him a new guest, and wanting to stay! Then she filled the mustard-pot, and, putting it with some stateliness upon a gold and black tea-tray, carried it into the parlour.

She rapped and entered promptly. As she did so her visitor moved quickly, so that she got but a glimpse of a white object disappearing behind the table. It would seem he was picking something from the floor. She rapped down the mustard-pot on the table, and then she noticed the overcoat and hat had been taken off and put over a chair in front of the fire. And a pair of wet boots threatened rust to her steel fender. She went to these things resolutely. 'I suppose I may have them to dry now?' she said, in a voice that brooked no denial.

'Leave the hat,' said her visitor in a muffled voice, and turning, she saw he had raised his head and was sitting and looking at her.

For a moment she stood gazing at him, too surprised to speak.

He held a white cloth—it was a serviette he had brought with him—over the lower part of the face, so that his mouth and jaws were completely hidden, and that was the reason of his muffled voice. But it was not that which startled Mrs Hall. It was the fact that all the forehead above his blue glasses was covered by a white bandage, and that another covered his ears, leaving not a scrap of his face exposed excepting only his pink, peaked nose. It was bright, pink, and shining, just as it had been at first. He wore a dark brown velvet jacket with a high, black, linen-lined collar turned up about his neck. The thick black hair, escaping as it could below and between the cross bandages, projected in curious tails and horns, giving him the strangest appearance conceivable. This muffled and bandaged head was so unlike what she had anticipated that for a moment she was rigid.

He did not remove the serviette, but remained holding it, as she saw now, with a brown gloved hand, and regarding her with his inscrutable blank glasses. 'Leave the hat,' he said, speaking indistinctly through the white cloth.

Her nerves began to recover from the shock they had received. She placed the hat on the chair again by the fire. 'I didn't know, sir,' she began, 'that—' And she stopped embarrassed.

'Thank you,' he said drily, glancing from her to the door, and then at her again.

'I'll have them nicely dried, sir, at once,' she said, and carried his clothes out of the room. She glanced at his white-swathed head and blank goggles again as she was going out of the door; but his napkin was still in front of his face. She shivered a little as she closed the door behind her, and her face was eloquent of her surprise and perplexity. 'I *never!*' she whispered. 'There!' She went quite softly to the kitchen, and was too preoccupied to ask Millie what she was messing about with *now*, when she got there.

The visitor sat and listened to her retreating feet. He glanced inquiringly at the window before he removed his serviette, and resumed his meal. He took a mouthful, glanced suspiciously at the window, took another mouthful; then rose, and taking the serviette in his hand, walked across the room and pulled the blind down to the top of the white muslin that obscured the lower panes. This plunged the room in twilight. He returned with an easier air to the table and his meal.

'The poor soul's had an accident, or an op'ration or somethin',' said Mrs Hall. 'What a turn them bandages did give me to be sure!'

She put on some more coal, unfolded the clothes-horse, and extended the traveller's coat upon this. 'And they goggles! Why, he looked more like a divin' 'elmet than a human man!' She hung his muffler on a corner of the horse. 'And holding that handkerchief over his mouth all the time. Talkin' through it! . . . Perhaps his mouth was hurt too— maybe.'

She turned round, as one who suddenly remembers. 'Bless my soul alive!' she said, going off at a tangent, 'ain't you done them taters *yet*, Millie?'

When Mrs Hall went to clear away the stranger's lunch her idea that his mouth must also have been cut or disfigured in the accident she supposed him to have suffered was confirmed, for he was smoking a pipe, and all the time that she was in the room he never loosened the silk muffler he had wrapped round the lower part of his face to put the mouthpiece to his lips. Yet it was not forgetfulness, for she saw he glanced at the tobacco as it smouldered out. He sat in the corner with his back to the window-blind, and spoke now, having eaten and drunk and being comfortably warmed through, with less aggressive brevity than before. The reflection of the fire lent a kind of red animation to his big spectacles they had lacked hitherto.

'I have some luggage,' he said, 'at Bramblehurst Station,' and he asked her how he could have it sent. He bowed his bandaged head quite politely in acknowledgment of her explanation. 'To-morrow!' he said. 'There is no speedier delivery?' and seemed disappointed when she answered 'No.' 'Was she quite sure? No man with a trap who would go over?'

Mrs Hall, nothing loth, answered his questions and then developed a conversation. 'It's a steep road by the down, sir,' she said in answer to the question about a trap; and then snatching at an opening said: 'It was there a carriage was upsettled, a year ago and more. A gentleman killed, besides his coachman. Accidents, sir, happen in a moment, don't they?'

But the visitor was not to be drawn so easily. 'They do,' he said, through his muffler, eyeing her quietly from behind his impenetrable glasses.

'But they take long enough to get well, sir, don't they? There was my sister's son, Tom, jest cut his arm with a scythe—tumbled on it in the 'ayfield—and bless me! he was three months tied up, sir. You'd hardly believe it. It's regular give me a dread of a scythe, sir.'

'I can quite understand that,' said the visitor.

'We was afraid, one time, that he'd have to have an op'ration, he was that bad, sir.'

The visitor laughed abruptly—a bark of a laugh that he seemed to bite and kill in his mouth. '*Was* he?' he said.

'He was, sir. And no laughing matter to them as had the doing for him as I had, my sister being took up with her little ones so much. There was bandages to do, sir, and bandages to undo. So that if I may make so bold as to say it, sir——'

'Will you get me some matches?' said the visitor quite abruptly. 'My pipe is out.'

Mrs Hall was pulled up suddenly. It was certainly rude of him after telling him all she had done. She gasped at him for a moment, and remembered the two sovereigns. She went for the matches.

'Thanks,' he said concisely, as she put them down, and turned his shoulder upon her and stared out of the window again. Evidently he was sensitive on the topic of operations and bandages. She did not 'make so bold as to say,' after all. But his snubbing way had irritated her, and Millie had a hot time of it that afternoon.

The visitor remained in the parlour until four o'clock, without giving the ghost of an excuse for an intrusion. For the most part he was quite still during that time: it would seem he sat in the growing darkness, smoking by the firelight—perhaps dozing.

Once or twice a curious listener might have heard him at the coals, and for the space of five minutes he was audible pacing the room. He seemed to be talking to himself. Then the arm-chair creaked as he sat down again.

II

AT four o'clock, when it was fairly dark, and Mrs Hall was screwing up her courage to go in and ask her visitor if he would take some tea, Teddy Henfrey, the clock-jobber,* came into the bar.

'My sakes! Mrs Hall,' said he, 'but this is terrible weather for thin boots!' The snow outside was falling faster.

Mrs Hall agreed, and then noticed he had his bag with him. 'Now you're here, Mr Teddy,' said she, 'I'd be glad if you'd give th' old clock in the parlour a bit of a look. 'Tis going, and it strikes well and hearty, but the hour hand won't do nuthin' but point at six.'

And leading the way, she went across to the parlour door and rapped and entered.

Her visitor, she saw, as she opened the door, was seated in the arm-chair before the fire, dozing, it would seem, with his bandaged head drooping on one side. The only light in the room was the red glow from the fire. Everything was ruddy, shadowy, and indistinct to her, the more so since she had just been lighting the bar lamp, and her eyes were dazzled. But for a second it seemed to her that the man she looked at had an enormous mouth wide open, a vast and incredible mouth that swallowed the whole of the lower portion of his face. It was the sensation of a moment; the white-bound head, the monstrous goggle eyes, and this huge yawn below it. Then he stirred, started up in his chair, put up his hand. She opened the door wide so that the room was lighter, and she saw him more clearly, with the muffler held to his face, just as she had seen him hold the serviette before. The shadows, she fancied, had tricked her.

'Would you mind, sir, this man a-coming to look at the clock, sir?' she said, recovering from her momentary disorder.

'Look at the clock?' he said, staring round in a drowsy manner, and speaking over his hand; and then, getting more fully awake, 'Certainly.'

Mrs Hall went away to get a lamp, and he rose and stretched himself. Then came the light, and Mr Teddy Henfrey, entering, was confronted by this bandaged person. He was, he says, 'taken aback.'

'Good afternoon,' said the stranger, regarding him—as Mr Henfrey says, with a vivid sense of the dark spectacles—'like a lobster.'

'I hope,' said Mr Henfrey, 'that it's no intrusion.'

'None whatever,' said the stranger. 'Though I understand,' he said, turning to Mrs Hall, 'that this room is really to be mine for my own private use.'

'I thought, sir,' said Mrs Hall, 'you'd prefer the clock——'

'Certainly,' said the stranger, 'certainly; but as a rule I like to be alone and undisturbed.'

He turned round with his back to the fireplace, and put his hands behind his back. 'And presently,' he said, 'when the clock-mending is over, I think I should like to have some tea. But not till the clock-mending is over.'

Mrs Hall was about to leave the room—she made no conversational advances this time, because she did not want to be snubbed in front of Mr Henfrey—when her visitor asked her if she had made any arrangements about his boxes at Bramblehurst. She told him she had mentioned the matter to the postman, and that the carrier could bring them over on the morrow.

'You are certain that is the earliest?' he said.

She was certain, with a marked coolness.

'I should explain,' he added, 'what I was really too cold and fatigued to do before, that I am an experimental investigator.'

'Indeed, sir,' said Mrs Hall, much impressed.

'And my baggage contains apparatus and appliances.'

'Very useful things indeed they are, sir,' said Mrs Hall.

'And I'm naturally anxious to get on with my inquiries.'

'Of course, sir.'

'My reason for coming to Iping,' he proceeded, with a certain deliberation of manner, 'was . . . a desire for solitude. I do not wish to be disturbed in my work. In addition to my work, an accident——'

'I thought as much,' said Mrs Hall to herself.

'Necessitates a certain retirement. My eyes are sometimes so weak and painful that I have to shut myself up in the dark for hours together—lock myself up. Sometimes—now and then. Not at present, certainly. At such times the slightest disturbance, the entry of a stranger into the room, is a source of excruciating annoyance to me. . . . It is well these things should be understood.'

'Certainly, sir,' said Mrs Hall. 'And if I might make so bold as to ask——'

'That, I think, is all,' said the stranger, with that quietly irresistible air of finality he could assume at will. Mrs Hall reserved her question and sympathy for a better occasion.

After Mrs Hall had left the room he remained standing in front of the fire, glaring, so Mr Henfrey puts it, at the clock-mending. Mr Henfrey worked with the lamp close to him, and the green shade threw a brilliant light upon his hands and upon the frame and wheels, and left the rest of the room shadowy. When he looked up coloured patches swam in his eyes. Being constitutionally of a curious nature, he had removed the works—a quite unnecessary proceeding—with the idea of delaying his departure and perhaps falling into conversation with the stranger. But the stranger stood there, perfectly silent and still. So still—it got on Henfrey's nerves. He felt alone in the room and looked up, and there, grey and dim, was the bandaged head and huge, dark lenses, staring fixedly, with a mist of green spots drifting in front of them. It was so uncanny to Henfrey that for a minute they remained staring blankly at one another. Then Henfrey looked down again. Very uncomfortable position! One would like to say something. Should he remark that the weather was very cold for the time of the year?

He looked up as if to take aim with that introductory shot. 'The weather——' he began.

'Why don't you finish and go?' said the rigid figure, evidently in a state of painfully suppressed rage. 'All you've got to do is to fix the hour hand on its—axle. You're simply humbugging.'

'Certainly sir—one minute more. I overlooked . . .' And Mr Henfrey finished and went.

But he went off feeling excessively annoyed. 'Damn it!' said Mr Henfrey to himself, trudging down the village through the falling snow, 'a man must do a clock at times, sure-*ly*.'

And again, 'Can't a man look at you? Ugly!'

And yet again, 'Seemingly not. If the police was wanting you, you couldn't be more wropped and bandaged.'

At Gleeson's corner he saw Hall, who had recently married the stranger's hostess at the 'Coach and Horses,' and who now drove the Iping conveyance, when occasional people required it, to Sidderbridge Junction, coming towards him on his return from that place. Hall had evidently been 'stopping a bit' at Sidderbridge, to judge by his driving. ''Ow do, Teddy?' he said, passing.

'You got a rum un up home!' said Teddy.

Hall very sociably pulled up. 'What's that?' he asked.

'Rum-looking customer stopping at the "Coach and Horses," ' said Teddy. 'My sakes!'

And he proceeded to give Hall a vivid description of his wife's grotesque guest. 'Looks a bit like a disguise, don't it? I'd like to see a man's face if I had him stopping in *my* place,' said Henfrey. 'But women are that trustful—where strangers are concerned. He's took your rooms, and he ain't even given a name, Hall.'

'You don't say so,' said Hall, who was a man of sluggish apprehension.

'Yes,' said Teddy. 'By the week. Whatever he is, you can't get rid of him under the week. And he's got a lot of luggage coming to-morrow, so he says. Let's hope it won't be stones in boxes, Hall.'

He told Hall how his aunt at Hastings had been swindled by a stranger with empty portmanteaux. Altogether he left Hall vaguely suspicious. 'Get up, old girl,' said Hall. 'I s'pose I must see 'bout this.'

Teddy trudged on his way with his mind considerably relieved.

Instead of 'seeing 'bout it,' however, Hall, on his return, was severely rated by his wife on the length of time he had spent in Sidderbridge, and his mild inquiries were answered snappishly and in a manner not to the point. But the seed of suspicion Teddy had sown germinated in the mind of Mr Hall in spite of these discouragements. 'You wim' don't know everything,' said Mr Hall, resolved to ascertain more about the personality of his guest at the earliest possible opportunity. And after the stranger had gone to bed, which he did about half-past nine, Mr Hall went very aggressively into the parlour and looked very hard at his wife's furniture, just to show that the stranger wasn't master there, and scrutinised a little contemptuously a sheet of mathematical computations the stranger had left. When retiring for the night he instructed Mrs Hall to look very closely at the stranger's luggage when it came next day.

'You mind your own business, Hall,' said Mrs Hall, 'and I'll mind mine.'

She was all the more inclined to snap at Hall because the stranger was undoubtedly an unusually strange sort of stranger, and she was by no means assured about him in her own mind. In the middle of the *night* she woke up dreaming of huge, white heads like turnips, that came *trailing* after her, at the end of interminable necks, and with vast black eyes. But being a sensible woman she subdued her terrors, and turned over and went to sleep again.

III

So it was that on the 29th day of February, at the beginning of the thaw, this singular person fell out of infinity into Iping village. Next day his luggage arrived through the slush—and very remarkable luggage it was. There were a couple of trunks, indeed, such as a rational man might have, but in addition there were a box of books—big, fat books, of which some were just in an incomprehensible handwriting—and a dozen or more crates, boxes, and cases, containing objects packed in straw—as it seemed to Hall, tugging with a casual curiosity at the straw—glass bottles. The stranger, muffled in hat, coat, gloves, and wrapper, came out impatiently to meet Fearenside's cart while Hall was having a word or so of gossip preparatory to helping bring them in. Out he came, not noticing Fearenside's dog, who was sniffing in a *dilettante* spirit at Hall's legs.

'Come along with those boxes,' he said. 'I've been waiting long enough.'

And he came down the steps towards the tail of the waggon, as if to lay hands on the smaller crate.

No sooner had Fearenside's dog caught sight of him, however, than it began to bristle and growl savagely, and when he rushed down the steps it gave an undecided hop, and then sprang straight at his hand. 'Whup!' cried Hall, jumping back, for he was no hero with dogs, and Fearenside howled 'Lie down!' and snatched his whip.

They saw the dog's teeth had slipped the hand, heard a kick, saw the dog execute a flanking jump and get home on the stranger's leg, and heard the rip of his trousering. Then the finer end of Fearenside's whip reached his property, and the dog, yelping with dismay, retreated under the wheels of the waggon. It was all the business of a swift half minute. No one spoke, every one shouted. The stranger glanced swiftly at his torn glove and at his leg, made as if he would stoop to the latter, then turned and rushed swiftly up the steps into the inn. They heard him go headlong across the passage and up the uncarpeted stairs to his bedroom.

'You brute, you!' said Fearenside, climbing off the waggon with his whip in his hand, while the dog watched him through the wheel.

'Come here!' said Fearenside. . . . 'You'd better.'

Hall had stood gaping. 'He wuz bit,' said Hall. 'I'd better go an' see to en.' And he trotted after the stranger. He met Mrs Hall in the passage. 'Carrier's darg,' he said, 'bit en.'

He went straight upstairs, and the stranger's door being ajar, he pushed it open, and was entering without any ceremony, being of a naturally sympathetic turn of mind.

The blind was down and the room dim. He caught a glimpse of a most singular thing, what seemed a handless arm waving towards him, and a face of three huge, indeterminate spots on white, very like the face of a pale pansy. Then he was struck violently in the chest, hurled back, and the door slammed in his face, and locked. It was so rapid that it gave him no time to observe. A waving of indecipherable shapes, a blow and a concussion. There he stood on the dark little landing, wondering what it might be that he had seen.

A couple of minutes after he rejoined the little group that had formed outside the 'Coach and Horses.' There was Fearenside telling about it all over again for the second time; there was Mrs Hall saying his dog didn't have no business to bite her guests; there was Huxter, the general dealer from over the road, interrogative; and Sandy Wadgers from the forge, judicial; besides women and children, all of them saying fatuities: 'Wouldn't let en bite *me*, I knows'; ''Tasn't right *have* such dargs'; 'Whad '*e* bite 'n for, than?' and so forth.

Mr Hall, staring at them from the steps and listening, found it incredible that he had seen anything so very remarkable happen upstairs. Besides, his vocabulary was altogether too limited for his impressions.

'He don't want no help, he says,' he said in answer to his wife's inquiry. 'We'd better be a-takin' of his luggage in.'

'He ought to have it cauterised at once,' said Mr Huxter, 'especially if it's at all inflamed.'

'I'd shoot en, that's what I'd do,' said a lady in the group.

Suddenly the dog began growling again.

'Come along,' cried an angry voice in the doorway, and there stood the muffled stranger, with his collar turned up and his hat brim bent down. 'The sooner you get those things in the better I'll be pleased.' It is stated by an anonymous bystander that his trousers and gloves had been changed.

'Was you hurt, sir?' said Fearenside. 'I'm rare sorry the darg——'

'Not a bit,' said the stranger. 'Never broke the skin. Hurry up with those things.'

He then swore to himself, so Mr Hall asserts.

Directly the first crate was, in accordance with his directions, carried into the parlour, the stranger flung himself upon it with extraordinary eagerness, and began to unpack it, scattering the straw with an utter disregard of Mrs Hall's carpet, and from it he began to produce bottles—little fat bottles containing powders, small and slender bottles containing coloured and white fluids, fluted blue bottles labelled *poison,* bottles with round bodies and slender necks, large green glass bottles, large white glass bottles, bottles with glass stoppers and frosted labels, bottles with fine corks, bottles with bungs, bottles with wooden caps, wine bottles, salad-oil bottles—putting them in rows on the chiffonnier,* on the mantel, on the table under the window, round the floor, on the bookshelf—everywhere. The chemist's shop in Bramblehurst could not boast half so many. Quite a sight it was. Crate after crate yielded bottles, until all six were empty and the table high with straw; the only things that came out of these crates besides the bottles were a number of test tubes and a carefully packed balance.

And directly the crates were unpacked the stranger went to the window and set to work, not troubling in the least about the litter of straw, the fire which had gone out, the box of books outside, nor for the trunks and other luggage that had gone upstairs.

When Mrs Hall took his dinner in to him, he was already so absorbed in his work, pouring little drops out of the bottles into test tubes, that he did not hear her until she had swept away the bulk of the straw and put the tray on the table, with some little emphasis perhaps, seeing the state that the floor was in. Then he half turned his head, and immediately turned it away again. But she saw he had removed his glasses; they were beside him on the table, and it seemed to her that his eye sockets were extraordinarily hollow. He put on his spectacles again, and then turned and faced her. She was about to complain of the straw on the floor when he anticipated her.

'I wish you wouldn't come in without knocking,' he said, in the tone of abnormal exasperation that seemed so characteristic of him.

'I knocked, but seemingly——'

'Perhaps you did. But in my investigations—my really very urgent and necessary investigations—the slightest disturbance, the jar of a door. . . . I must ask you——'

'Certainly, sir. You can turn the lock if you're like that, you know. Any time.'

'A very good idea,' said the stranger.

'This stror, sir. If I might make so bold as to remark——'

'Don't. If the straw makes trouble put it down in the bill.' And he mumbled at her—words suspiciously like curses.

He was so odd, standing there, so aggressive and explosive, bottle in one hand and test tube in the other, that Mrs Hall was quite alarmed. But she was a resolute woman. 'In which case, I should like to know, sir, what you consider——'

'A shilling—put down a shilling. Surely a shilling's enough?'

'So be it,' said Mrs Hall, taking up the table-cloth and beginning to spread it over the table. 'If you're satisfied, of course——'

He turned and sat down with his coat collar towards her.

All the afternoon he worked with the door locked, and, as Mrs Hall testifies, for the most part in silence. But once there was a concussion and a sound of bottles ringing together, as though the table had been hit, and the smash of glass flung violently down, and then a rapid pacing athwart the room. Fearing something was the matter, she went to the door and listened, not caring to knock.

'I can't go on,' he was raving; 'I *can't* go on! Three hundred thousand, four hundred thousand! The huge multitude! Cheated! All my life it may take me! . . . Patience! Patience indeed! . . . Fool! fool!'

There was a noise of hobnails on the bricks in the bar, and Mrs Hall had very reluctantly to leave the rest of his soliloquy. When she returned the room was silent again, save for the faint crepitation of his chair and the occasional clink of a bottle. It was all over; the stranger had resumed work.

When she took in his tea she saw broken glass in the corner of the room under the concave mirror, and a golden stain that had been carelessly wiped. She called attention to it.

'Put it down in the bill,' snapped her visitor. 'For God's sake don't worry me! If there's damage done, put it down in the bill,' and he went on ticking a list in the exercise-book before him.

* * * *

'I'll tell you something,' said Fearenside mysteriously. It was late in the afternoon, and they were in the little beershop of Iping Hanger.

'Well?' said Teddy Henfrey.

'This chap you're speaking of, what my darg bit. Well—he's black. Leastways his legs are.

'I seed through the tear of his trousers and the tear of his glove. You'd have expected a sort of pinky to show, wouldn't you? Well— there wasn't none. Just blackness. I tell you he's as black as my hat.'

'My sakes!' said Henfrey. 'It's a rummy case altogether. Why, his nose is as pink as paint!'

'That's true,' said Fearenside. 'I knows that. And I tell 'ee what I'm thinking. That marn's a piebald, Teddy; black here and white there—in patches. And he's ashamed of it. He's a kind of half-breed, and the colour's come off patchy instead of mixing. I've heard of such things before. And it's the common way with harrses, as any one can see.'

IV

I HAVE told the circumstances of the stranger's arrival in Iping with a certain fulness of detail, in order that the curious impression he created may be understood by the reader. But excepting two odd incidents, the circumstances of his stay until the extraordinary day of the club festival may be passed over very cursorily. There were a number of skirmishes with Mrs Hall on matters of domestic discipline, but in every case until late in April, when the first signs of penury began, he overrode her by the easy expedient of an extra payment. Hall did not like him, and whenever he dared he talked of the advisability of getting rid of him; but he showed his dislike mainly by concealing it ostentatiously, and avoiding his visitor as much as possible. 'Wait till the summer,' said Mrs Hall sagely, 'when the artisks* are beginning to come. Then we'll see. He may be a bit overbearing, but bills settled punctual is bills settled punctual, whatever you likes to say.'

The stranger did not go to church, and indeed made no difference between Sunday and the irreligious days, even in costume. He worked, as Mrs Hall thought, very fitfully. Some days he would come down early and be continuously busy. On others he would rise late, pace his room, fretting audibly for hours together, smoke, or sleep in the armchair by the fire. Communication with the world beyond the village he had none. His temper continued very uncertain; for the most part his manner was that of a man suffering under almost unendurable provocation, and once or twice things were snapped, torn, crushed, or broken in spasmodic gusts of violence. His habit of talking to himself in a low voice grew steadily upon him, but though Mrs Hall listened conscientiously she could make neither head nor tail of what she heard.

He rarely went abroad by day, but at twilight he would go out muffled up invisibly, whether the weather was cold or not, and he chose the loneliest paths and those most overshadowed by trees and banks. His goggling spectacles and ghastly, bandaged face under the penthouse of his hat, came with a disagreeable suddenness out of the darkness upon one or two home-going labourers; and Teddy Henfrey, tumbling out of the 'Scarlet Coat' one night at half-past nine, was scared shamefully by the stranger's skull-like head (he was walking hat in hand) lit by the sudden light of the opened inn door. Such children as saw him at nightfall dreamt of bogies, and it seemed doubtful whether he disliked boys more than they disliked him, or the reverse; but there was certainly a vivid enough dislike on either side.

It was inevitable that a person of so remarkable an appearance and bearing should form a frequent topic in such a village as Iping. Opinion was greatly divided about his occupation. Mrs Hall was sensitive on the point. When questioned, she explained very carefully that he was an 'experimental investigator,' going gingerly over the syllables as one who dreads pitfalls. When asked what an experimental investigator was, she would say with a touch of superiority that most educated people knew such things as that, and would thus explain that he 'discovered things.' Her visitor had had an accident, she said, which temporarily discoloured his face and hands, and being of a sensitive disposition was averse to any public notice of the fact.

Out of her hearing there was a view largely entertained that he was a criminal trying to escape from justice by wrapping himself altogether from the eye of the police. This idea sprang from the brain of Mr Teddy Henfrey. No crime of any magnitude dating from the middle or end of February* was known to have occurred. Elaborated in the imagination of Mr Gould, the probationary assistant in the National School,* this theory took the form that the stranger was an anarchist* in disguise, preparing explosives, and he resolved to undertake such detective operations as his time permitted. These consisted for the most part in looking very hard at the stranger whenever they met, or in asking people who had never seen the stranger leading questions about him. But he detected nothing.

Another school of opinion followed Mr Fearenside, and either accepted the piebald view or some modification of it. As, for instance, Silas Durgan who was heard to assert that 'if he chose to show enself at fairs he'd make his fortune in no time,' and being a bit of a theologian compared the stranger to the man with the one talent.* Yet another view explained the entire matter by regarding the stranger as a harmless lunatic. That had the advantage of accounting for everything straight away. Between these main groups there were waverers and compromisers. Sussex folk have few superstitions, and it was only after the events of early April that the thought of the supernatural was first whispered in the village. Even then it was only credited among the women folk.

But whatever they thought of him, people in Iping on the whole agreed in disliking him. His irritability, though it might have been comprehensible to an urban brain-worker,* was an amazing thing to these quiet Sussex villagers. The frantic gesticulations they surprised now and then, the headlong pace after nightfall that swept him upon them round quiet corners, the inhuman bludgeoning of all the tentative advances of curiosity, the taste for twilight that led to the closing of doors, the pulling down of blinds, the extinction of candles and lamps—who could agree with such goings on? They drew aside as he passed down the village, and when he had gone by, young humorists would up with coat collars and down with hat brims, and go pacing nervously after him in imitation of his occult bearing. There was a song popular at that time called 'The Bogey Man!'* Miss Satchell sang it at the schoolroom concert—in aid of the church lamps—and thereafter, whenever one or two of the villagers were gathered together and the stranger appeared, a bar or so of this tune, more or less sharp or flat, was whistled in the midst of them. Also belated little children would call 'Bogey Man!' after him, and make off tremulously elated.

Cuss, the general practitioner, was devoured by curiosity. The bandages excited his professional interest; the report of the thousand-and-one bottles aroused his jealous regard. All through April and May he coveted an opportunity of talking to the stranger, and at last, towards Whitsuntide, he could stand it no longer, but hit upon the subscription-list for a village nurse as an excuse. He was surprised to find that Mr Hall did not know his guest's name.

'He give a name,' said Mrs Hall—an assertion which was quite unfounded—'but I didn't rightly hear it.' She thought it seemed so silly not to know the man's name.

Cuss rapped at the parlour door and entered. There was a fairly audible imprecation from within.

'Pardon my intrusion,' said Cuss, and then the door closed and cut Mrs Hall off from the rest of the conversation.

She could hear the murmur of voices for the next ten minutes, then a cry of surprise, a stirring of feet, a chair flung aside, a bark of laughter, quick steps to the door, and Cuss appeared, his face white, his eyes staring over his shoulder. He left the door open behind him, and, without looking at her, strode across the hall and went down the steps, and she heard his feet hurrying along the road. He carried his hat in his hand. She stood behind the bar, looking at the open door of the parlour. Then she heard the stranger laughing quietly, and his footsteps came across the room. She could not see his face where she stood. The parlour door slammed, and the place was silent again.

Cuss went straight up the village to Bunting, the vicar.

'Am I mad?' Cuss began abruptly, as he entered the shabby little study. 'Do I look like an insane person?'

'What's happened?' said the vicar, putting the ammonite* on the loose sheets of his forthcoming sermon.

'That chap at the inn——'

'Well?'

'Give me something to drink,' said Cuss, and he sat down.

When his nerves had been steadied by a glass of cheap sherry—the only drink the good vicar had available—he told him of the interview he had just had.

'Went in,' he gasped, 'and began to demand a subscription for that nurse fund. He'd stuck his hands in his pockets as I came in, and he sat down lumpily in his chair. Sniffed. I told him I'd heard he took an interest in scientific things. He said, 'Yes.' Sniffed again. Kept on sniffing all the time, evidently recently caught an infernal cold. No wonder—wrapped up like that. I developed the nurse idea, and all the while kept my eyes open. Bottles—chemicals—everywhere. Balance, test tubes, in stands, and a smell of—evening primrose. Would he subscribe? Said he'd consider it. Asked him point blank was he researching. Said he was. A long research? Got quite cross, a 'damnable long research,' said he, blowing the cork out, so to speak. 'Oh?' said I. And out came the grievance. The man was just on the boil, and my question boiled him over. He had been given a prescription—most valuable prescription—what for he wouldn't say. Was it medical? 'Damn you! what are you fishing after?' I apologised. Dignified sniff and cough. He resumed. He'd read it. Five ingredients. Put it down; turned his head. Draught of air from window lifted the paper. Swish, rustle. He was working in a room with an open fireplace, he said. Saw a flicker, and there was the prescription burning and lifting chimneyward. Rushed towards it just as it whisked up chimney. So! Just at that point, to illustrate his story, out came his arm.'

'Well?'

'No hand. Just an empty sleeve. Lord! I thought, *that's* a deformity! Got a cork arm,* I suppose, and has taken it off. Then, I thought, there's something odd in that. What the devil keeps that sleeve up and open if there's nothing in it? There was nothing in it, I tell you. Nothing down it, right down to the joint. I could see right down it to the elbow, and there was a glimmer of light shining through a tear of the cloth. "Good God!" I said. Then he stopped. Stared at me with those blank, goggled eyes of his, and then at his sleeve.'

'Well?'

'That's all. He never said a word, just glared and put his sleeve back in his pocket quickly, "I was saying," said he, "that there was the prescription burning, wasn't I?" Interrogative cough. "How the devil," said I, "can you move an empty sleeve like that?" "Empty sleeve?" "Yes," said I, "an empty sleeve."

' "It's an empty sleeve, is it? You saw it was an empty sleeve?" He stood up right away. I stood up, too. He came towards me in three very slow steps, and stood quite close. Sniffed venomously. I didn't flinch, though I'm hanged if that bandaged knob of his, and those blinkers, aren't enough to unnerve any one, coming quietly up to you.

' "You said it was an empty sleeve?" he said. "Certainly," I said. At staring and saying nothing a bare-faced man, unspectacled, starts scratch. Then very quietly he pulled his sleeve out of his pocket again, and raised his arm towards me, as though he would show it to me again. He did it very, very slowly. I looked at it. Seemed an age. "Well?" said I, clearing my throat; "there's nothing in it."

'Had to say something. I was beginning to feel frightened. I could see right down it. He extended it straight towards me, slowly, slowly—just like that—until the cuff was six inches from my face. Queer thing to see an empty sleeve come at you like that! And then——'

'Well?'

'Something—exactly like a finger and a thumb it felt—nipped my nose.'

Bunting began to laugh.

'There wasn't anything there!' said Cuss—his voice running up into a shriek at the 'there.' 'It's all very well for you to laugh, but I tell you I was so startled, I hit his cuff hard, and turned round and cut out of the room—I left him——'

Cuss stopped. There was no mistaking the sincerity of his panic. He turned round in a helpless way, and took a second glass of the excellent vicar's very inferior sherry. 'When I hit his cuff,' said Cuss, 'I tell you, it felt exactly like hitting an arm.

'And there wasn't an arm! There wasn't the ghost of an arm!'

Mr Bunting thought it over. He looked suspiciously at Cuss. 'It's a most remarkable story,' he said. He looked very wise and grave indeed. 'It's really,' said Mr Bunting with judicial emphasis, 'a most remarkable story.'

V

THE BURGLARY AT THE VICARAGE

THE facts of the burglary at the Vicarage come to us chiefly through the medium of the vicar and his wife. It occurred in the small hours of Whit Monday, the day devoted in Iping to the Club festivities.* Mrs Bunting, it seems, woke up suddenly in the stillness that comes before the dawn, with a strong impression that the door of their bedroom had opened and closed. She did not arouse her husband at first, but sat up in bed listening. She then distinctly heard the pad, pad, pad of bare feet coming out of the adjoining dressing-room and walking along the passage towards the staircase. So soon as she felt assured of this, she aroused the Rev. Mr Bunting as quietly as possible. He did not strike a light, but putting on his spectacles, her dressing gown, and his bath slippers, went out on the landing to listen. He heard quite distinctly a fumbling going on at his study desk downstairs, and then a violent sneeze.

At that he returned to his bedroom, armed himself with the most obvious weapon, the poker, and descended the staircase as noiselessly as possible. Mrs Bunting came out on the landing.

The hour was about four, and the ultimate darkness of the night was passed. There was a faint shimmer of light in the hall, but the study doorway yawned impenetrably black. Everything was still, except the faint creaking of the stairs under Mr Bunting's tread, and the slight movements in the study. Then something snapped, the drawer was opened, and there was a rustle of papers. Then came an imprecation, and a match was struck, and the study was flooded with yellow light. Mr Bunting was now in the hall, and through the crack of the door he could see the desk and the open drawer, and a candle burning on the desk. But the robber he could not see. He stood there in the hall undecided what to do, and Mrs Bunting, her face white and intent, crept slowly downstairs after him. One thing kept up Mr Bunting's courage. The persuasion that this burglar was a resident in the village.

They heard the chink of money, and realised that the robber had found the housekeeping reserve of gold—two pounds ten in half sovereigns* altogether. At that sound Mr Bunting was nerved to abrupt action. Gripping the poker firmly he rushed into the room, closely followed by Mrs Bunting.

'Surrender!' cried Mr Bunting fiercely, and then stopped amazed. Apparently the room was perfectly empty.

Yet their conviction that they had that very moment heard somebody moving in the room had amounted to a certainty. For half a minute perhaps they stood gasping, then Mrs Bunting went across the room and looked behind the screen, while Mr Bunting, by a kindred impulse, peered under the desk. Then Mrs Bunting turned back the window curtains, and Mr Bunting looked up the chimney, and probed it with the poker. Then Mrs Bunting scrutinised the waste-paper basket, and Mr Bunting opened the coal-scuttle. Then they came to a stop, and stood with eyes interrogating one another.

'I could have sworn——' said Mr Bunting.

'The candle!' said Mr Bunting. 'Who lit the candle?'

'The drawer!' said Mrs Bunting. 'And the money's gone!'

She went hastily to the doorway.

'Of all the extraordinary occurrences——'

There was a violent sneeze in the passage. They rushed out, and as they did so the kitchen door slammed. 'Bring the candle!' said Mr Bunting, and led the way. They both heard the sound of bolts being hastily shot back.

As he opened the kitchen door he saw through the scullery that the back door was just opening, and the faint light of early dawn displayed the dark masses of the garden beyond. He was certain that nothing went out of the door. It opened, stood open for a moment, and then closed with a slam. As it did so, the candle Mrs Bunting was bringing from the study flickered and flared. . . . It was a minute or more before they entered the kitchen.

The place was empty. They refastened the back door, examined the kitchen, pantry, and scullery thoroughly, and at last went down into the cellar. There was not a soul to be found in the house, search as they would.

Daylight found the vicar and his wife, a quaintly costumed little couple, still marvelling about on their own ground floor by the unnecessary light of a guttering candle.

'Of all the extraordinary affairs,' began the vicar for the twentieth time.

'My dear,' said Mrs Bunting, 'there's Susie coming down. Just wait here until she has gone into the kitchen, and then slip upstairs.'

VI

THE FURNITURE THAT WENT MAD

Now it happened that in the early hours of Whit Monday, before Millie was hunted out for the day, Mr Hall and Mrs Hall both rose and went noiselessly down into the cellar. Their business there was of a private nature, and had something to do with the specific gravity of their beer.

They had hardly entered the cellar when Mrs Hall found she had forgotten to bring down a bottle of sarsaparilla* from their joint room. As she was the expert and principal operator in this affair, Hall very properly went upstairs for it.

On the landing he was surprised to see that the stranger's door was ajar. He went on into his own room and found the bottle as he had been directed.

But returning with the bottle, he noticed that the bolts on the front door had been shot back—that the door was, in fact, simply on the latch. And, with a flash of inspiration, he connected this with the stranger's room upstairs and the suggestions of Mr Teddy Henfrey. He distinctly remembered holding the candle while Mrs Hall shot these bolts overnight. At the sight he stopped, gaping; then, with the bottle still in his hands, went upstairs again. He rapped at the stranger's door. There was no answer. He rapped again; then pushed the door wide open and entered.

It was as he expected. The bed, the room also, was empty. And what was queerer, even to his heavy intelligence, on the bedroom chair and along the rail of the bed were scattered the garments, the only garments so far as he knew, and the bandages of their guest. His big slouch hat* even was cocked jauntily over the bedpost.

As Hall stood there he heard his wife's voice coming out of the depth of the cellar, and with that rapid telescoping of the syllables and interrogative cocking up of the final words to a high note, by which the West Sussex villager is wont to indicate a brisk impatience. 'Gearge! You gart whad a wand?'

At that he turned and hurried down to her. 'Janny,' he said over the rail of the cellar steps, ''tas the truth what Henfrey sez. 'E's not in uz room, 'e en't. And the front door's onbolted.'

At first Mrs Hall did not understand, and so soon as she did she resolved to see the empty room for herself. Hall, still holding the bottle, went first. 'If 'e en't there,' he said, "is close are. And what's 'e doin' 'ith-out 'is close, than? 'Tas a most curius basness.'

As they came up the cellar steps they both, it was afterwards ascertained, fancied they heard the front door open and shut, but, seeing it closed and nothing there, neither said a word to the other about it at the time. Mrs Hall passed her husband in the passage, and ran on first upstairs. Some one sneezed on the staircase. Hall, following six steps behind, thought that he heard her sneeze; she, going on first, was under the impression that Hall was sneezing. She flung open the door and stood regarding the room. 'Of all the curious!' she said.

She heard a sniff close behind her head, as it seemed, and, turning, was surprised to see Hall a dozen feet off on the topmost stair. But in another moment he was beside her. She bent forward and put her hand on the pillow and then under the clothes.

'Cold,' she said. 'He's been up this hour or more.'

As she did so a most extraordinary thing happened. The bed-clothes gathered themselves together, leapt up suddenly into a sort of peak, and then jumped headlong over the bottom rail. It was exactly as if a hand had clutched them in the centre and flung them aside. Immediately after, the stranger's hat hopped off the bedpost, described a whirling flight in the air through the better part of a circle, and then dashed straight at Mrs Hall's face. Then as swiftly came the sponge from the washstand, and then the chair, flinging the stranger's coat and trousers carelessly aside, and laughing drily in a voice singularly like the stranger's, turned itself up with its four legs at Mrs Hall, seemed to take aim at her for a moment, and charged at her. She screamed and turned, and then the chair legs came gently but firmly against her back and impelled her and Hall out of the room. The door slammed violently, and was locked. The chair and bed seemed to be executing a dance of triumph for a moment, and then abruptly everything was still.

Mrs Hall was left almost in a fainting condition in Mr Hall's arms on the landing. It was with the greatest difficulty that Mr Hall and Millie, who had been roused by her scream of alarm, succeeded in getting her downstairs, and applying the restoratives customary in such cases.

"Tas sperits,' said Mrs Hall. 'I know 'tas sperits. I've read in papers of en. Tables and chairs leaping and dancing . . .'

'Take a drop more, Janny,' said Hall. ''Twill steady ye.'

'Lock him out,' said Mrs Hall. 'Don't let him come in again. I half guessed . . . I might ha' known. With them goggling eyes and bandaged head, and never going to church of a Sunday. And all they bottles—more'n it's right for any one to have. He's put the sperits into the furniture. . . . My good old furniture! 'Twas in that very chair my poor dear mother used to sit when I was a little girl. To think it should rise up against me now . . .'

'Just a drop more, Janny,' said Hall. 'Your nerves is all upset.'

They sent Millie across the street through the golden five o'clock sunshine to rouse up Mr Sandy Wadgers, the blacksmith.

Mr Hall's compliments, and the furniture upstairs was behaving most extraordinary. Would Mr Wadgers come round?

He was a knowing man, was Mr Wadgers, and very resourceful. He took quite a grave view of the case. 'Arm darmed if thet ent witchcraft,' was the view of Mr Sandy Wadgers. 'You warnt horseshoes* for such gentry as he.'

He came round greatly concerned. They wanted him to lead the way upstairs to the room; but he didn't seem to be in any hurry. He preferred to talk in the passage. Over the way Huxter's apprentice came out, and began taking down the shutters of the tobacco window. He was called over to join the discussion. Mr Huxter naturally followed over in the course of a few minutes. The Anglo–Saxon genius for parliamentary government asserted itself: there was a great deal of talk and no decisive action.

'Let's have the facts first,' insisted Mr Sandy Wadgers. 'Let's be sure we'd be acting perfectly right in bustin' that there door open. A door onbust is always open to bustin', but ye can't onbust a bust door once you've busted en.'

And suddenly and most wonderfully the door of the room upstairs opened of its own accord, and as they looked up in amazement, they saw descending the stairs the muffled figure of the stranger, staring more blackly and blankly than ever with those unreasonably large glass eyes of his. He came down stiffly and slowly, staring all the time; he walked across the passage, staring, then stopped.

'Look there!' he said, and their eyes followed the direction of his gloved finger, and saw a bottle of sarsaparilla hard by the cellar door. Then he entered the parlour, and suddenly, swiftly, viciously, slammed the door in their faces.

Not a word was spoken until the last echoes of the slam had died away. They stared at one another.

'Well, if that don't lick everything!' said Mr Wadgers, and left the alternative unsaid.

'I'd go in and ask'n 'bout it,' said Wadgers to Mr Hall. 'I'd d'mand an explanation.'

It took some time to bring the landlady's husband up to that pitch. At last he rapped, opened the door, and got as far as:

'Excuse me——'

'Go to the devil!' said the stranger in a tremendous voice, and 'Shut that door after you.'

So this brief interview terminated.

VII

THE stranger went into the little parlour of the 'Coach and Horses' about half-past five in the morning, and there he remained until near midday, the blinds down, the door shut, and none, after Hall's repulse, venturing near him.

All that time he must have fasted. Thrice he rang his bell, the third time furiously and continuously, but no one answered him. 'Him and his "Go to the devil," indeed!' said Mrs Hall. Presently came an imperfect rumour of the burglary at the Vicarage, and two and two were put together. Hall, assisted by Wadgers, went off to find Mr Shuckleforth, the magistrate, and take his advice. No one ventured upstairs. How the stranger occupied himself is unknown. Now and then he would stride violently up and down, and twice came an outburst of curses, a tearing of paper, and a violent smashing of bottles.

The little group of scared but curious people increased. Mrs Huxter came over; some gay young fellows resplendent in black, ready-made jackets and *piqué* paper ties*—for it was Whit Monday*—joined the group with confused and confusing interrogations. Young Archie Harker distinguished himself by going up the yard and trying to peep under the drawn blinds. He could see nothing, but gave reason for supposing that he did, and others of the Iping youth presently joined him.

It was the finest of all possible Whit Mondays, and down the village street stood a row of nearly a dozen booths, a shooting-gallery, and on the grass by the forge were three yellow and chocolate waggons, and some picturesque strangers of both sexes putting up a cocoanut shy. The gentlemen wore blue jerseys, the ladies white aprons and quite fashionable hats with heavy plumes. Woodyer, of the 'Purple Fawn,' and Mr Jaggers, the cobbler, who also sold second-hand ordinary bicycles,* were stretching a string of union jacks and royal ensigns, which had originally celebrated the first Victorian Jubilee,* across the road.

And inside in the artificial darkness of the parlour, into which only one thin jet of sunlight penetrated, the stranger, hungry we must suppose, and fearful, hidden in his uncomfortable hot wrappings, pored through his dark glasses upon his paper, or chinked his dirty little bottles, and occasionally swore savagely at the boys, audible, if invisible, outside the windows. In the corner by the fireplace lay the fragments of half a dozen smashed bottles, and a pungent twang of chlorine tainted the air. So much we know from what was heard at the time, and from what was subsequently seen in the room.

About noon he suddenly opened his parlour door and stood glaring fixedly at the three or four people in the bar. 'Mrs Hall,' he said. Somebody went sheepishly and called for Mrs Hall.

Mrs Hall appeared after an interval, a little short of breath, but all the fiercer for that. Hall was still out. She had deliberated over this scene, and she came holding a little tray with an unsettled bill upon it. 'Is it your bill you're wanting, sir?' she said.

'Why wasn't my breakfast laid? Why haven't you prepared my meals and answered my bell? Do you think I live without eating?'

'Why isn't my bill paid?' said Mrs Hall. 'That's what I want to know.'

'I told you three days ago I was awaiting a remittance——'

'I told you three days ago I wasn't going to await no remittances. You can't grumble if your breakfast waits a bit, if my bill's been waiting these five days, can you?'

The stranger swore briefly but vividly.

'Nar, nar!' from the bar.

'And I'd thank you kindly, sir, if you'd keep your swearing to yourself, sir,' said Mrs Hall.

The stranger stood looking more like an angry diving helmet than ever. It was universally felt in the bar that Mrs Hall had the better of him. His next words showed as much.

'Look here, my good woman——' he began.

'Don't "good woman" *me*,' said Mrs Hall.

'I've told you my remittance hasn't come.'

'Remittance, indeed!' said Mrs Hall.

'Still, I daresay in my pocket——'

'You told me three days ago that you hadn't anything but a sovereign's worth of silver upon you.'

'Well, I've found some more.'

''Ul-*lo*!' from the bar.

'I wonder where you found it?' said Mrs Hall.

That seemed to annoy the stranger very much. He stamped his foot. 'What do you mean?' he said.

'That I wonder where you found it,' said Mrs Hall. 'And before I take any bills, or get any breakfasts, or do any such things whatsoever, you got to tell me one or two things I don't understand, and what nobody don't understand, and what everybody is very anxious to understand. I want know what you been doing t'my chair upstairs, and I want know how 'tis your room was empty and how you got in again? Them as stops in this house comes in by the doors—that's the rule of this house, and that you *didn't* do, and what I want know is how you *did* come. And I want know——'

Suddenly the stranger raised his gloved hands clenched, stamped his foot, and said 'Stop!' with such extraordinary violence that he silenced her instantly.

'You don't understand,' he said, 'who I am or what I am. I'll show you. By heaven! I'll show you.' Then he put his open palm over his face and withdrew it. The centre of his face became a black cavity. 'Here,' he said. He stepped forward and handed Mrs Hall something which she, staring at his metamorphosed face, accepted automatically. Then, when she saw what it was, she screamed loudly, dropped it, and staggered back. The nose—it was the stranger's nose! pink and shining—rolled on the floor with a sound of hollow cardboard.

Then he removed his spectacles, and every one in the bar gasped. He took off his hat, and with a violent gesture tore at his whiskers and bandages. For a moment they resisted him. A flash of horrible anticipation passed through the bar. 'Oh, my Gard!' said some one. Then off they came.

It was worse than anything. Mrs Hall, standing open-mouthed and horror-struck, shrieked at what she saw, and made for the door of the house. Every one began to move. They were prepared for scars, disfigurement, tangible horrors—but *nothing!* The bandages and false hair flew across the passage into the bar, making a hobbledehoy jump to avoid them. Every one tumbled on every one else down the steps. For the man who stood there shouting some incoherent explanation was a solid, gesticulating figure up to the coat-collar of him, and then—nothingness, no visible thing at all!

People down the village heard shouts and shrieks, and looking up the street saw the 'Coach and Horses' violently firing out its humanity. They saw Mrs Hall fall down and Mr Teddy Henfrey jump to avoid tumbling over her, and then they heard the frightful screams of Millie, who, emerging suddenly from the kitchen at the noise of the tumult had come upon the headless stranger from behind. These ceased suddenly.

Forthwith every one all the way down the street—the sweetstuff-seller, cocoanut-shy proprietor and his assistant, the swing man, little boys and girls, rustic dandies, smart wenches, smocked elders, and aproned gipsies—began running towards the inn, and in a miraculously short space of time a crowd of perhaps forty people, and rapidly increasing, swayed, and hooted, and inquired, and exclaimed, and suggested in front of Mrs Hall's establishment. Everybody seemed eager to talk at once, and the result was Babel. A small group supported Mrs Hall, who was picked up in a state of collapse. There was a confusion, and the incredible evidence of a vociferous eye-witness. 'O Bogie.' 'What's he been doin', then?' 'Ain't hurt the girl, 'as 'e?' 'Run at en with a knife, I believe.' 'No—'ed, I tell ye. I don't mean no manner of speaking, I mean Marn 'ithout a 'Ed!' 'Narnsense! 'tis some conjuring trick.' 'Fetched off 'is wrappings, 'e did——'

In its struggles to see in through the open door the crowd formed itself into a struggling wedge, with the more adventurous apex nearest the inn. 'He stood for a moment, I heerd the gal scream, and he turned. I saw her skirts whisk, and he went after her. Didn't take ten seconds. Back he comes with a knife in his hand and a loaf, stood just as if he was staring. Not a moment ago. Went in that there door. I tell 'e, 'e ain't gart no 'ed 'tall. You just missed en——'

There was a disturbance behind, and the speaker stopped to step aside for a little procession that was marching very resolutely towards the house; first Mr Hall, very red and determined, then Mr Bobby Jaffers, the village constable, and then the wary Mr Wadgers. They had come now armed with a warrant.

People shouted conflicting information of the recent circumstances. ''Ed or no 'ed,' said Jaffers. 'I got to 'rest en, and 'rest en I *will*.'

Mr Hall marched up the steps, marched straight to the door of the parlour and found it open. 'Constable,' he said, 'do your duty.'

Jaffers marched in, Hall next, Wadgers last. They saw in the dim light the headless figure facing them, with a gnawed crust of bread in one gloved hand and a chunk of cheese in the other.

'That's him,' said Hall.

'What the devil's this?' came in a tone of angry expostulation from above the collar of the figure.

'You're a darmed rum customer, mister,' said Mr Jaffers. 'But 'ed or no 'ed, the warrant says "body," and duty's duty——'

'Keep off!' said the figure, starting back.

Abruptly he whipped down the bread and cheese, and Mr Hall just grasped the knife on the table in time to save it. Off came the stranger's left glove, and was slapped in Jaffers' face. In another moment Jaffers, cutting short some statement concerning a warrant, had gripped him by the handless wrist, and caught his invisible throat. He got a sound-ing* kick on the shin that made him shout, but he kept his grip. Hall sent the knife sliding along the table to Wadgers, who acted as goal-keeper for the offensive, so to speak, and then stepped forward as Jaffers and the stranger swayed and staggered towards him, clutching and hitting in. A chair stood in the way, and went aside with a crash as they came down together.

'Get the feet,' said Jaffers between his teeth.

Mr Hall, endeavouring to act on instructions, received a sounding kick in the ribs that disposed of him for a moment; and Mr Wadgers, seeing the decapitated stranger had rolled over and got the upper side of Jaffers, retreated towards the door, knife in hand, and so collided with Mr Huxter and the Sidderbridge carter coming to the rescue of law and order. At the same moment down came three or four bottles from the chiffonnier and shot a web of pungency into the air of the room.

'I'll surrender,' cried the stranger, though he had Jaffers down, and in another moment he stood up panting, a strange figure, headless and handless—for he had pulled off his right glove now as well as his left. 'It's no good,' he said, as if sobbing for breath.

It was the strangest thing in the world to hear that voice coming as if out of empty space, but the Sussex peasants are perhaps the most matter-of-fact people under the sun. Jaffers got up also, and produced a pair of handcuffs. Then he stared.

'I say!' said Jaffers, brought up short by a dim realisation of the incon-gruity of the whole business. 'Darm it! Can't use 'em as I can see.'

The stranger ran his arm down his waistcoat, and, as if by a mir-acle, the buttons to which his empty sleeve pointed became undone. Then he said something about his shin, and stooped down. He seemed to be fumbling with his shoes and socks.

'Why!' said Huxter suddenly, 'that's not a man at all. It's just empty clothes. Look! You can see down his collar and the linings of his clothes. I could put my arm——'

He extended his hand; it seemed to meet something in mid-air, and he drew it back with a sharp exclamation. 'I wish you'd keep your fingers out of my eye,' said the aerial voice in a tone of savage expostulation. 'The fact is, I'm all here—head, hands, legs, and all the rest of it, but it happens I'm invisible. It's a confounded nuisance, but I am. That's no reason why I should be poked to pieces by every stupid bumpkin in Iping, is it?'

The suit of clothes, now all unbuttoned and hanging loosely upon its unseen supports, stood up, arms akimbo.

Several other of the men folk had now entered the room, so that it was closely crowded. 'Invisible, eh?' said Huxter, ignoring the stranger's abuse. 'Who ever heard the likes of that?'

'It's strange, perhaps, but it's not a crime. Why am I assaulted by a policeman in this fashion——'

'Ah! that's a different matter,' said Jaffers. 'No doubt you are a bit difficult to see in this light, but I got a warrant and it's all correct. What I'm after ain't no invisibility, it's burglary. There's a house been broke into, and money took.'

'Well?'

'And circumstances certainly point——'

'Stuff and nonsense!' said the Invisible Man.

'I hope so, sir. But I've got my instructions——'

'Well,' said the stranger, 'I'll come. I'll *come*. But no handcuffs.'

'It's the regular thing,' said Jaffers.

'No handcuffs,' stipulated the stranger.

'Pardon me,' said Jaffers.

Abruptly the figure sat down, and before any one could realise what was being done, the slippers, socks, and trousers had been kicked off under the table. Then he sprang up again and flung off his coat.

'Here, stop that,' said Jaffers, suddenly realising what was happening. He gripped the waistcoat, it struggled, and the shirt slipped out of it and left it limp and empty in his hand. 'Hold him!' said Jaffers loudly. 'Once he gets the things off——'

'Hold him!' cried every one, and there was a rush at the fluttering white shirt, which was now all that was visible of the stranger.

The shirt sleeve planted a shrewd blow in Hall's face that stopped his open-armed advance and sent him backward into old Toothsome, the sexton, and in another moment the garment was lifted up, and became convulsed and vacantly flapping about the arms, even as a shirt that is being thrust off over a man's head. Jaffers clutched at it, and only helped to pull it off. He was struck in the mouth out of the air, and incontinently drew his truncheon and smote Teddy Henfrey savagely upon the crown of his head.

'Look out!' said everybody, fencing at random and hitting at nothing. 'Hold him! Shut the door! Don't let him loose. I got something! Here he is!' A perfect Babel of noises they made. Everybody, it seemed, was being hit all at once, and Sandy Wadgers, knowing as ever, and his wits sharpened by a frightful blow on the nose, reopened the door and led the rout. The others, following incontinently, were jammed for a moment in the corner by the doorway. The hitting continued. Phipps, the Unitarian, had a front tooth broken, and Henfrey was injured in the cartilage of his ear. Jaffers was struck under the jaw, and, turning, caught at something that intervened between him and Huxter in the *mêlée*, and prevented their coming together. He felt a muscular chest, and in another moment the whole mass of struggling, excited men shot out into the crowded hall.

'I got him!' shouted Jaffers, choking and reeling through them all, and wrestling with purple face and swelling veins against his unseen enemy.

Men staggered right and left as the extraordinary conflict swayed swiftly towards the house door and went spinning down the half-dozen steps of the inn. Jaffers cried in a strangled voice, holding tight nevertheless, and making play with his knee, spun round and fell heavily undermost with his head on the gravel. Only then did his fingers relax.

There were excited cries of 'Hold him!' 'Invisible!' and so forth, and a young fellow, a stranger in the place, whose name did not come to light, rushed in at once, caught something, missed his hold, and fell over the constable's prostrate body. Half-way across the road a woman screamed as something pushed by her, a dog, kicked apparently, yelped and ran howling into Huxter's yard, and with that the transit of the Invisible Man was accomplished. For a space people stood amazed and gesticulating, and then came panic, and scattered them abroad through the village as a gust scatters dead leaves. But Jaffers lay quite still, face upward and knees bent, at the foot of the steps of the inn.

VIII

IN TRANSIT

THE eighth chapter is exceedingly brief, and relates that Gibbins, the amateur naturalist of the district, while lying out on the spacious open downs without a soul within a couple of miles of him as he thought, and almost dozing, heard close to him the sound as of a man coughing, sneezing, and then swearing savagely to himself, and looking, beheld nothing. Yet the voice was indisputable. It continued to swear with that breadth and variety that distinguishes the swearing of a cultivated man. It grew to a climax, diminished again and died away in the distance, going, as it seemed to him, in the direction of Adderdean. It lifted to a spasmodic sneeze, and ended. Gibbins had heard nothing of the morning's occurrences, but the phenomenon was so striking and disturbing, that his philosophical tranquillity vanished; he got up hastily and hurried down the steepness of the hill, towards the village, as fast as he could go.

IX

You must picture Mr Thomas Marvel as a person of copious, flexible visage, a nose of cylindrical protrusion, a liquorish, ample, fluctuating mouth, and a beard of bristling eccentricity. His figure inclined to *embonpoint*,* his short limbs accentuated this inclination. He wore a furry silk hat, and the frequent substitution of twine and shoe-laces for buttons, apparent at critical points of his costume, marked a man essentially bachelor.

Mr Thomas Marvel was sitting with his feet in a ditch by the roadside over the down towards Adderdean, about a mile and a half out of Iping. His feet, save for socks of irregular open-work, were bare, his big toes were broad, and pricked like the ears of a watchful dog. In a leisurely manner—he did everything in a leisurely manner—he was contemplating trying on a pair of boots. They were the soundest boots he had come across for a long time, but too large for him, whereas the ones he had were, in dry weather, a very comfortable fit, but too thin soled for damp. Mr Thomas Marvel hated roomy boots, but then he hated damp. He had never properly thought out which he hated most, and it was a pleasant day, and there was nothing better to do. So he put the four boots in a graceful group on the turf, and looked at them. And seeing them there among the grass and springing agrimony,* it suddenly occurred to him that both pairs were exceedingly ugly to see. He was not at all startled by a voice behind him.

'They're boots, anyhow,' said the Voice.

'They are—Charity Boots,' said Mr Thomas Marvel with his head on one side regarding them distastefully; 'and which is the ugliest pair in the whole blessed universe, I'm darned if I know!'

'H'm,' said the Voice.

'I've worn worse—in fact, I've worn none. But none so owdacious ugly—if you'll allow the expression. I've been cadging boots—in particular—for days, because I was sick of *them*. They're sound enough, of course. But a gentleman on tramp sees such a thundering lot of his boots. And if you'll believe me, I've raised nothing in the whole blessed county, try as I would, but *them*. Look at 'em! And a good county for boots, too, in a general way. But it's just my promiscuous luck. I've got my boots in this county ten years or more. And then they treat you like this.'

'It's a beast of a county,' said the Voice, 'and pigs for people.'

'Ain't it?' said Mr Thomas Marvel. 'Lord! But them boots! It beats it.'

He turned his head over his shoulder to the right, to look at the boots of his interlocutor, with a view to comparisons, and lo! where the boots of his interlocutor should have been were neither legs nor boots. He turned his head over his shoulder to the left, and there also were neither legs nor boots. He was irradiated by the dawn of a great amazement. 'Where *are* yer?' said Mr Thomas Marvel over his shoulder, and coming on all fours. He saw a stretch of empty down, with the wind swaying the remote green-pointed furze bushes.

'Am I drunk?' said Mr Marvel. 'Have I had visions? Was I talking to myself? What the——'

'Don't be alarmed,' said a Voice.

'None of your ventriloquising *me*,' said Mr Thomas Marvel, rising sharply to his feet. 'Where *are* yer? Alarmed, indeed!'

'Don't be alarmed,' repeated the Voice.

'*You'll* be alarmed in a minute, you silly fool,' said Mr Thomas Marvel. 'Where *are* yer? Lemme get my mark on yer . . .

'Are yer *buried*?' said Mr Thomas Marvel after an interval.

There was no answer. Mr Thomas Marvel stood bootless and amazed, his jacket nearly thrown off.

'Peewit,' said a peewit very remote.

'Peewit, indeed!' said Mr Thomas Marvel. 'This ain't no time for foolery.' The down was desolate east and west, north and south; the road, with its shallow ditches and white bordering stakes, ran smooth and empty north and south, and, save for that peewit, the blue sky was empty too. 'So help me,' said Mr Thomas Marvel, shuffling his coat on to his shoulders again. 'It's the drink. I might ha' known.'

'It's not the drink,' said the Voice. 'You keep your nerves steady.'

'Ow!' said Mr Marvel, and his face grew white amidst its patches. 'It's the drink,' his lips repeated noiselessly. He remained staring about him, rotating slowly backwards. 'I could have *swore* I heard a voice,' he whispered.

'Of course you did.'

'It's there again,' said Mr Marvel, closing his eyes and clasping his hand on his brow with a tragic gesture. He was suddenly taken by the collar and shaken violently, and left more dazed than ever. 'Don't be a fool!' said the Voice.

'I'm—off—my—blooming—chump!' said Mr Marvel. 'It's no good. It's fretting about them blarsted boots. I'm off my blessed, blooming chump. Or it's spirits!'

'Neither one thing nor the other,' said the Voice. 'Listen!'

'Chump!' said Mr Marvel.

'One minute,' said the Voice penetratingly, tremulous with self-control.

'Well?' said Mr Thomas Marvel, with a strange feeling of having been dug in the chest by a finger.

'You think I'm just imagination—just imagination?'

'What else *can* you be?' said Mr Thomas Marvel, rubbing the back of his neck.

'Very well,' said the Voice in a tone of relief. 'Then I'm going to throw flints at you till you think differently.'

'But where *are* yer?'

The Voice made no answer. Whizz came a flint, apparently out of the air, and missed Mr Marvel's shoulder by a hair's breadth. Mr Marvel, turning, saw a flint jerk up into the air, trace a complicated path, hang for a moment, and then fall at his feet with almost invisible rapidity. He was too amazed to dodge. Whizz it came, and ricocheted from a bare toe into the ditch. Mr Thomas Marvel jumped a foot, and howled aloud. Then he started to run, tripped over an unseen obstacle, and came head over heels into a sitting position.

'*Now*,' said the Voice, as a third stone curved upward and hung in the air above the tramp, 'am I imagination?'

Mr Marvel, by way of reply, struggled to his feet, and was immediately rolled over again. He lay quiet for a moment.

'If you struggle any more,' said the Voice, 'I shall throw the flint at your head.'

'It's a fair do,' said Mr Thomas Marvel, sitting up, taking his wounded toe in hand, and fixing his eye on the third missile. 'I don't understand it. Stones flinging themselves. Stones talking. Put yourself down. Rot away. I'm done.'

The third flint fell.

'It's very simple,' said the Voice. 'I'm an invisible man.'

'Tell us something I don't know,' said Mr Marvel, gasping with pain. 'Where you've hid—how you do it—I *don't* know. I'm beat.'

'That's all,' said the Voice. 'I'm invisible. That's what I want you to understand.'

'Any one could see that. There is no need for you to be so confounded impatient, mister. *Now*, then. Give us a notion. How are you hid?'

'I'm invisible. That's the great point. And what I want you to understand is this——'

'But whereabouts?' interrupted Mr Marvel.

'Here—six yards in front of you.'

'Oh, *come!* I ain't blind. You'll be telling me next you're just thin air. I'm not one of your ignorant tramps——'

'Yes. I am—thin air. You're looking through me.'

'What! Ain't there any stuff to you? *Vox et**—what is it?—jabber. Is it that?'

'I am just a human being—solid, needing food and drink, needing covering, too. . . . But I'm invisible. You see? Invisible. Simple idea. Invisible.'

'What, real like?'

'Yes, real.'

'Let's have a hand of you,' said Marvel, 'if you *are* real. It won't be so darn out-of-the-way like, then——

'*Lord!*' he said, 'how you made me jump!—gripping me like that!'

He felt the hand that had closed round his wrist with his disengaged fingers, and his fingers went timorously up the arm, patted a muscular chest, and explored a bearded face. Marvel's face was astonishment.

'I'm dashed!' he said. 'If this don't beat cock-fighting! Most remarkable!—And there I can see a rabbit clean through you arf a mile away! Not a bit of you visible—except——'

He scrutinised the apparently empty space keenly. 'You 'aven't been eatin' bread and cheese?' he asked, holding the invisible arm.

'You are quite right. It's not assimilated into the system.'

'Ah!' said Mr Marvel. 'Sort of ghostly, though.'

'Of course all this isn't half so wonderful as you think.'

'It's quite wonderful enough for *my* modest wants,' said Mr Thomas Marvel. 'Howjer manage it? How the dooce* is it done?'

'It's too long a story. And besides——'

'I tell you, the whole business fair beats me,' said Mr Marvel.

'What I want to say at present is this: I need help. I have come to that. I came upon you suddenly. I was wandering, mad with rage, naked, impotent. I could have murdered. . . . And I saw you——'

'*Lord!*' said Mr Marvel.

'I came up behind you—hesitated—went on.'

Mr Marvel's expression was eloquent.

'Then stopped. "Here," I said, "is an out-cast like myself. This is the man for me." So I turned back and came to you. You. And——'

'*Lord!*' said Mr Marvel. 'But I'm all in a dizzy. May I ask: How is it?—and what you may be requiring in the way of help? Invisible!'

'I want you to help me get clothes and shelter, and then with other things. I've left them long enough. If you won't—well! . . . But you *will—must.*'

'Look here,' said Mr Marvel. 'I'm too flabbergasted. Don't knock me about any more. And leave me go. I must get steady a bit. And you've pretty near broken my toe. It's all so unreasonable. Empty downs, empty sky. Nothing visible for miles except the bosom of Nature. And then comes a voice. A voice out of heaven!* And stones. And a fist. Lord!'

'Pull yourself together,' said the Voice, 'for you have to do the job I've chosen for you.'

Mr Marvel blew out his cheeks, and his eyes were round.

'I've chosen you,' said the Voice. 'You are the only man, except some of those fools down there, who knows there is such a thing as an Invisible Man. You have to be my helper. Help me—and I will do great things for you. An Invisible Man is a man of power.' He stopped for a moment to sneeze violently.

'But if you betray me,' he said, 'if you fail to do as I direct you——'

He paused and tapped Mr Marvel's shoulder smartly. Mr Marvel gave a yelp of terror at the touch. 'I don't want to betray you,' said Mr Marvel, edging away from the direction of the fingers. 'Don't you go a-thinking that, whatever you do. All I want to do is to help you—just tell me what I got to do. (Lord!) Whatever you want done, that I'm most willing to do.'

MR MARVEL'S VISIT TO IPING

AFTER the first gusty panic had spent itself Iping became argumentative. Scepticism suddenly reared its head—rather nervous scepticism, not at all assured of its back, but scepticism nevertheless. It is so much easier not to believe in an Invisible Man, and those who had actually seen him dissolve into air or felt the strength of his arm could be counted on the fingers of two hands. And of these witnesses Mr Wadgers was presently missing, having retired impregnably behind the bolts and bars of his own house, and Jaffers was lying stunned in the parlour of the 'Coach and Horses.' Great and strange ideas transcending experience often have less effect upon men and women than smaller, more tangible considerations. Iping was gay with bunting, and everybody was in gala dress. Whit Monday had been looked forward to for a month or more. By the afternoon even those who believed in the Unseen were beginning to resume their little amusements in a tentative fashion, on the supposition that he had quite gone away, and with the sceptics he was already a jest. But people—sceptics and believers alike—were remarkably sociable all that day.

Haysman's meadow was gay with a tent, in which Mrs Bunting and other ladies were preparing tea, while without the Sunday-school children ran races and played games under the noisy guidance of the curate and the Misses Cuss and Sackbut. No doubt there was a slight uneasiness in the air, but people for the most part had the sense to conceal whatever imaginative qualms they experienced. On the village green an inclined string, down which, clinging the while to a pulley-swung handle, one could be hurled violently against a sack at the other end, came in for considerable favour among the adolescent, as also did the swings and the cocoanut-shies. There was also promenading, and the steam organ attached to a small roundabout filled the air with a pungent flavour of oil and with equally pungent music. Members of the club, who had attended church in the morning, were splendid in badges of pink and green, and some of the gayer minded had also adorned their bowler hats with brilliant coloured favours of ribbon. Old Fletcher, whose conceptions of holiday-making were severe, was visible through the jasmine about his window or through the open door (whichever way you chose to look) poised delicately on a plank supported on two chairs, and whitewashing the ceiling of his front room.

About four o'clock a stranger entered the village from the direction of the downs. He was a short, stout person in an extraordinarily shabby top hat, and he appeared to be very much out of breath. His cheeks were alternately limp and tightly puffed. His mottled face was apprehensive, and he moved with a sort of reluctant alacrity. He turned the corner by the church and directed his way to the 'Coach and Horses.' Among others, old Fletcher remembers seeing him, and indeed the old gentleman was so struck by his peculiar agitation that he inadvertently allowed a quantity of whitewash to run down the brush into the sleeve of his coat while regarding him.

This stranger, to the perceptions of the proprietor of the cocoanut-shy, appeared to be talking to himself, and Mr Huxter remarked the same thing. He stopped at the foot of the 'Coach and Horses' steps, and, according to Mr Huxter, appeared to undergo a severe internal struggle before he could induce himself to enter the house. Finally he marched up the steps, and was seen by Mr Huxter to turn to the left and open the door of the parlour. Mr Huxter heard voices from within the room and from the bar apprising the man of his error.

'That room's private!' said Hall, and the stranger shut the door clumsily and went into the bar.

In the course of a few minutes he reappeared, wiping his lips with the back of his hand, with an air of quiet satisfaction that somehow impressed Mr Huxter as assumed. He stood looking about him for some moments, and then Mr Huxter saw him walk in an oddly furtive manner towards the gates of the yard, upon which the parlour window opened. The stranger, after some hesitation, leant against one of the gate-posts, produced a short clay pipe, and prepared to fill it. His fingers trembled while doing so. He lit it clumsily, and, folding his arms, began to smoke in a languid attitude, an attitude which his occasional quick glances up the yard altogether belied.

All this Mr Huxter saw over the canisters* of the tobacco window, and the singularity of the man's behaviour prompted him to maintain his observation.

Presently the stranger stood up abruptly and put his pipe in his pocket. Then he vanished into the yard. Forthwith Mr Huxter, conceiving he was witness of some petty larceny, leapt round his counter and ran out into the road to intercept the thief. As he did so, Mr Marvel reappeared, his hat askew, a big bundle in a blue tablecloth in one hand, and three books tied together—as it proved afterwards with the vicar's braces—in the other. Directly he saw Huxter he gave a sort of gasp, and turning sharply to the left, began to run. 'Stop thief!' cried Huxter, and set off after him.

Mr Huxter's sensations were vivid but brief. He saw the man just before him, and sprinting briskly for the church corner and the down road. He saw the village flags and festivities beyond, and only a face or two turned towards him. He bawled 'Stop thief' again, and set off gallantly. He had hardly gone ten strides before his shin was caught in some mysterious fashion, and he was no longer running but flying with incredible velocity through the air. He saw the ground suddenly close to his head. The world seemed to splash into a million whirling specks of light, and 'subsequent proceedings interested him no more.'*

Now, in order to clearly understand what had happened in the inn, it is necessary to go back to the moment when Mr Marvel first came into view of Mr Huxter's window.

At that precise moment Mr Cuss and Mr Bunting were in the parlour. They were seriously investigating the strange occurrences of the morning, and were, with Mr Hall's permission, making a thorough examination of the Invisible Man's belongings. Jaffers had partially recovered from his fall and had gone home in the charge of his sympathetic friends. The stranger's scattered garments had been removed by Mrs Hall, and the room tidied up. And on the table under the window, where the stranger had been wont to work, Cuss had hit almost at once on three big books in manuscript labelled 'Diary.'

'Diary!' said Cuss, putting the three books on the table. 'Now, at any rate, we shall learn something.' The vicar stood with his hands on the table.

'Diary,' repeated Cuss, sitting down, putting two volumes to support the third, and opening it. 'H'm—no name on the fly leaf. Bother! . . . Cypher. And figures.'

The vicar came round to look over his shoulder.

Cuss turned the pages over with a face suddenly disappointed. 'I'm—dear me! It's all cypher, Bunting.'

'There are no diagrams?' asked Mr Bunting. 'No illustrations throwing light——'

'See for yourself,' said Mr Cuss. 'Some of it's mathematical, and some of it's Russian or some such language (to judge by the letters), and some of it's Greek. Now the Greek I thought *you*——'

'Of course,' said Mr Bunting, taking out and wiping his spectacles, and feeling suddenly very uncomfortable—for he had no Greek left in his mind worth talking about. 'Yes—the Greek, of course, may furnish a clue.'

'I'll find you a place.'

'I'd rather glance through the volumes first,' said Mr Bunting, still wiping. 'A general impression first, Cuss, and *then*, you know, we can go looking for clues.'

He coughed, put on his glasses, arranged them fastidiously, coughed again, and wished something would happen to avert the seemingly inevitable exposure. Then he took the volume Cuss handed him in a leisurely manner. And then something did happen.

The door opened suddenly.

Both men started violently, looked round, and were relieved to see a sporadically rosy face beneath a furry silk hat. 'Tap?'* asked the face, and stood staring.

'No,' said both gentlemen at once.

'Over the other side, my man,' said Mr Bunting. 'And please shut that door,' said Mr Cuss irritably.

'All right,' said the intruder, as it seemed in a low voice, curiously different from the huskiness of its first inquiry. 'Right you are,' said the intruder in the former voice. 'Stand clear,' and he vanished and closed the door.

'A sailor, I should judge,' said Mr Bunting. 'Amusing fellows they are. Stand clear, indeed. A nautical term, referring to his getting back out of the room, I suppose.'

'I daresay so,' said Cuss. 'My nerves are all loose to-day. It quite made me jump—the door opening like that.'

Mr Bunting smiled as if he had not jumped. 'And now,' he said with a sigh, 'these books.'

'One minute,' said Cuss, and went and locked the door. 'Now I think we are safe from interruption.'

Some one sniffed as he did so.

'One thing is indisputable,' said Bunting, drawing up a chair next to that of Cuss. 'There certainly have been very strange things happen in Iping during the last few days—very strange. I cannot, of course, believe in this absurd invisibility story——'

'It's incredible,' said Cuss—'incredible. But the fact remains that I saw—I certainly saw right down his sleeve——'

'But did you—are you sure . . . ? Suppose a mirror, for instance . . . Hallucinations are so easily produced. I don't know if you have ever seen a really good conjuror——'

'I won't argue again,' said Cuss. 'We've thrashed that out, Bunting. And just now there's these books . . . Ah! here's some of what I take to be Greek! Greek letters, certainly.'

He pointed to the middle of the page. Mr Bunting flushed slightly, and brought his face nearer, apparently finding some difficulty with his glasses. The little man's Greek was of the flimsiest, and he firmly believed that every one outside the Church credited him with a knowledge of Greek and Hebrew originals. And now—Should he confess? Should he vamp?* Suddenly he became aware of a strange feeling at the nape of his neck. He tried to move his head, and encountered an immovable resistance.

The feeling was a curious pressure—the grip of a heavy, firm hand, and it bore his chin irresistibly to the table. '*Don't move, little men,*' whispered a voice, '*or I'll brain you both!*'

He looked into the face of Cuss, close to his own, and saw a horrified reflection of his own sickly astonishment.

'I'm sorry to handle you roughly,' said the Voice, 'but it's unavoidable.

'Since when did you learn to pry into an investigator's private memoranda?' said the Voice, and two chins struck the table simultaneously, and two sets of teeth rattled.

'Since when did you learn to invade the private rooms of a man in misfortune?' and the concussion was repeated.

'Where have they put my clothes?

'Listen,' said the Voice. 'The windows are fastened, and I've taken the key out of the door. I am a fairly strong man, and I have the poker handy—besides being invisible. There's not the slightest doubt that I could kill you both and get away quite easily if I wanted to—do you understand? Very well. If I let you go, will you promise not to try any nonsense, and do what I tell you?'

The vicar and the doctor looked at one another, and the doctor pulled a face. 'Yes,' said Mr Bunting, and the doctor repeated it. Then the pressure on the necks relaxed, and the doctor and vicar sat up, both very red in the face, and wriggling their heads.

'Please keep sitting where you are,' said the Invisible Man. 'Here's the poker, you see.

'When I came into this room,' continued the Invisible Man, after presenting the poker to the tip of the nose of each of his visitors, 'I did not expect to find it occupied; and I expected to find, in addition to my books of memoranda, an outfit of clothing. Where is it? No—don't rise. I can see it's gone. Now just at present, though the days are quite warm enough for an invisible man to run about stark—the evenings are chilly. I want clothing—and other accommodation. And I must also have those three books.'

THE INVISIBLE MAN LOSES HIS TEMPER

IT is unavoidable that at this point the narrative should break off again, for a certain very painful reason that will presently be apparent. And while these things were going on in the parlour, and while Mr Huxter was watching Mr Marvel smoking his pipe against the gate, not a dozen yards away were Mr Hall and Teddy Henfrey discussing in a state of cloudy puzzlement the one Iping topic.

Suddenly there came a violent thud against the door of the parlour, a sharp cry, and then—silence.

'*Hul*-lo!' said Teddy Henfrey.

'Hul-*lo!*' from the tap.

Mr Hall took things in slowly but surely. 'That ain't right,' he said, and came round from behind the bar towards the parlour door.

He and Teddy approached the door together, with intent faces. Their eyes considered. 'Summat wrong,' said Hall, and Henfrey nodded agreement. Whiffs of an unpleasant chemical odour met them, and there was a muffled sound of conversation, very rapid and subdued.

'You all raight thur?' asked Hall, rapping.

The muttered conversation ceased abruptly, for a moment silence, then the conversation was resumed in hissing whispers, then a sharp cry of 'No! no you don't!' There came a sudden motion and the oversetting of a chair, a brief struggle. Silence again.

'What the dooce!' exclaimed Henfrey *sotto voce*.

'You—all—raight—thur?' asked Mr Hall sharply again.

The vicar's voice answered with a curious jerking intonation. 'Quite ri-ight. Please don't—interrupt.'

'Odd!' said Mr Henfrey.

'Odd!' said Mr Hall.

'Says, "Don't interrupt," ' said Henfrey.

'I heerd'n,' said Hall.

'And a sniff,' said Henfrey.

They remained listening. The conversation was rapid and subdued. 'I *can't*,' said Mr Bunting, his voice rising; 'I tell you, sir, I *will* not.'

'What was that?' asked Henfrey.

'Says he wi' nart,' said Hall. 'Warn't speakin' to us, wuz he?'

'Disgraceful!' said Mr Bunting within.

'"Disgraceful,"' said Mr Henfrey. 'I heard it—*distinct*.'

'Who's that speaking now?' asked Henfrey.

'Mr Cuss, I s'pose,' said Hall. 'Can you hear—anything?'

Silence. The sounds within indistinct and perplexing.

'Sounds like throwing the tablecloth about,' said Hall.

Mrs Hall appeared behind the bar. Hall made gestures of silence and invitation. This roused Mrs Hall's wifely opposition.

'What yer listenin' there for, Hall?' she asked. 'Ain't you nothin' better to do—busy day like this?'

Hall tried to convey everything by grimaces and dumb show, but Mrs Hall was obdurate. She raised her voice. So Hall and Henfrey, rather crestfallen, tiptoed back to the bar, gesticulating, to explain to her.

At first she refused to see anything in what they had heard at all. Then she insisted on Hall keeping silence, while Henfrey told her his story. She was inclined to think the whole business nonsense— perhaps they were just moving the furniture about.

'I heerd'n say "disgraceful"; *that* I did,' said Hall.

'*I* heard that, Mis' Hall,' said Henfrey.

'Like as not,' began Mrs Hall.

'Hsh!' said Mr Teddy Henfrey. 'Didn't I hear the window?'

'What window?' asked Mrs Hall.

'Parlour window,' said Henfrey.

Every one stood listening intently. Mrs Hall's eyes, directed straight before her, saw, without seeing, the brilliant oblong of the inn door, the road, white and vivid, and Huxter's shop-front blistering in the June sun. Abruptly Huxter's door opened, and Huxter appeared, eyes staring with excitement, arms gesticulating.

'*Yap!*' cried Huxter. 'Stop thief!' and he ran obliquely across the oblong towards the yard gates and vanished.

Simultaneously came a tumult from the parlour, and a sound of windows being closed.

Hall, Henfrey, and the human contents of the tap rushed out at once pell-mell into the street. They saw some one whisk round the corner towards the down road, and Mr Huxter executing a compli- cated leap in the air that ended on his face and shoulder. Down the street people were standing astonished or running towards them.

Mr Huxter was stunned. Henfrey stopped to discover this, but Hall and the two labourers from the tap rushed at once to the corner, shouting incoherent things, and saw Mr Marvel vanishing by the corner of the church wall. They appear to have jumped to the impossible conclusion that this was the Invisible Man suddenly become visible, and set off at once along the lane in pursuit. But Hall had hardly run a dozen yards before he gave a loud shout of astonishment and went flying headlong sideways, clutching one of the labourers and bringing him to the ground. He had been charged just as one charges a man at football. The second labourer came round in a circle, stared, and conceiving that Hall had tumbled over of his own accord, turned to resume the pursuit, only to be tripped by the ankle just as Huxter had been. Then as the first labourer struggled to his feet he was knocked sideways by a blow that might have felled an ox.

As he went down, the rush from the direction of the village green came round the corner. The first to appear was the proprietor of the cocoanut-shy, a burly man in a blue jersey. He was astonished to see the lane empty save for three men sprawling absurdly on the ground. And then something happened to his rear-most foot, and he went headlong and rolled sideways just in time to snare the feet of his brother and partner, following headlong. The two were then kicked, knelt on, fallen over, and cursed by quite a number of over-hasty people.

Now when Hall and Henfrey and the labourers ran out of the house, Mrs Hall, who had been disciplined by years of experience, remained in the bar next the till. And suddenly the parlour door was opened, and Mr Cuss appeared, and, without glancing at her, rushed at once down the steps towards the corner. 'Hold him!' he cried, 'don't let him drop that parcel! You can see him so long as he holds the parcel.'

He knew nothing of the existence of Marvel; for the Invisible Man had handed over the books and bundle in the yard. The face of Mr Cuss was angry and resolute, but his costume was defective—a sort of limp, white kilt that could only have passed muster in Greece. 'Hold him!' he bawled. 'He's got my trousers!—and every stitch of the vicar's clothes!'

''Tend to him in a minute!' he cried to Henfrey as he passed the prostrate Huxter, and coming round the corner to join the tumult was promptly knocked off his feet into an indecorous sprawl. Somebody in full flight trod heavily on his finger. He yelled, struggled to regain his feet, was knocked against and thrown on all-fours again, and became aware that he was involved not in a capture but in a rout. Every one was running back to the village. He rose again, and was hit severely behind the ear. He staggered, and set off back to the 'Coach and Horses' forthwith, leaping over the deserted Huxter, who was now sitting up, on his way.

Behind him, as he was half-way up the inn steps, he heard a sudden yell of rage, rising sharply out of the confusion of cries, and a sounding smack in some one's face. He recognised the voice as that of the Invisible Man, and the note was that of a man suddenly infuriated by a painful blow.

In another moment Mr Cuss was back in the parlour.

'He's coming back, Bunting!' he said, rushing in. 'Save yourself!'

Mr Bunting was standing in the window, engaged in an attempt to clothe himself in the hearthrug and a *West Surrey Gazette.*

'Who's coming?' he said, so startled that his costume narrowly escaped disintegration.

'Invisible Man!' said Cuss, and rushed to the window. 'We'd better clear out from here! He's fighting mad! Mad!'

In another moment he was out in the yard.

'Good heavens!' said Mr Bunting, hesitating between two horrible alternatives. He heard a frightful struggle in the passage of the inn, and his decision was made. He clambered out of the window, adjusted his costume hastily, and fled up the village as fast as his fat little legs would carry him.

*   *   *   *

From the moment when the Invisible Man screamed with rage and Mr Bunting made his memorable flight up the village, it became impossible to give a consecutive account of affairs in Iping. Possibly the Invisible Man's original intention was simply to cover Marvel's retreat with the clothes and books. But his temper, at no time very good, seems to have gone completely at some chance blow, and forthwith he set to smiting and overthrowing for the mere satisfaction of hurting.

You must figure the street full of running figures, of doors slamming, and fights for hiding-places. You must figure the tumult suddenly striking on the unstable equilibrium of old Fletcher's plank and two chairs—with cataclysmal results. You must figure an appalled couple caught dismally in a swing. And then the whole tumultuous rush has passed, and the Iping Street, with its gauds and flags, is deserted, save for the still raging unseen, and littered with cocoanuts, overthrown canvas screens, and the scattered stock-in-trade of a sweetstuff stall. Everywhere there is a sound of closing shutters and shooting bolts, and the only visible humanity is an occasional flitting eye under a raised eyebrow in the corner of a window-pane.

The Invisible Man amused himself for a little while by breaking all the windows in the 'Coach and Horses,' and then he thrust a street lamp through the parlour window of Mrs Grogram. He it must have been who cut the telegraph wire to Adderdean just beyond Higgins' cottage on the Adderdean Road. And after that, as his peculiar qualities allowed, he passed out of human perceptions altogether, and he was neither heard, seen, nor felt in Iping any more. He vanished absolutely.

But it was the best part of two hours before any human being ventured out again into the desolation of Iping Street.

XIII

MR MARVEL DISCUSSES HIS RESIGNATION

WHEN the dusk was gathering, and Iping was just beginning to peep timorously forth again upon the shattered wreckage of its Bank Holiday, a short, thickset man in a shabby silk hat was marching painfully through the twilight behind the beechwoods on the road to Bramblehurst. He carried three books, bound together by some sort of ornamental elastic ligature, and a bundle wrapped in a blue tablecloth. His rubicund face expressed consternation and fatigue, he appeared to be in a spasmodic sort of hurry. He was accompanied by a Voice other than his own, and ever and again he winced under the touch of unseen hands.

'If you give me the slip again,' said the Voice; 'if you attempt to give me the slip again——'

'Lord!' said Mr Marvel. 'That shoulder's a mass of bruises as it is.'

'On my honour,' said the Voice, 'I will kill you.'

'I didn't try to give you the slip,' said Marvel, in a voice that was not far remote from tears. 'I swear I didn't. I didn't know the blessed turning, that was all! How the devil was I to know the blessed turning? As it is, I've been knocked about——'

'You'll get knocked about a great deal more if you don't mind,' said the Voice, and Mr Marvel abruptly became silent. He blew out his cheeks, and his eyes were eloquent of despair.

'It's bad enough to let these floundering yokels explode my little secret, without *your* cutting off with my books. It's lucky for some of them they cut and ran when they did! Here am I . . . No one knew I was invisible! And now what am I to do?'

'What am *I* to do?' asked Marvel, *sotto voce*.

'It's all about. It will be in the papers! Everybody will be looking for me. Every one on their guard——'

The Voice broke off into vivid curses and ceased. The despair of Mr Marvel's face deepened, and his pace slackened.

'Go on,' said the Voice.

Mr Marvel's face assumed a greyish tint between the ruddier patches.

'Don't drop those books, stupid!' said the Voice sharply.

'The fact is,' said the Voice, 'I shall have to make use of you. . . . You're a poor tool, but I must.'

'I'm a *miserable* tool,' said Marvel.

'You are,' said the Voice.

'I'm the worst possible tool you could have,' said Marvel.

'I'm not strong,' he said, after a discouraging silence.

'I'm not over strong,' he repeated.

'No?'

'And my heart's weak. That little business—I pulled it through, of course. But, bless you! I could have dropped.'

'Well?'

'I haven't the nerve and strength for the sort of thing you want——'

'*I'll* stimulate you.'

'I wish you wouldn't. I wouldn't like to mess up your plans, you know. But I might. Out of sheer funk and misery——'

'You'd better not,' said the Voice, with quiet emphasis.

'I wish I was dead,' said Marvel.

'It ain't justice,' he said. 'You must admit. . . . It seems to me I've a perfect right——'

'*Get* on,' said the Voice.

Mr Marvel mended his pace, and for a time they went in silence again.

'It's devilish hard,' said Mr Marvel.

This was quite ineffectual. He tried another tack.

'What do I make by it?' he began, again in a tone of unendurable wrong.

'Oh! *shut up!*' said the Voice, with sudden amazing vigour. 'I'll see to you all right. You do what you're told. You'll do it all right. You're a fool and all that, but you'll do——'

'I tell you, sir, I'm not the man for it. Respectfully—but it *is* so——'

'If you don't shut up I shall twist your wrist again,' said the Invisible Man. 'I want to think.'

Presently two oblongs of yellow light appeared through the trees, and the square tower of a church loomed through the gloaming. 'I shall keep my hand on your shoulder,' said the Voice, 'all through this village. Go straight through and try no foolery. It will be the worse for you if you do.'

'I know that,' sighed Mr Marvel; 'I know all that.'

The unhappy-looking figure in the obsolete silk hat passed up the street of the little village with his burdens, and vanished into the gathering darkness beyond the lights of the windows.

XIV

AT PORT STOWE

TEN o'clock the next morning found Mr Marvel unshaven, dirty, and travel-stained, sitting with his hands deep in his pockets, looking very weary, nervous, and uncomfortable, and inflating his cheeks at frequent intervals, on the bench outside a little inn on the outskirts of Port Stowe. Beside him were the books, but now they were tied with string. The bundle had been abandoned in the pine-woods beyond Bramblehurst, in accordance with a change in the plans of the Invisible Man. Mr Marvel sat on the bench, and although no one took the slightest notice of him, his agitation remained at fever heat. His hands would go ever and again to his various pockets with a curious, nervous fumbling.

When he had been sitting for the best part of an hour, however, an elderly mariner, carrying a newspaper, came out of the inn and sat down beside him.

'Pleasant day,' said the mariner.

Mr Marvel glanced about him with something very like terror. 'Very,' he said.

'Just seasonable weather for the time of year,' said the mariner, taking no denial.

'Quite,' said Mr Marvel.

The mariner produced a toothpick, and (saving his regard)* was engrossed thereby for some minutes. His eyes meanwhile were at liberty to examine Mr Marvel's dusty figure and the books beside him. As he had approached Mr Marvel he had heard a sound like the dropping of coins into a pocket. He was struck by the contrast of Mr Marvel's appearance with this suggestion of opulence. Thence his mind wandered back again to a topic that had taken a curiously firm hold of his imagination.

'Books?' he said suddenly, noisily finishing with the toothpick.

Mr Marvel started and looked at them. 'Oh, yes,' he said. 'Yes, they're books.'

'There's some extra-ordinary things in books,' said the mariner.

'I believe you,' said Mr Marvel.

'And some extra-ordinary things out of 'em,' said the mariner.

'True, likewise,' said Mr Marvel. He eyed his interlocutor, and then glanced about him.

'There's some extra-ordinary things in newspapers, for example,' said the mariner.

'There are.'

'In *this* newspaper,' said the mariner.

'Ah!' said Mr Marvel.

'There's a story,' said the mariner, fixing Mr Marvel with an eye that was firm and deliberate; 'there's a story about an Invisible Man, for instance.'

Mr Marvel pulled his mouth askew and scratched his cheek and felt his ears glowing. 'What will they be writing next?' he asked faintly. 'Ostria or America?'

'Neither,' said the mariner. '*Here*.'

'Lord!' said Mr Marvel, starting.

'When I say *here*,' said the mariner to Mr Marvel's intense relief, 'I don't of course mean here in this place, I mean hereabouts.'

'An Invisible Man!' said Mr Marvel. 'And what's *he* been up to?'

'Everything,' said the mariner, controlling Marvel with his eye, and then amplifying, 'every—blessed—thing.'

'I ain't seen a paper these four days,' said Marvel.

'Iping's the place he started at,' said the mariner.

'In-*deed!*' said Mr Marvel.

'He started there. And where he came from nobody don't seem to know. Here it is: 'Pe-culiar Story from Iping.' And it says in this paper that the evidence is extraordinary strong, extra-ordinary.'

'Lord!' said Mr Marvel.

'But then it's a extra-ordinary story. There is a clergyman and a medical gent witnesses—saw 'im all right and proper—or leastways, didn't see him. He was staying, it says, at the 'Coach an' Horses,' and no one don't seem to have been aware of his misfortune, it says, aware of his misfortune, until in an Alteration* in the inn, it says, his bandages on his head was torn off. It was then observed that his head was invisible. Attempts were At Once made to secure him, but, casting off his garments, it says, he succeeded in escaping, but not until after a desperate struggle, In Which he had inflicted serious injuries, it says, on our worthy and able constable, Mr J. A. Jaffers. Pretty straight story, eh? Names and everything.'

'Lord!' said Mr Marvel, looking nervously about him, trying to count the money in his pockets by his unaided sense of touch, and full of a strange and novel idea. 'It sounds most astonishing.'

'Don't it? Extra-ordinary, *I* call it. Never heard tell of Invisible Men before, I haven't, but nowadays one hears such a lot of extra-ordinary things—that——'

'That all he did?' asked Marvel, trying to seem at his ease.

'It's enough, ain't it?' said the mariner.

'Didn't go back by any chance?' asked Marvel. 'Just escaped, and that's all, eh?'

'All!' said the mariner. 'Why!—ain't it enough?'

'Quite enough,' said Marvel.

'I should think it was enough,' said the mariner. 'I should think it was enough.'

'He didn't have any pals—it don't say he had any pals, does it?' asked Mr Marvel, anxious.

'Ain't one of a sort enough for you?' asked the mariner. 'No, thank heaven, as one might say, he didn't.'

He nodded his head slowly. 'It makes me regular uncomfortable, the bare thought of that chap running about the country!——He is at present at Large, and from certain evidence, it is supposed that he has—taken—*took*, I suppose they mean—the road to Port Stowe. You see we're right *in* it! None of your American wonders this time. And just think of the things he might do! Where'd you be if he took a drop over and above, and had a fancy to go for you? Suppose he wants to rob—who can prevent him? He can trespass, he can burgle, he can walk through a cordon of policemen as easy as me or you could give the slip to a blind man! Easier! For these here blind chaps hear uncommon sharp, I'm told. And wherever there was liquor he fancied——'

'He's got a tremenjous advantage, certainly,' said Mr Marvel. 'And—well . . .'

'You're right,' said the mariner; 'he *has*.'

All this time Mr Marvel had been glancing about him intently, listening for faint footfalls, trying to detect imperceptible movements. He seemed on the point of some great resolution; he coughed behind his hand.

He looked about him again—listened—bent towards the mariner, and lowered his voice.

'The fact of it is, I happen—to know just a thing or two about this Invisible Man. From private sources.'

'Oh!' said the mariner. '*You?*'

'Yes,' said Mr Marvel—'me.'

'Indeed!' said the mariner. 'And may I ask—?'

'You'll be astonished,' said Mr Marvel, behind his hand. 'It's tremenjous.'

'Indeed!' said the mariner.

'The fact is,' began Mr Marvel eagerly, in a confidential undertone. Suddenly his expression changed marvellously. 'Ow!' he said. He rose stiffly in his seat; his face was eloquent of physical suffering. 'Wow!' he said.

'What's up?' said the mariner, concerned.

'Toothache,' said Mr Marvel, and put his hand to his ear. He caught hold of his books. 'I must be getting on, I think,' he said. He edged in a curious way along the seat away from his interlocutor.

'But you was just a-going to tell me about this here Invisible Man,' protested the mariner.

Mr Marvel seemed to consult with himself.

'Hoax,' said a Voice.

'It's a hoax,' said Mr Marvel.

'But it's in the paper,' said the mariner.

'Hoax all the same,' said Marvel. 'I know the chap that started the lie. There ain't no Invisible Man whatsoever. . . . Blimey.'

'But how 'bout this paper? D'you mean to say——?'

'Not a word of it,' said Mr Marvel stoutly.

The mariner stared, paper in hand. Mr Marvel jerkily faced about. 'Wait a bit,' said the mariner, rising and speaking slowly. 'D'you mean to say——?'

'I do,' said Mr Marvel.

'Then why did you let me go on and tell you all this Blarsted stuff, then? What d'yer mean by letting a man make a fool of himself like that for, eh?'

Mr Marvel blew out his cheeks. The mariner was suddenly very red indeed, he clenched his hands. 'I been talking here this ten minutes,' he said; 'and you, you little pot-bellied, leathery-faced son of an old boot, couldn't have the elementary manners——'

'Don't you come bandying words with *me*,' said Mr Marvel.

'Bandying words! I've a jolly good mind——'

'Come up,' said a Voice, and Mr Marvel was suddenly whirled about and started marching off in a curious, spasmodic manner. 'You'd better move on,' said the mariner. '*Who's* moving on?' said Mr Marvel. He was receding obliquely with a curious, hurrying gait, with occasional violent jerks forward. Some way along the road he began a muttered monologue, protests and recriminations.

'Silly devil,' said the mariner, legs wide apart, arms akimbo, watching the receding figure. 'I'll show you, you silly fool, hoaxing *me!* It's here in the paper!'

Mr Marvel retorted incoherently, and receding was hidden by a bend in the road; but the mariner still stood magnificent in the midst of the way, until the approach of a butcher's cart dislodged him. Then he turned himself towards Port Stowe. 'Full of extra-ordinary fools,' he said softly to himself. 'Just to take me down a bit—that was his silly game . . . It's on the paper!'

And there was another extraordinary thing he was presently to hear that had happened quite close to him. And that was a vision of a 'fist full of money' (no less) travelling without visible agency, along by the wall at the corner of St Michael's Lane. A brother mariner had seen this wonderful sight that very morning. He had snatched the money forthwith, and had been knocked headlong, and when he had got to his feet the butterfly money had vanished. Our mariner was in the mood to believe anything, he declared, but that was a bit *too* stiff. Afterwards, however, he began to think things over.

The story of the flying money was true. And all about that neighbourhood, even from the august London and County Banking Company,* from the tills of shops and inns—doors standing that sunny weather entirely open—money had been quietly and dexterously making off that day in handfuls and rouleaux,* floating quietly along by walls and shady places, dodging quickly from the approaching eyes of men. And it had, though no man had traced it, invariably ended its mysterious flight in the pocket of that agitated gentleman in the obsolete silk hat, sitting outside the little inn on the outskirts of Port Stowe.

It was ten days after—and indeed only when the Burdock story was already old—that the mariner collated these facts and began to understand how near he had been to the wonderful Invisible Man.

XV

THE MAN WHO WAS RUNNING

IN the early evening time Dr Kemp was sitting in his study in the belvedere on the hill overlooking Burdock. It was a pleasant little room, with three windows—north, west, and south—and bookshelves covered with books and scientific publications, and a broad writing-table, and, under the north window, a microscope, glass slips, minute instruments, some cultures, and scattered bottles of reagents. Dr Kemp's solar lamp* was lit, albeit the sky was still bright with the sunset light, and his blinds were up because there was no offence of peering outsiders to require them pulled down. Dr Kemp was a tall and slender young man, with flaxen hair and a moustache almost white, and the work he was upon would earn him, he hoped, the fellowship of the Royal Society,* so highly did he think of it.

And his eye, presently wandering from his work, caught the sunset blazing at the back of the hill that is over against his own. For a minute, perhaps, he sat, pen in mouth, admiring the rich golden colour above the crest, and then his attention was attracted by the little figure of a man, inky black, running over the hill brow towards him. He was a shortish little fellow, and he wore a high hat, and he was running so fast that his legs verily twinkled.

'Another of those asses,' said Dr Kemp. 'Like that ass who ran into me this morning round a corner, with his "'Visible Man a-coming, sir!" I can't imagine what possesses people. One might think we were in the thirteenth century.'

He got up, went to the window, and stared at the dusky hillside and the dark little figure tearing down it. 'He seems in a confounded hurry,' said Dr Kemp, 'but he doesn't seem to be getting on. If his pockets were full of lead he couldn't run heavier.

'Spurted, sir!' said Dr Kemp.

In another moment the higher of the villas that had clambered up the hill from Burdock had occulted the running figure. He was visible again for a moment, and again and then again, three times between the three detached houses that came next, and then the terrace hid him.

'Asses!' said Dr Kemp, swinging round on his heel and walking back to his writing-table.

But those who saw the fugitive nearer, and perceived the abject terror on his perspiring face, being themselves in the open roadway, did not share in the doctor's contempt. By the man pounded, and as he ran he chinked like a well-filled purse that is tossed to and fro. He looked neither to the right nor left, but his dilated eyes stared straight down hill to where the lamps were being lit and the people were crowded in the street. And his ill-shaped mouth fell apart, and a glairy foam lay on his lips, and his breath came hoarse and noisy. All he passed stopped and began staring up the road and down, and interrogating one another with an inkling of discomfort for the reason of his haste.

And then presently, far up the hill, a dog playing in the road yelped and ran under a gate, and as they still wondered, something—a wind— a pad, pad, pad, a sound like a panting breathing, rushed by.

People screamed. People sprang off the pavement. It passed in shouts, it passed by instinct down the hill. They were shouting in the street before Marvel was halfway there. They were bolting into houses and slamming the doors behind them, with the news. He heard it, and made one last desperate spurt. Fear came striding by, rushed ahead of him, and in a moment had seized the town.

'The Invisible Man is coming! *The Invisible Man!*'

XVI

IN THE 'JOLLY CRICKETERS'

THE 'Jolly Cricketers' is just at the bottom of the hill, where the tram-lines begin. The barman leant his fat red arms on the counter and talked of horses with an anæmic cabman, while a black-bearded man in grey snapped up biscuit and cheese, drank Burton,* and conversed in American with a policeman off duty.

'What's the shouting about?' said the anæmic cabman, going off at a tangent, trying to see up the hill over the dirty yellow blind in the low window of the inn. Somebody ran by outside.

'Fire, perhaps,' said the barman.

Footsteps approached, running heavily, the door was pushed open violently, and Marvel, weeping and dishevelled, his hat gone, the neck of his coat torn open, rushed in, made a convulsive turn, and attempted to shut the door. It was held half open by a strap.

'Coming!' he bawled, his voice shrieking with terror. 'He's coming. The 'Nvisible Man! After me. For Gawd's sake. 'Elp! 'Elp! 'Elp!'

'Shut the doors,' said the policeman. 'Who's coming? What's the row?' He went to the door, released the strap, and it slammed. The American closed the other door.

'Lemme go inside,' said Marvel, staggering and weeping, but still clutching the books. 'Lemme go inside. Lock me in—somewhere. I tell you he's after me. I give him the slip. He said he'd kill me, and he will.'

'*You're* safe,' said the man with the black beard. 'The door's shut. What's it all about?'

'Lemme go inside,' said Marvel, and shrieked aloud as a blow suddenly made the fastened door shiver, and was followed by a hurried rapping and a shouting outside.

'Hullo,' cried the policeman, 'who's there?'

Mr Marvel began to make frantic dives at panels that looked like doors. 'He'll kill me—he's got a knife or something. For Gawd's sake——!'

'Here you are,' said the barman. 'Come in here.' And he held up the flap of the bar.

Mr Marvel rushed behind the bar as the summons outside was repeated. 'Don't open the door,' he screamed. '*Please* don't open the door. *Where* shall I hide?'

'This, this Invisible Man, then?' asked the man with the black beard with one hand behind him. 'I guess it's about time we saw him.'

The window of the inn was suddenly smashed in, and there was a screaming and running to and fro in the street. The policeman had been standing on the settee staring out, craning to see who was at the door. He got down with raised eyebrows. 'It's that,' he said. The barman stood in front of the bar-parlour door, which was now locked on Mr Marvel, stared at the smashed window, and came round to the two other men.

Everything was suddenly quiet. 'I wish I had my truncheon,' said the policeman, going irresolutely to the door. 'Once we open, in he comes. There's no stopping him.'

'Don't you be in too much hurry about that door,' said the anæmic cabman anxiously.

'Draw the bolts,' said the man with the black beard, 'and if he comes . . .' He showed a revolver in his hand.

'That won't do,' said the policeman, 'that's murder.'

'I know what country I'm in,' said the man with the beard. 'I'm going to let off at his legs. Draw the bolts.'

'Not with that thing going off behind me,' said the barman, craning over the blind.

'Very well,' said the man with the black beard, and stooping down, revolver ready, drew them himself. Barman, cabman, and policeman faced about.

'Come in,' said the bearded man in an undertone, standing back and facing the unbolted doors with his pistol behind him. No one came in, the door remained closed. Five minutes afterwards, when a second cabman pushed his head in cautiously, they were still waiting, and an anxious face peered out of the bar-parlour and supplied information.

'Are all the doors of the house shut?' asked Marvel. 'He's going round—prowling round. He's as artful as the devil.'

'Good Lord!' said the burly barman. 'There's the back! Just watch them doors! I say——!' He looked about him helplessly. The bar-parlour door slammed and they heard the key turn. 'There's the yard door and the private door. The yard door——'

He rushed out of the bar.

In a minute he reappeared with a carving knife in his hand. 'The yard door was open,' he said, and his fat underlip dropped.

'He may be in the house now,' said the first cabman.

'He's not in the kitchen,' said the barman. 'There's two women there, and I've stabbed every inch of it with this little beef slicer. And they don't think he's come in. They haven't noticed——'

'Have you fastened it?' asked the first cabman.

'I'm out o' frocks,'* said the barman.

The man with the beard replaced his revolver. And even as he did so the flap of the bar was shut down and the bolt clicked, and then with a tremendous thud the catch of the door snapped and the bar-parlour door burst open. They heard Marvel squeal like a caught leveret,* and forthwith they were clambering over the bar to his rescue. The bearded man's revolver cracked, and the looking-glass at the back of the parlour starred and came smashing and tinkling down.

As the barman entered the room, he saw Marvel curiously crumpled up and struggling against the door that led to the yard and kitchen. The door flew open while the barman hesitated, and Marvel was lugged into the kitchen. There was a scream and a clatter of pans. Marvel, head down, and lugging back obstinately, was forced to the kitchen door, and the bolts were drawn.

The policeman, who had been trying to pass the barman, rushed in, followed by one of the cabmen, gripped the wrist of the invisible hand that collared Marvel, was hit in the face and went reeling back. The door opened, and Marvel made a frantic effort to obtain a lodgment behind it. Then the cabman collared something.

'I got him,' said the cabman.

The barman's red hands came clawing at the unseen.

'Here he is!' said the barman.

Mr Marvel, released, suddenly dropped to the ground, and made an attempt to crawl behind the legs of the fighting men. The struggle blundered round the edge of the door. The voice of the Invisible Man was heard for the first time, yelling out sharply as the policeman trod on his foot. Then he cried out passionately, and his fists flew round like flails. The cabman suddenly whooped and doubled up, kicked under the diaphragm. The door into the bar-parlour from the kitchen slammed and covered Mr Marvel's retreat. The men in the kitchen found themselves clutching at and struggling with empty air.

'Where's he gone?' cried the man with the beard. 'Out?'

'This way,' said the policeman, stepping into the yard and stopping.

A piece of tile whizzed by his head, and smashed among the crockery on the kitchen table.

'I'll show him,' shouted the man with the black beard, and suddenly a steel barrel shone over the policeman's shoulder, and five bullets had followed one another into the twilight whence the missile had come. As he fired, the man with the beard moved his hand in a horizontal curve, so that his shots radiated out into the narrow yard like spokes from a wheel.

A silence followed. 'Five cartridges,' said the man with the black beard. 'That's best of all. Four aces and the joker. Get a lantern, some one, and come and feel about for his body.'

XVII

DR KEMP'S VISITOR

DR KEMP had continued writing in his study until the shots aroused him. Crack, crack, crack, they came one after the other.

'Hullo!' said Dr Kemp, putting his pen into his mouth again and listening. 'Who's letting off revolvers in Burdock? What are the asses at now?'

He went to the south window, threw it up, and leaning out stared down on the network of windows, beaded gas-lamps and shops with its black interstices of roof and yard that made up the town at night. 'Looks like a crowd down the hill,' he said, 'by "The Cricketers,"' and remained watching. Thence his eyes wandered over the town to far away where the ships' lights shone and the pier glowed—a little illuminated, facetted pavilion like a gem of yellow light. The moon in its first quarter hung over the westward hill, and the stars were clear and almost tropically bright.

After five minutes, during which his mind had travelled into a remote speculation of social conditions of the future,* and lost itself at last over the time dimension, Dr Kemp roused himself with a sigh, pulled down the window again, and returned to his writing-desk.

It must have been about an hour after this that the front door-bell rang. He had been writing slackly, and with intervals of abstraction, since the shots. He sat listening. He heard the servant answer the door, and waited for her feet on the staircase, but she did not come. 'Wonder what that was?' said Dr Kemp.

He tried to resume his work, failed, got up, went downstairs from his study to the landing, rang, and called over the balustrade to the housemaid, as she appeared in the hall below. 'Was that a letter?' he asked.

'Only a runaway ring,* sir,' she answered.

'I'm restless to-night,' he said to himself. He went back to his study, and this time attacked his work resolutely.

In a little while he was hard at work again, and the only sounds in the room were the ticking of the clock and the subdued shrillness of his quill, hurrying in the very centre of the circle of light his lamp-shade threw on his table.

It was two o'clock before Dr Kemp had finished his work for the night. He rose, yawned, and went upstairs to bed. He had already removed his coat and vest,* when he noticed that he was thirsty. He took a candle and went down to the dining-room in search of a syphon and whisky.

Dr Kemp's scientific pursuits had made him a very observant man, and as he re-crossed the hall he noticed a dark spot on the linoleum near the mat at the foot of the stairs. He went on upstairs, and then it suddenly occurred to him to ask himself what the spot on the lino-leum might be. Apparently some subconscious element was at work. At any rate, he turned with his burthen, went back to the hall, put down the syphon and whisky, and bending down, touched the spot. Without any great surprise he found it had the stickiness and colour of drying blood.

He took up his burden again, and returned upstairs looking about him and trying to account for the blood spot. On the landing he saw something, and stopped astonished. The door-handle of his room was bloodstained.

He looked at his own hand. It was quite clean, and then he remembered that the door of his room had been open when he came down from his study, and that consequently he had not touched the handle at all. He went straight into his own room, his face quite calm—perhaps a trifle more resolute than usual. His glance, wandering inquisitively, fell on the bed. On the counterpane was a mess of blood, and the sheet had been torn. He had not noticed this when he had entered the room before, because then he had walked straight to the dressing-table. On the further side the bed-clothes were depressed as if some one had recently been sitting there.

Then he had an odd impression that he had heard a low voice say, 'Good Heavens!—Kemp!' But Dr Kemp was no believer in voices.

He stood staring at the tumbled sheets. Was that really a voice? He looked about again, but noticed nothing further than the disordered and blood-stained bed. Then he distinctly heard a movement across the room, near the washhand-stand. All men, however highly educated, retain some superstitious inklings. The feeling that is called 'eerie'* came upon him. He closed the door of the room, came forward to the dressing-table, and put down his burden. Suddenly, with a start, he perceived a coiled and blood-stained bandage of linen rag hanging in mid-air, between him and the washhand-stand.

He stared at this in amazement. It was an empty bandage—a bandage properly tied, but quite empty. He would have advanced to grasp it, but a touch arrested him and a voice speaking quite close to him.

'Kemp!' said the Voice.

'Eh?' said Kemp, with his mouth open.

'Keep your nerve,' said the Voice. 'I'm an Invisible Man.'

Kemp made no answer for a space, simply stared at the bandage. 'Invisible Man?' he said.

'I am an Invisible Man,' repeated the Voice.

The story he had been active to ridicule only that morning rushed through Kemp's brain. He does not appear to have been either very much frightened or very greatly surprised at the moment. Realisation came later.

'I thought it was all a lie,' he said. The thought uppermost in his mind was the reiterated arguments of the morning. 'Have you a bandage on?' he asked.

'Yes,' said the Invisible Man.

'Oh!' said Kemp, and then roused himself. 'I say!' he said. 'But this is nonsense. It's some trick.' He stepped forward suddenly, and his hand extended towards the bandage met invisible fingers.

He recoiled at the touch, and his colour changed.

'Keep steady, Kemp, for God's sake! I want help badly. Stop!'

The hand gripped his arm. He struck at it. 'Kemp!' cried the Voice. 'Kemp, keep steady!' and the grip tightened.

A frantic desire to free himself took possession of Kemp. The hand of the bandaged arm gripped his shoulder, and he was suddenly tripped and flung backwards upon the bed. He opened his mouth to shout, and the corner of the sheet was thrust between his teeth. The Invisible Man had him down grimly, but his arms were free, and he struck and tried to kick savagely.

'Listen to reason, will you?' said the Invisible Man, sticking to him in spite of a pounding in the ribs. 'By heaven, you'll madden me in a minute!

'Lie still, you fool!' bawled the Invisible Man in Kemp's ear.

Kemp struggled for another moment, and then lay still.

'If you shout, I'll smash your face,' said the Invisible Man, relieving his mouth. 'I'm an Invisible Man. It is no foolishness and no magic. I am really an Invisible Man. And I want your help. I don't want to hurt you, but if you behave like a frantic rustic I must. Don't you remember me, Kemp? Griffin, of University College.'*

'Let me get up,' said Kemp. 'I'll stop where I am. And let me sit quiet for a minute.'

He sat up and felt his neck.

'I am Griffin, of University College, and I have made myself invisible. I am just an ordinary man—a man you have known—made invisible.'

'Griffin?' said Kemp.

'Griffin,' answered the Voice. 'A younger student than you were, almost an albino, six feet high, and broad—with a pink and white face and red eyes, who won the medal for chemistry.'

'I'm confused,' said Kemp. 'My brain is rioting. What has this to do with Griffin?'

'I *am* Griffin.'

Kemp thought. 'It's horrible,' he said. 'But what devilry must happen to make a man invisible?'

'It's no devilry. It's a process, sane and intelligible enough——'

'It's horrible!' said Kemp. 'How on earth——?'

'It's horrible enough. But I'm wounded and in pain, and tired . . . Great God! Kemp, you are a man. Take it steady. Give me some food and drink, and let me sit down here.'

Kemp stared at the bandage as it moved across the room, then saw a basket chair dragged along the floor and come to rest near the bed. It creaked, and the seat was depressed* a quarter of an inch or so. He rubbed his eyes and felt his neck again. 'This beats ghosts,' he said, and laughed stupidly.

'That's better. Thank Heaven, you're getting sensible!'

'Or silly,' said Kemp, and knuckled his eyes.

'Give me some whisky. I'm near dead.'

'It didn't feel so. Where are you? If I get up shall I run into you? *There!* All right. Whisky. . . . Here. Where shall I give it you?'

The chair creaked, and Kemp felt the glass drawn away from him. He left go by an effort; his instinct was all against it. It came to rest poised twenty inches above the front edge of the chair. He stared at it in infinite perplexity.

'This is—this *must* be—hypnotism. You must have suggested you are invisible.'

'Nonsense!' said the Voice.

'It's frantic!'

'Listen to me.'

'I demonstrated conclusively this morning,' began Kemp, 'that invisibility——'

'Never mind what you've demonstrated! I'm starving,' said the Voice, 'and the night is chilly to a man without clothes.'

'Food?' said Kemp.

The tumbler of whisky tilted itself. 'Yes,' said the Invisible Man, rapping it down. 'Have you got a dressing-gown?'

Kemp made some exclamation in an undertone. He walked to a wardrobe, and produced a robe of dingy scarlet. 'This do?' he asked. It was taken from him. It hung limp for a moment in mid-air, fluttered weirdly, stood full and decorous buttoning itself, and sat down in his chair.

'Drawers, socks, slippers would be a comfort,' said the Unseen, curtly. 'And food.'

'Anything. But this is the insanest thing I was ever in, in my life!'

He turned out his drawers for the articles, and then went downstairs to ransack his larder. He came back with some cold cutlets and bread, pulled up a light table, and placed them before his guest.

'Never mind knives,' said his visitor, and a cutlet hung in mid-air with a sound of gnawing.

'I always like to get something about me before I eat,' said the Invisible Man, with a full mouth, eating greedily. 'Queer fancy.'

'I suppose that wrist is all right?' said Kemp.

'Trust me,' said the Invisible Man.

'Of all the strange and wonderful——'

'Exactly. But it's odd I should blunder into *your* house to get my bandaging. My first stroke of luck! Anyhow, I meant to sleep in this house to-night. You must stand that! It's a filthy nuisance, my blood showing, isn't it? Quite a clot over there. Gets visible as it coagulates, I see. It's only the living tissue I've changed, and only for as long as I'm alive . . . I've been in the house three hours.'

'But how's it done?' began Kemp, in a tone of exasperation. 'Confound it! The whole business—it's unreasonable from beginning to end.'

'Quite reasonable,' said the Invisible Man; 'perfectly reasonable.'

He reached over and secured the whisky bottle. Kemp stared at the devouring dressing-gown. A ray of candle-light penetrating a torn patch in the right shoulder made a triangle of light under the left ribs.

'What were the shots?' he asked. 'How did the shooting begin?'

'There was a fool of a man—a sort of confederate of mine, curse him!—who tried to steal my money. Has done so.'

'Is he invisible, too?'

'No.'

'Well?'

'Can't I have some more to eat before I tell all that? I'm hungry—in pain. And you want me to tell stories!'

Kemp got up. '*You* didn't do any shooting?' he asked.

'Not me,' said his visitor. 'Some fool I'd never seen fired at random. A lot of them got scared. They all got scared at me. Curse them! I say—I want more to eat than this, Kemp.'

'I'll see what there is more to eat downstairs,' said Kemp. 'Not much, I'm afraid.'

After he had done eating—and he made a heavy meal—the Invisible Man demanded a cigar. He bit the end savagely, before Kemp could find a knife, and cursed when the outer leaf loosened.

It was strange to see him smoking: his mouth and throat, pharynx and nares,* became visible as a sort of whirling smoke cast.

'This blessed gift of smoking,' he said, and puffed vigorously. 'I'm lucky to have fallen upon you, Kemp. You must help me. Fancy tumbling on you just now! I'm in a devilish scrape—I've been mad, I think. The things I have been through! But we will do things yet, let me tell you.'

He helped himself to more whisky and soda. Kemp got up, looked about him, and fetched himself a glass from his spare room.

'It's wild—but I suppose I may drink.'

'You haven't changed much, Kemp, these dozen years. You fair men don't. Cool and methodical. . . . I must tell you. We will work together!'

'But how was it all done?' said Kemp, 'and how did you get like this?'

'For God's sake let me smoke in peace for a little while, and then I will begin to tell you.'

But the story was not told that night. The Invisible Man's wrist was growing painful; he was feverish, exhausted, and his mind came round to brood upon his chase down the hill and the struggle about the inn. He began his story and fell away from it. He spoke in fragments of Marvel, he smoked faster, his voice grew angry. Kemp tried to gather what he could.

'He was afraid of me—I could see he was afraid of me,' said the Invisible Man many times over. 'He meant to give me the slip—he was always casting about! What a fool I was!

'The cur!

'I was furious. I should have killed him——'

'Where did you get the money?' asked Kemp abruptly.

The Invisible Man was silent for a space. 'I can't tell you to-night.'

He groaned suddenly and leaned forward, supporting his invisible head on invisible hands.

'Kemp,' he said, 'I've had no sleep for near three days, except a couple of dozes of an hour or so. I must sleep soon.'

'Well, have my room—have this room.'

'But how can I sleep? If I sleep—he will get away. Ugh! What does it matter?'

'What's the shot wound?' asked Kemp.

'Nothing—scratch and blood. Oh, God! How I want sleep!'

'Why not?'

The Invisible Man appeared to be regarding Kemp. 'Because I've a particular objection to being caught by my fellow-men,' he said slowly.

Kemp started.

'Fool that I am!' said the Invisible Man, striking the table smartly. 'I've put the idea into your head.'

XVIII

EXHAUSTED and wounded as the Invisible Man was, he refused to accept Kemp's word that his freedom should be respected. He examined the two windows of the bedroom, drew up the blinds and opened the sashes to confirm Kemp's statement that a retreat by them would be possible. Outside the night was very quiet and still, and the new moon* was setting over the down. Then he examined the keys of the bedroom and the two dressing-room doors, to satisfy himself that these also could be made an assurance of freedom. Finally he expressed himself satisfied. He stood on the hearthrug and Kemp heard the sound of a yawn.

'I'm sorry,' said the Invisible Man, 'if I cannot tell you all that I have done to-night. But I am worn out. It's grotesque, no doubt. It's horrible! But, believe me, Kemp, in spite of your arguments of this morning, it is quite a possible thing. I have made a discovery. I meant to keep it to myself. I can't. I must have a partner. And you . . . We can do such things . . . But to-morrow. Now, Kemp, I feel as though I must sleep or perish.'

Kemp stood in the middle of the room staring at the headless garment. 'I suppose I must leave you,' he said. 'It's—incredible. Three things happening like this, overturning all my preconceptions—would make me insane. But it's real! Is there anything more that I can get you?'

'Only bid me good-night,' said Griffin.

'Good-night,' said Kemp, and shook an invisible hand. He walked sideways to the door.

Suddenly the dressing-gown walked quickly towards him. 'Understand me!' said the dressing-gown. 'No attempts to hamper me or capture me! Or——'

Kemp's face changed a little. 'I thought I gave you my word,' he said.

Kemp closed the door softly behind him, and the key was turned upon him forthwith. Then as he stood with an expression of passive amazement on his face, the rapid feet came to the door of the dressing-room, and that too was locked. Kemp slapped his brow with his hand.

'Am I dreaming? Has the world gone mad, or have I?'

He laughed, and put his hand to the locked door. 'Barred out of my own bedroom by a flagrant absurdity!' he said.

He walked to the head of the staircase, turned, and stared at the locked doors. 'It's fact,' he said. He put his fingers to his slightly bruised neck. 'Undeniable fact!

'But——'

He shook his head hopelessly, turned and went downstairs.

He lit the dining-room lamp, got out a cigar, and began pacing the room, ejaculating. Now and then he would argue with himself.

'Invisible!' he said.

'Is there such a thing as an invisible animal? . . . In the sea—yes. Thousands—millions. All the larvæ, all the little nauplii and tornarias,* all the microscopic things—the jelly-fish! In the sea there are more things invisible than visible! I never thought of that before. . . . And in the ponds too! All those little pond-life things—specks of colourless, translucent jelly! . . . But in air! No!

'It can't be.

'But after all—why not?

'If a man were made of glass he would still be visible.'

His meditation became profound. The bulk of three cigars had diffused as a white ash over the carpet before he spoke again. Then it was merely an exclamation. He turned aside, walked out of the room, went into his little consulting-room and lit the gas there. It was a little room, because Dr Kemp did not live by practice, and in it were the day's newspapers. The morning's paper lay carelessly opened and thrown aside. He caught it up, turned it over, and read the account of a 'Strange Story from Iping' that the mariner at Port Stowe had spelt over so painfully to Marvel. Kemp read it swiftly.

'Wrapped up!' said Kemp. 'Disguised! Hiding it! "No one seems to have been aware of his misfortune." What the devil *is* his game?'

He dropped the paper and his eye went seeking. 'Ah!' he said, and caught up the *St James's Gazette*,* lying folded up as it arrived. 'Now we shall get at the truth,' said Dr Kemp. He rent the paper open. A couple of columns confronted him. 'An Entire Village in Sussex Goes Mad,' was the heading.

'Good heavens!' said Kemp, reading eagerly an incredulous account of the events in Iping of the previous afternoon, that have already been described. Over the leaf the report in the morning paper had been reprinted.

He re-read it. 'Ran through the streets striking right and left. Jaffers insensible. Mr Huxter in great pain—still unable to describe what he saw. Painful humiliation—vicar. Woman ill with terror. Windows smashed. This extraordinary story probably a fabrication. Too good not to print—*cum grano*.'*

He dropped the paper and stared blankly in front of him. 'Probably a fabrication!'

He caught up the paper again, and re-read the whole business.

'But when does the Tramp come in? Why the deuce was he chasing a tramp?'

He sat down abruptly on the surgical couch.

'He's not only invisible,' he said, 'but he's mad! Homicidal! . . .'

When dawn came to mingle its pallor with the lamplight and cigar-smoke of the dining-room, Kemp was still pacing up and down, trying to grasp the incredible.

He was altogether too excited to sleep. His servants, descending sleepily, discovered him, and were inclined to think that over-study had worked this ill on him. He gave them extraordinary but quite explicit instructions to lay breakfast for two in the belvedere study, and then to confine themselves to the basement and ground floor. Then he continued to pace the dining-room until the morning's paper came. That had much to say and little to tell, beyond the confirmation of the evening before, and a very badly written account of another remarkable tale from Port Burdock. This gave Kemp the essence of the happenings at the 'Jolly Cricketers,' and the name of Marvel. 'He has made me keep with him twenty-four hours,' Marvel testified. Certain minor facts were added to the Iping story, notably the cutting of the village telegraph wire. But there was nothing to throw light on the connection between the Invisible Man and the tramp—for Mr Marvel had supplied no information about the three books or the money with which he was lined. The incredulous tone had vanished, and a shoal of reporters and inquirers were already at work elaborating the matter.

Kemp read every scrap of the report, and sent his housemaid out to get every one of the morning papers she could. These also he devoured.

'He is invisible!' he said. 'And it reads like rage growing to mania! The things he may do! The things he may do! And he's upstairs free as the air. What on earth ought I to do?

'For instance, would it be a breach of faith if——No.'

He went to a little untidy desk in the corner, and began a note. He tore this up half written, and wrote another. He read it over and considered it. Then he took an envelope and addressed it to 'Colonel Adye, Port Burdock.'

The Invisible Man awoke even as Kemp was doing this. He awoke in an evil temper, and Kemp, alert for every sound, heard his pattering feet rush suddenly across the bedroom overhead. Then a chair was flung over and the washhand-stand tumbler smashed. Kemp hurried upstairs and rapped eagerly.

XIX

CERTAIN FIRST PRINCIPLES

'What's the matter?' asked Kemp, when the Invisible Man admitted him.

'Nothing,' was the answer.

'But, confound it! The smash?'

'Fit of temper,' said the Invisible Man. 'Forgot this arm; and it's sore.'

'You're rather liable to that sort of thing.'

'I am.'

Kemp walked across the room and picked up the fragments of broken glass. 'All the facts are out about you,' said Kemp, standing up with the glass in his hand. 'All that happened in Iping and down the hill. The world has become aware of its invisible citizen. But no one knows you are here.'

The Invisible Man swore.

'The secret's out. I gather it was a secret. I don't know what your plans are, but of course I'm anxious to help you.'

The Invisible Man sat down on the bed.

'There's breakfast upstairs,' said Kemp, speaking as easily as possible, and he was delighted to find his strange guest rose willingly. Kemp led the way up the narrow staircase to the belvedere.

'Before we can do anything else,' said Kemp, 'I must understand a little more about this invisibility of yours.' He had sat down, after one nervous glance out of the window, with the air of a man who has talking to do. His doubts of the sanity of the entire business flashed and vanished again as he looked across to where Griffin sat at the breakfast-table, a headless, handless dressing-gown, wiping unseen lips on a miraculously held serviette.

'It's simple enough—and credible enough,' said Griffin, putting the serviette aside.

'No doubt to you, but—' Kemp laughed.

'Well, yes, to me it seemed wonderful at first, no doubt. But now, Great God! . . . But we will do great things yet! I came on the stuff first at Chesilstowe.'

'Chesilstowe?'

'I went there after I left London. You know I dropped medicine and took up physics? No; well, I did. *Light* fascinated me.'

'Ah!'

'Optical density! The whole subject is a network of riddles—a network with solutions glimmering elusively through. And being but two-and-twenty and full of enthusiasm, I said: 'I will devote my life to this. This is worth while.' You know what fools we are at two-and-twenty?'

'Fools then or fools now,' said Kemp.

'As though knowing could be any satisfaction to a man!

'But I went to work—like a nigger. And I had hardly worked and thought about the matter six months before light came through one of the meshes suddenly—blindingly! I found a general principle of pigments and refraction—a formula, a geometrical expression involving four dimensions. Fools, common men—even common mathematicians, do not know anything of what some general expression may mean to the student of molecular physics. In the books—the books that tramp has hidden—there are marvels, miracles! But this was not a method, it was an idea that might lead to a method by which it would be possible without changing any other property of matter—except in some instances colours—to lower the refractive index* of a substance, solid or liquid, to that of air—so far as all practical purposes are concerned.'

'Phew!' said Kemp. 'That's odd! But still I don't see quite . . . I can understand that thereby you could spoil a valuable stone, but personal invisibility is a far cry.'

'Precisely,' said Griffin. 'But consider, visibility depends on the action of the visible bodies on light. Let me put the elementary facts to you as if you did not know. It will make my meaning clearer. You know quite well that either a body absorbs light or it reflects or refracts it or does all these things. If it neither reflects or refracts nor absorbs light, it cannot of itself be visible. You see an opaque red box, for instance, because the colour absorbs some of the light and reflects the rest, all the red part of the light to you. If it did not absorb any particular part of the light, but reflected it all, then it would be a shining white box. Silver! A diamond box would neither absorb much of the light nor reflect much from the general surface, but just here and there where the surfaces are favourable the light would be reflected and refracted, so that you would get a brilliant appearance of flashing reflections and translucencies. A sort of skeleton of light. A glass box would not be so brilliant, not so clearly visible as a diamond box, because there would be less refraction and reflection. See that? From certain points of view you would see quite clearly through it. Some kinds of glass would be more visible than others—a box of flint glass would be brighter than a box of ordinary window glass. A box of very thin, common glass would be hard to see in a bad light, because it would absorb hardly any light and refract and reflect very little. And if you put a sheet of common white glass in water, still more if you put it in some denser liquid than water, it would vanish almost altogether, because light passing from water to glass is only slightly refracted or reflected, or, indeed, affected in any way. It is almost as invisible as a jet of coal gas or hydrogen is in air. And for precisely the same reason!'

'Yes,' said Kemp, 'that is plain sailing. Any schoolboy nowadays knows all that.'

'And here is another fact any schoolboy will know. If a sheet of glass is smashed, Kemp, and beaten into a powder, it becomes much more visible while it is in the air; it becomes at last an opaque, white powder. This is because the powdering multiplies the surfaces of the glass at which refraction and reflection occur. In the sheet of glass there are only two surfaces, in the powder the light is reflected or refracted by each grain it passes through, and very little gets right through the powder. But if the white, powdered glass is put into water it forthwith vanishes. The powdered glass and water have much the same refractive index, that is, the light undergoes very little refraction or reflection in passing from one to the other.

'You make the glass invisible by putting it into a liquid of nearly the same refractive index; a transparent thing becomes invisible if it is put in any medium of almost the same refractive index. And if you will consider only a second, you will see also that the powder of glass might be made to vanish in air, if its refractive index could be made the same as that of air. For then there would be no refraction or reflection as the light passed from glass to air.'

'Yes, yes,' said Kemp. 'But a man's not powdered glass!'

'No,' said Griffin. '*He's more transparent!*'

'Nonsense!'

'That's from a doctor! How one forgets! Have you already forgotten your physics in ten years? Just think of all the things that are transparent and seem not to be so! Paper, for instance, is made up of

transparent fibres, and it is white and opaque only, for the same reason that a powder of glass is white and opaque. Oil white paper, fill up
the interstices between the particles with oil, so that there is no longer
refraction or reflection except at the surfaces, and it becomes as transparent as glass. And not only paper, but cotton fibre, linen fibre, wool
fibre, woody fibre, and *bone*, Kemp, *flesh*, Kemp, *hair*, Kemp, *nails* and
nerves, Kemp; in fact, the whole fabric of a man, except the red of his
blood and the dark pigment of hair, are all made up of transparent,
colourless tissue—so little suffices to make us visible one to the other.
For the most part, the fibres of a living creature are no more opaque
than water.'

'Of course, of course!' cried Kemp. 'I was thinking only last night
of the sea larvæ and jelly-fish!'

'*Now* you have me! And all that I knew and had in mind a year after
I left London—six years ago. But I kept it to myself. I had to do
my work under frightful disadvantages. Hobbema, my professor, was
a scientific bounder, a thief of ideas—he was always prying! And you
know the knavish system of the scientific world.* I simply would not
publish and let him share my credit. I went on working; I got nearer
and nearer making my formula into an experiment—a reality. I told
no living soul, because I meant to flash my work upon the world with
crushing effect and become famous at a blow. I took up the question
of pigments to fill up certain gaps, and suddenly—not by design, but
by accident—I made a discovery in physiology.'

'Yes?'

'You know the red colouring matter of blood—it can be made
white—colourless—and remain with all the functions it has now!'

Kemp gave a cry of incredulous amazement.

The Invisible Man rose and began pacing the little study. 'You may
well exclaim. I remember that night. It was late at night—in the day-
time one was bothered with the gaping, silly students—and I worked
there sometimes till dawn. It came suddenly, splendid and complete,
into my mind. I was alone, the laboratory was still, with the tall lights
burning brightly and silently. . . . "One could make an animal—
a tissue—transparent! One could make it invisible! All except the pigments. I could be Invisible," I said, suddenly realising what it meant
to be an albino* with such knowledge. It was overwhelming. I left the
filtering I was doing, and went and stared out of the great window at
the stars. "I could be Invisible," I repeated.

'To do such a thing would be to transcend magic. And I beheld, unclouded by doubt, a magnificent vision of all that Invisibility might mean to a man. The mystery, the power, the freedom. Drawbacks I saw none. You have only to think! And I, a shabby, poverty-struck, hemmed-in demonstrator, teaching fools in a provincial college, might suddenly become—this. I ask you, Kemp, if *you* . . . Any one, I tell you, would have flung himself upon that research. And I worked three years, and every mountain of difficulty I toiled over showed another from its summit. The infinite details! And the exasperation! A professor, a provincial professor, always prying. 'When are you going to publish this work of yours?' was his everlasting question. And the students, the cramped means! Three years I had of it——

'And after three years of secrecy and trouble, I found that to complete it was impossible—impossible.'

'How?' asked Kemp.

'Money,' said the Invisible Man, and went again to stare out of the window.

He turned round abruptly. 'I robbed the old man—robbed my father.

'The money was not his, and he shot himself.'

XX

FOR a moment Kemp sat in silence, staring at the back of the headless figure at the window. Then he started, struck by a thought, rose, took the Invisible Man's arm, and turned him away from the outlook.

'You are tired,' he said, 'and while I sit you walk about. Have my chair.'

He placed himself between Griffin and the nearest window.

For a space Griffin sat silent, and then he resumed abruptly:

'I had left the Chesilstowe College already,' he said, 'when that happened. It was last December. I had taken a room in London, a large unfurnished room in a big, ill-managed lodging-house in a slum near Great Portland Street.* The room was soon full of the appliances I had bought with his money, and the work was going on steadily, successfully, drawing near an end. I was like a man emerging from a thicket, and suddenly coming on some unmeaning tragedy. I went to bury my father. My mind was still on this research, and I did not lift a finger to save his character. I remember the funeral, the cheap hearse, the scant ceremony, the windy, frost-bitten hillside, and the old college friend of his who read the service over him—a shabby, black, bent old man with a snivelling cold.

'I remember walking back to the empty home, through the place that had once been a village and was now patched and tinkered by the jerry builders* into the ugly likeness of a town. Every way the roads ran out at last into the desecrated fields and ended in rubble heaps and rank, wet weeds. I remember myself as a gaunt, black figure, going along the slippery, shiny side-walk, and the strange sense of detachment I felt from the squalid respectability, the sordid commercialism of the place. . . .

'I did not feel a bit sorry for my father. He seemed to me to be the victim of his own foolish sentimentality. The current cant required my attendance at his funeral, but it was really not my affair.

'But going along the High Street my old life came back to me for a space. I met the girl I had known ten years since. Our eyes met. . . .

'Something moved me to turn back and talk to her. She was a very ordinary person.

'It was all like a dream, that visit to the old place. I did not feel then that I was lonely, that I had come out from the world into a desolation. I appreciated my loss of sympathy, but I put it down to the general inanity of life. Re-entering my room seemed like the recovery of reality. There were the things I knew and loved. There stood the apparatus, the experiments arranged and waiting. And now there was scarcely a difficulty left, beyond the planning of details.

'I will tell you, Kemp, sooner or later, all the complicated processes. We need not go into that now. For the most part, saving certain gaps I chose to remember, they are written in cypher in those books that tramp has hidden. We must hunt him down. We must get those books again. But the essential phase was to place the transparent object whose refraction index was to be lowered, between two radiating centres of a sort of ethereal vibration, of which I will tell you more fully later. No—not these Röntgen vibrations,* I don't know that these others of mine have been described, yet they are obvious enough. I needed two little dynamos—principally, and these I worked with a cheap gas-engine. . . . My first experiment was with a bit of white wool fabric. It was the strangest thing in the world to see it soft and white in the flicker of the flashes, and then to watch it fade like a wreath of smoke and vanish.

'I could scarcely believe I had done it. I put my hand into the emptiness and there was the thing as solid as ever. I felt it awkwardly, and threw it on the floor. I had a little trouble finding it again.

'And then came a curious experience. I heard a miaow behind me, and, turning, saw a lean white cat,* very dirty, on the cistern cover outside the window. A thought came into my head. "Everything ready for you," I said, and went to the window, opened it, and called softly. She came in, purring—the poor beast was starving—and I gave her some milk. All my food was in a cupboard in the corner of the room. After that she went smelling round the room, evidently with the idea of making herself at home. The invisible rag upset her a bit; you should have seen her spit at it! But I made her comfortable on the pillow of my truckle-bed,* and I gave her butter* to get her to wash.'

'And you processed her?'

'I processed* her. But giving drugs to a cat is no joke, Kemp! And the process failed.'

'Failed?'

'In two particulars. These were the claws and the pigment stuff—what is it? At the back of the eye in a cat. You know?'

'*Tapetum*.'*

'Yes, the *tapetum*. It didn't go. After I'd given the stuff to bleach the blood and done certain other things to her, I gave the beast opium, and put her and the pillow she was sleeping on, on the apparatus. And after all the rest had faded and vanished, there remained the two little ghosts of her eyes.'

'Odd.'

'I can't explain it. She was bandaged and clamped of course—so I had her safe, but she awoke while she was still misty, and miawled* dismally, and some one came knocking. It was an old woman from downstairs, who suspected me of vivisecting*—a drink-sodden old creature, with only a cat to care for in all the world. I whipped out some chloroform, applied it, and answered the door. "Did I hear a cat?" she asked. "My cat?" "Not here," said I, very politely. She was a little doubtful, and tried to peer past me into the room—strange enough to her, no doubt, bare walls, uncurtained windows, truckle-bed, with the gas-engine vibrating, and the seethe of the radiant points, and that faint stinging of chloroform in the air. She had to be satisfied at last, and went away again.'

'How long did it take?' asked Kemp.

'Three or four hours—the cat. The bones and sinews and the fat were the last to go, and the tips of the coloured hairs. And, as I say, the back part of the eye, tough, iridescent stuff it is, wouldn't go at all.

'It was night outside long before the business was over, and nothing was to be seen but the dim eyes and the claws. I stopped the gas-engine, felt for and stroked the beast, which was still insensible, released its fastenings, and then, being tired, left it sleeping on the invisible pillow and went to bed. I found it hard to sleep. I lay awake thinking weak, aimless stuff, going over the experiment again and again, or dreaming feverishly of things growing misty and vanishing about me until everything, the ground I stood on, vanished, and so I came to that sickly, falling nightmare one gets. About two the cat began miawling about the room. I tried to hush it by talking to it, and then I decided to turn it out. I remember the shock I had striking a light—there were just the round eyes shining green—and nothing round them. I would have given it milk, but I hadn't any. It wouldn't be quiet, it just sat down and miaowed at the door. I tried to catch it, with an idea of putting it out of the window, but it wouldn't be caught, it vanished. It kept on miaowing in different parts of the room. At last

I opened the window and made a bustle. I suppose it went out at last. I never saw nor heard any more of it.

'Then—Heaven knows why—I fell thinking of my father's funeral again, and the dismal, windy hillside, until the day had come. I found sleep was hopeless, and, locking my door after me, wandered out into the morning streets.'

'You don't mean to say there's an Invisible Cat at large in the world?' said Kemp.

'If it hasn't been killed,' said the Invisible Man. 'Why not?'

'Why not?' said Kemp. 'I didn't mean to interrupt.'

'It's very probably been killed,' said the Invisible Man. 'It was alive four days after, I know, and down a grating in Great Tichfield Street, because I saw a crowd round the place trying to see whence the miaowing came.'

He was silent for the best part of a minute. Then he resumed abruptly: 'I remember that morning before the change very vividly.

'I must have gone up Great Portland Street—for I remember the barracks in Albany Street* and the horse soldiers coming out, and at last I found myself sitting in the sunshine and feeling very ill and strange on the summit of Primrose Hill. It was a sunny day in January— one of those sunny, frosty days that came before the snow this year. My weary brain tried to formulate the position, to plot out a plan of action.

'I was surprised to find, now that my prize was within my grasp, how inconclusive its attainment seemed. As a matter of fact I was worked out, the intense stress of nearly four years' continuous work left me incapable of any strength or feeling. I was apathetic, and I tried in vain to recover the enthusiasm of my first inquiries, the passion of discovery that had enabled me to compass even the downfall of my father's grey hairs. Nothing seemed to matter. I saw pretty clearly this was a transient mood, due to overwork and want of sleep, and that either by drugs or rest it would be possible to recover my energies.

'All I could think clearly was that the thing had to be carried through; the fixed idea still ruled me. And soon, for the money I had was almost exhausted. I looked about me at the hillside with children playing and girls watching them, and tried to think of all the fantastic advantages an invisible man would have in the world. After a time I crawled home, took some food and a strong dose of strychnine, and went to sleep in my clothes on my unmade bed. . . . Strychnine* is a grand tonic, Kemp, to take the flabbiness out of a man.'

'It's the devil,' said Kemp. 'It's the palæolithic in a bottle.'

'I awoke vastly invigorated and rather irritable. You know?'

'I know the stuff.'

'And there was some one rapping at the door. It was my landlord with threats and inquiries, an old Polish Jew in a long grey coat and greasy slippers. I had been tormenting a cat in the night, he was sure—the old woman's tongue had been busy. He insisted on knowing all about it. The laws of this country against vivisection were very severe—he might be liable. I denied the cat. Then the vibration of the little gas-engine could be felt all over the house, he said. That was true, certainly. He edged round me into the room, peering about over his German silver spectacles, and a sudden dread came into my mind that he might carry away something of my secret. I tried to keep between him and the concentrating apparatus I had arranged, and that only made him more curious. What was I doing? Why was I always alone and secretive? Was it legal? Was it dangerous? I paid nothing but the usual rent. His had always been a most respectable house—in a disreputable neighbourhood. Suddenly my temper gave way. I told him to get out. He began to protest, to jabber of his right of entry. In a moment I had him by the collar—something ripped—and he went spinning out into his own passage. I slammed and locked the door and sat down quivering.

'He made a fuss outside, which I disregarded, and after a time he went away.

'But this brought matters to a crisis. I did not know what he would do, nor even what he had the power to do. To move to fresh apartments would have meant delay—altogether I had barely twenty pounds left in the world, for the most part in a bank—and I could not afford that. Vanish! It was irresistible. Then there would be an inquiry, the sacking of my room.

'At the thought of the possibility of my work being exposed or interrupted at its very climax, I became angry and active. I hurried out with my three books of notes, my cheque book—the tramp has them now—and directed them from the nearest Post Office to a house of call for letters and parcels in Great Portland Street. I tried to go out noiselessly. Coming in, I found my landlord going quietly upstairs—he had heard the door close, I suppose. You would have laughed to see him jump aside on the landing as I came tearing after him. He glared at me as I went by him, and I made the house quiver with the slamming of my door. I heard him come shuffling up to my floor, hesitate, and go down. I set to work upon my preparations forthwith.

'It was all done that evening and night. While I was still sitting under the sickly, drowsy influence of the drugs that decolorise blood, there came a repeated knocking at the door. It ceased, footsteps went away and returned, and the knocking was resumed. There was an attempt to push something under the door—a blue paper. Then in a fit of irritation I rose, and went and flung the door wide open. "Now then?" said I.

'It was my landlord, with a notice of ejectment or something. He held it out to me, saw something odd about my hands, I expect, and lifted his eyes to my face.

'For a moment he gaped. Then he gave a sort of inarticulate cry, dropped candle and writ together, and went blundering down the dark passage to the stairs.

'I shut the door, locked it, and went to the looking-glass. Then I understood his terror. . . . My face was white—like white stone.

'But it was all horrible. I had not expected the suffering. A night of racking anguish,* sickness, and fainting. I set my teeth, though my skin was presently afire, all my body afire, but I lay there like grim death. I understood now how it was the cat had howled until I chloroformed it. Lucky it was I lived alone and untended in my room. There were times when I sobbed, and groaned, and talked. But I stuck to it. . . . I became insensible, and woke languid in the darkness.

'The pain had passed. I thought I was killing myself, and I did not care. I shall never forget that dawn, and the strange horror of seeing that my hands had become as clouded glass, and watching them grow clearer and thinner as the day went by, until at last I could see the sickly disorder of my room through them, though I closed my transparent eyelids. My limbs became glassy, the bones and arteries faded, vanished, and the little white nerves went last. I gritted my teeth and stayed there to the end. . . . At last only the dead tips of the fingernails remained, pallid and white, and the brown stain of some acid upon my fingers.

'I struggled up. At first I was as incapable as a swathed infant—stepping with limbs I could not see. I was weak and very hungry. I went and stared at nothing in my shaving-glass—at nothing, save where an attenuated pigment still remained behind the retina of my eyes, fainter than mist. I had to hang on to the table and press my forehead to the glass.

'It was only by a frantic effort of will that I dragged myself back to the apparatus, and completed the process.

'I slept during the forenoon, pulling a sheet over my eyes to shut out the light, and about midday I was awakened again by a knocking. My strength had returned. I sat up and listened and heard a whispering. I sprang to my feet, and as noiselessly as possible began to detach the connections of my apparatus, and to distribute it about the room so as to destroy the suggestions of its arrangement. Presently the knocking was renewed and voices called, first my landlord's and then two others. To gain time I answered them. The invisible rag and pillow came to hand, and I opened the window and pitched them out on to the cistern cover. As the window opened a heavy crash came at the door. Some one had charged it with the idea of smashing the lock. But the stout bolts I had screwed up some days before stopped him. That startled me—made me angry. I began to tremble and do things hurriedly.

'I tossed together some loose paper, straw, packing-paper, and so forth, in the middle of the room, and turned on the gas. Heavy blows began to rain upon the door. I could not find the matches. I beat my hands on the wall with rage. I turned down the gas again, stepped out of the window on the cistern cover, very softly lowered the sash, and sat down, secure and invisible, but quivering with anger, to watch events. They split a panel, I saw, and in another moment they had broken away the staples of the bolts and stood in the open doorway. It was the landlord and his two step-sons—sturdy young men of three or four and twenty. Behind them fluttered the old hag of a woman from downstairs.

'You may imagine their astonishment at finding the room empty. One of the younger men rushed to the window at once, flung it open and stared out. His staring eyes, and thick-lipped, bearded face came a foot from my face. I was half-minded to hit his silly countenance, but I arrested my doubled fist.

'He stared right through me. So did the others as they joined him. The old man went and peered under the bed, and then they all made a rush for the cupboard. They had to argue about it at length in Yiddish and Cockney English. They concluded I had not answered them, that their imagination had deceived them. A feeling of extraordinary elation took the place of my anger as I sat outside the window and watched these four people—for the old lady came in, glancing suspiciously about her like a cat—trying to understand the riddle of my existence.

'The old man, so far as I could understand his polyglot, agreed with the old lady that I was a vivisectionist. The sons protested in garbled English that I was an electrician, and appealed to the dynamos and radiators. They were all nervous against my arrival, although I found subsequently that they had bolted the front door. The old lady peered into the cupboard and under the bed. One of my fellow-lodgers, a costermonger,* who shared the opposite room with a butcher, appeared on the landing, and he was called in, and told incoherent things.

'It occurred to me that the peculiar radiators I had, if they fell into the hands of some acute, well-educated person, would give me away too much, and, watching my opportunity, I descended from the window-sill into the room and dodging the old woman tilted one of the little dynamos off its fellow on which it was standing, and smashed both apparatus. How scared they were! . . . Then, while they were trying to explain the smash, I slipped out of the room and went softly downstairs.

'I went into one of the sitting-rooms and waited until they came down, still speculative and argumentative, all a little disappointed at finding no "horrors,"* and all a little puzzled how they stood legally towards me. As soon as they had gone on down to the basement, I slipped up again with a box of matches, fired my heap of paper and rubbish, put the chairs and bedding thereby, led the gas to the affair by means of an indiarubber tube. . . .'

'You fired the house?' exclaimed Kemp.

'Fired the house! It was the only way to cover my trail, and no doubt it was insured. . . . I slipped the bolts of the front door quietly and went out into the street. I was invisible, and I was only just beginning to realise the extraordinary advantage my invisibility gave me. My head was already teeming with plans of all the wild and wonderful things I had now impunity to do.'

XXI

IN OXFORD STREET

'In going downstairs the first time I found an unexpected difficulty because I could not see my feet; indeed, I stumbled twice, and there was an unaccustomed clumsiness in gripping the bolt. By not looking down, however, I managed to walk on the level passably well.

'My mood, I say, was one of exaltation. I felt as a seeing man might do, with padded feet and noiseless clothes, in a city of the blind.* I experienced a wild impulse to jest, to startle people, to clap them on the back, fling people's hats astray, and generally revel in my extraordinary advantage.

'But hardly had I emerged upon Great Portland Street, however (my lodging was close to the big draper's shop there), when I heard a clashing concussion, and was hit violently behind, and turning, saw a man carrying a basket of soda-water syphons, and looking in amazement at his burden. Although the blow had really hurt me I found something so irresistible in his astonishment that I laughed aloud. "The devil's in the basket," I said, and suddenly twisted it out of his hand. He left go incontinently, and I swung the whole weight up into the air.

'But a fool of a cabman, standing outside a public-house, made a sudden rush for this, and his extended fingers took me with excruciating violence under the ear. I let the whole down with a smash on the cabman, and then, with shouts and the clatter of feet about me, people coming out of shops, vehicles pulling up, I realised what I had done for myself, and cursing my folly, backed against a shop window and prepared to dodge out of the confusion. In a moment I should be wedged into a crowd and inevitably discovered. I pushed by a butcher boy, who luckily did not turn to see the nothingness that shoved him aside, and dodged behind the cabman's four-wheeler. I do not know how they settled the business. I hurried straight across the road, which was happily clear, and hardly heeding which way I went in the fright of detection the incident had given me, plunged into the afternoon throng of Oxford Street.

'I tried to get into the stream of people, but they were too thick for me, and in a moment my heels were being trodden upon. I took the gutter, the roughness of which I found painful to my feet, and forthwith the shaft of a crawling hansom dug me forcibly under the shoulder blade, reminding me that I was already bruised severely. I staggered out of the way of the cab, avoided a perambulator by a convulsive movement, and found myself behind the hansom. A happy thought saved me, and as this drove slowly along I followed in its immediate wake, trembling and astonished at the turn of my adventure, and not only trembling but shivering. It was a bright day in January, and I was stark naked, and the thin slime of mud that covered the road was near freezing. Foolish as it seems to me now, I had not reckoned that, transparent or not, I was still amenable to the weather and all its consequences.

'Then suddenly a bright idea came into my head. I ran round and got into the cab. And so, shivering, scared, and sniffing with the first intimations of a cold, and with the bruises in the small of my back growing upon my attention, I drove slowly along Oxford Street and past Tottenham Court Road. My mood was as different from that in which I had sallied forth ten minutes since as it is possible to imagine. *This* invisibility, indeed! The one thought that possessed me now was how to get out of the scrape I was in?

'We crawled past Mudie's,* and there a tall woman, with five or six yellow-labelled books,* hailed my cab, and I sprang out just in time to escape her, shaving a railway van narrowly in my flight. I made off up the roadway to Bloomsbury Square, intending to strike north beyond the Museum,* and so get into the quiet district. I was now cruelly chilled, and the strangeness of my situation so unnerved me that I whimpered as I ran. At the westward corner of the square a little white dog ran out of the Pharmaceutical Society's offices,* and incontinently made for me, nose down.

'I had never realised it before, but the nose is to the mind of a dog what the eye is to the mind of a seeing man. Dogs perceive the scent of a man moving as men perceive his visible appearance. This brute began barking and leaping, showing, as it seemed to me only too plainly, that he was aware of me. I crossed Great Russell Street, glancing over my shoulder as I did so, and went some way along Montague Street before I realised what I was running towards.

'Then I became aware of a blare of music, and looking along the street saw a number of people advancing out of Russell Square, red jerseys and the banner of the Salvation Army* to the fore. Such a crowd, chanting in the roadway and scoffing on the pavement, I could not hope to penetrate, and dreading to go back and farther from home again, and, deciding on the spur of the moment, I ran up the white steps of a house facing the Museum railings, and stood there until the crowd should have passed. Happily the dog stopped at the noise of the band, hesitated, and turned tail, running back to Bloomsbury Square again.

'On came the band, bawling with unconscious irony some hymn about "When shall we see His face?"* and it seemed an interminable time to me before the tide of the crowd washed along the pavement by me. Thud, thud, thud, came the drum with a vibrating resonance, and for the moment I did not notice two urchins stopping at the railings by me. "See 'em," said one. "See what?" said the other. "Why—them footmarks—bare. Like what you makes in mud."

'I looked down and saw the youngsters had stopped and were gaping at the muddy footmarks I had left behind me, up the newly whitened steps. The passing people elbowed and jostled them, but their confounded intelligence was arrested. "Thud, thud, thud, when, thud, shall we see, thud, His face, thud, thud." "There's a barefoot man gone up them steps, or I don't know nothing," said one. "And he ain't never come down again. And his foot was a-bleeding."

'The thick of the crowd had already passed. "Looky there, Ted," quoth the younger of the detectives* with the sharpness of surprise in his voice, and pointed straight at my feet. I looked down and saw at once the dim suggestion of their outline sketched in splashes of mud. For a moment I was paralysed.

'"Why, that's rum!" said the elder. "Dashed rum! It's just like the ghost of a foot, ain't it?" He hesitated and advanced with outstretched hand. A man pulled up short to see what he was catching, and then a girl. In another moment he would have touched me. Then I saw what to do. I made a step, the boy started back with an exclamation, and with a rapid movement I swung myself over into the portico of the next house. But the smaller boy was sharp enough to follow the movement, and before I was well down the steps and upon the pavement he had recovered from his momentary astonishment, and was shouting out that the feet had gone over the wall.

'They rushed round and saw my new footmarks flash into being on the lower step and upon the pavement.

'"What's up?" asked some one.

' "Feet! Look! Feet running!"

'Everybody in the road, except my three pursuers, was pouring along after the Salvation Army, and this flow not only impeded me but them. There was an eddy of surprise and interrogation. At the cost of bowling over one young fellow I got through, and in another moment I was running headlong round the circuit of Russell Square, with six or seven astonished people following my footmarks. There was no time for explanation, or else the whole host would have been after me.

'Twice I doubled round corners, thrice I crossed the road and came back on my tracks, and then as my feet grew hot and dry the damp impressions began to fade. At last I had a breathing space, and rubbed my feet clean with my hands, and so got away altogether. The last I saw of the chase was a little group of a dozen people, perhaps, studying with infinite perplexity a slowly drying footprint that had resulted from a puddle in Tavistock Square, a footprint as isolated and incomprehensible to them as Crusoe's solitary discovery.*

'This running warmed me to a certain extent, and I went on with a better courage through the maze of less frequented roads that runs thereabout. My back had now become very stiff and sore, my tonsils were painful from the cabman's fingers, and the skin of my neck had been scratched by his nails; my feet hurt exceedingly, and I was lame from a little cut on one foot. I saw in time a blind man approaching me, and fled limping, for I feared his subtle intuitions. Once or twice accidental collisions occurred, and I left people amazed with unaccountable curses ringing in their ears. Then came something silent and quiet upon my face, and across the square fell a thin veil of slowly falling flakes of snow. I had caught a cold, and do as I would I could not avoid an occasional sneeze. And every dog that came in sight, with its pointing nose and curious sniffing, was a terror to me.

'Then came men and boys running, first one then others, and shouting as they ran. It was a fire. They ran in the direction of my lodging, and looking back down a street I saw a mass of black smoke streaming up above the roofs and telephone wires. It was, I felt assured, my lodging that was burning; my clothes, apparatus, all my resources, indeed, except my cheque-book and the three volumes of memoranda that awaited me in Great Portland Street, were there. Burning! I had burnt my boats—if ever a man did! The place was blazing.'

The Invisible Man paused and thought. Kemp glanced nervously out of the window. 'Yes!' he said, 'go on.'

XXII

IN THE EMPORIUM

'So last January, with the beginning of a snowstorm in the air about me—and if it settled on me it would betray me!—weary, cold, painful, inexpressibly wretched, and still but half convinced of my invisible quality, I began this new life to which I am committed. I had no refuge, no appliances, no human being in the whole world in whom I could confide. To have told my secret would have given me away—made a mere show and rarity of me. Nevertheless I was half-minded to accost some passer-by and throw myself upon his mercy. But I knew too clearly the terror and brutal cruelty my advances would evoke. I made no plans in the street. My sole object was to get shelter from the snow, to get myself covered and warm, then I might hope to plan. But even to me, an Invisible Man, the rows of London houses stood latched, barred, and bolted impregnably.

'Only one thing could I see clearly before me—the cold, exposure and misery of the snowstorm and night.

'And then I had a brilliant idea. I turned down one of the roads leading from Gower Street to Tottenham Court Road, and found myself outside Omniums,* the big establishment where everything is to be bought—you know the place: meat, grocery, linen, furniture, clothing, oil paintings even—a huge, meandering collection of shops rather than a shop. I had thought I should find the doors open, but they were closed, and as I stood in the wide entrance a carriage stopped outside, and a man in uniform—you know the kind of personage with "*Omnium*" on his cap—flung open the door. I contrived to enter, and walking down the shop—it was a department where they were selling ribbons and gloves and stockings and that sort of thing—came to a more spacious region, devoted to picnic baskets and wicker furniture.

'I did not feel safe there, however, people were going to and fro, and I prowled restlessly about until I came upon a huge section in an upper floor containing multitudes of bedsteads, and over these I clambered, and found a resting-place at last among a huge pile of folded flock mattresses. The place was already lit up and agreeably warm, and I decided to remain in hiding where I was, keeping a cautious eye on the two or three sets of shopmen and customers who were meandering through the place, until closing time came. Then I should be able, I thought, to rob the place for food and clothing and disguise, prowl through it, and examine its resources, perhaps sleep on some of the bedding. That seemed an acceptable plan. My idea was to procure clothing to make myself a muffled but acceptable figure, to get money, and then to recover my books and parcels, where they awaited me, take a lodging somewhere, and elaborate plans for the complete realisation of the advantages my invisibility gave me (as I still imagined) over my fellow-men.

'Closing time arrived quickly enough. It could not have been more than an hour after I took up my position on the mattresses before I noticed the blinds of the windows being drawn, and customers being marched doorward. And then a number of brisk young men began with remarkable alacrity to tidy up the goods that remained disturbed. I left my lair as the crowds diminished and prowled cautiously out into the less desolate parts of the shop. I was really surprised to observe how rapidly the young men and women whipped away the goods displayed for sale during the day. All the boxes of goods, the hanging fabrics, the festoons of lace, the boxes of sweets in the grocery section, the displays of this and that, were being taken down, folded up, slapped into tidy receptacles, and everything that could not be taken down and put away had sheets of some coarse stuff like sacking flung over them. Finally all the chairs were turned up on the counters, leaving the floors clear. Directly each of these young people had done he or she made promptly for the door with such an expression of animation as I have rarely observed in a shop-assistant before. Then came a lot of youngsters, scattering sawdust and carrying pails and brooms. I had to dodge to get out the way, and as it was my ankle got stung with the sawdust. For some time, wandering through the swathed and darkened departments, I could hear the brooms at work. And at last, a good hour or more after the shop had been closed, came a noise of locking doors. Silence came upon the place, and I found myself wandering through the vast and intricate shops, galleries, showrooms of the place alone. It was very still—in one place I remember passing near one of the Tottenham Court Road entrances and listening to the tapping boot-heels of the passers-by.

'My first visit was to the place where I had seen stockings and gloves for sale. It was dark, and I had the devil of a hunt after matches, which I found at last in a drawer of the little cash desk. Then I had to get a candle. I had to tear down wrappers and ransack a number of boxes and drawers, but at last I managed to turn out what I sought: the box label called them lambswool pants and lambswool vests. Then socks, a thick comforter, and then I went to the clothing place and got trousers, a lounge jacket, an overcoat, and a slouch hat—a clerical sort of hat with the brim turned down. I began to feel a human being again, and my next thought was food.

'Upstairs was a refreshment department, and there I got cold meat. There was coffee still in the urn, and I lit the gas and warmed it up again, and altogether I did not do badly. Afterwards, prowling through the place in search of blankets—I had to put up at last with a heap of down quilts—I came upon a grocery section with a lot of chocolate and crystallised fruits, more than was good for me, indeed, and some white burgundy. And near that was a toy department, and I had a brilliant idea. I found some artificial noses—dummy noses, you know, and I thought of dark spectacles. But Omniums had no optical department. My nose had been a difficulty indeed. I had thought of paint. But the discovery set my mind running on wigs and masks, and the like. Finally I went to sleep in a heap of down quilts, very warm and comfortable.

'My last thoughts before sleeping were the most agreeable I had had since the change. I was in a state of physical serenity, and that was reflected in my mind. I thought that I should be able to slip out unobserved in the morning with my clothes upon me, muffling my face with a white wrapper I had taken, purchase spectacles with the money I had stolen, and so complete my disguise. I lapsed into disorderly dreams of all the fantastic things that had happened during the last few days. I saw the ugly little Jew of a landlord vociferating in his rooms, I saw his two sons marvelling, and the wrinked* old woman's gnarled face as she asked for her cat. I experienced again the strange sensation of seeing the cloth disappear, and so I came round to the windy hillside and the sniffing old clergyman mumbling, "Earth to earth, ashes to ashes, dust to dust," at my father's open grave.

' "You also," said a voice, and suddenly I was being forced towards the grave. I struggled, shouted, appealed to the mourners, but they continued stonily following the service; the old clergyman, too, never faltered, droning and sniffing through the ritual. I realised I was invisible and inaudible, that overwhelming forces had their grip on me.

I struggled in vain, I was forced over the brink, the coffin rang hollow as I fell upon it, and the gravel came flying after me in spadefuls. Nobody heeded me, nobody was aware of me. I made convulsive struggles and awoke.

'The pale London dawn had come, the place was full of a chilly grey light that filtered round the edges of the window-blinds. I sat up, and for a time I could not think where this ample apartment, with its counters, its piles of rolled stuff, its heap of quilts and cushions, its iron pillars, might be. Then, as recollection came back to me, I heard voices in conversation.

'Then far down the place, in the brighter light of some department which had already raised its blinds, I saw two men approaching. I scrambled to my feet, looking about me for some way of escape, and even as I did so the sound of my movement made them aware of me. I suppose they saw merely a figure moving quietly and quickly away. "Who's that?" cried one, and "Stop there!" shouted the other. I dashed round a corner and came full tilt—a faceless figure, mind you!—on a lanky lad of fifteen. He yelled and I bowled him over, rushed past him, turned another corner, and by a happy inspiration threw myself flat behind a counter. In another moment feet went running past and I heard voices shouting, "All hands to the doors!" asking what was "up," and giving one another advice how to catch me.

'Lying on the ground, I felt scared out of my wits. But, odd as it may seem, it did not occur to me at the moment to take off my clothes, as I should have done. I had made up my mind, I suppose, to get away in them, and that ruled me. And then down the vista of the counters came a bawling of, "Here he is!"

'I sprang to my feet, whipped a chair off the counter, and sent it whirling at the fool who had shouted, turned, came into another round a corner, sent him spinning, and rushed up the stairs. He kept his footing, gave a view hallo, and came up the staircase hot after me. Up the staircase were piled a multitude of those bright-coloured pot things—what are they?'

'Art pots,' suggested Kemp.

'That's it! Art pots. Well, I turned at the top step and swung round, plucked one out of a pile, and smashed it on his silly head as he came at me. The whole pile of pots went headlong, and I heard shouting and footsteps running from all parts. I made a mad rush for the refreshment place, and there was a man in white like a man cook, who took up the chase. I made one last desperate turn and found myself among lamps and ironmongery. I went behind the counter of this and waited for my cook, and as he bolted in at the head of the chase, I doubled him up with a lamp. Down he went, and I crouched down behind the counter, began whipping off my clothes as fast as I could. Coat, jacket, trousers, shoes, were all right, but a lambswool vest fits a man like a skin. I heard more men coming, my cook was lying quiet on the other side of the counter, stunned or scared speechless, and I had to make another dash for it, like a rabbit hunted out of a wood pile.

'"This way, Policeman," I heard some one shouting. I found myself in my bedstead storeroom again, and at the end a wilderness of wardrobes. I rushed among them, went flat, got rid of my vest after infinite wriggling, and stood a free man again, panting and scared, as the policeman and three of the shopmen came round the corner. They made a rush for the vest and pants and collared the trousers. "He's dropping his plunder," said one of the young men. "He *must* be somewhere here."

'But they did not find me all the same.

'I stood watching them hunt for me for a time, and cursing my ill-luck in losing the clothes. Then I went into the refreshment-room, drank a little milk I found there, and sat down by the fire to consider my position.

'In a little while two assistants came in and began to talk over the business very excitedly, and like the fools they were. I heard a magnified account of my depredations, and other speculations as to my whereabouts. Then I fell to scheming again. The insurmountable difficulty of the place, especially now it was alarmed, was to get any plunder out of it. I went down into the warehouse to see if there was any chance of packing and addressing a parcel, but I could not understand the system of checking. About eleven o'clock, the snow having thawed as it fell, and the day being finer and a little warmer than the previous one, I decided that the Emporium was hopeless, and went out again exasperated at my want of success, and with only the vaguest plans of action in my mind.'

XXIII

'But you begin now to realise,' said the Invisible Man, 'the full disadvantage of my condition. I had no shelter—no covering—to get clothing was to forego all my advantage, to make of myself a strange and terrible thing. I was fasting; for to eat, to fill myself with unassimilated matter, would be to become grotesquely visible again.'

'I never thought of that,' said Kemp.

'Nor had I. And the snow had warned me of other dangers. I could not go abroad in snow—it would settle on me and expose me. Rain, too, would make me a watery outline, a glistening surface of a man—a bubble. And fog—I should be like a fainter bubble in a fog, a surface, a greasy glimmer of humanity. Moreover, as I went abroad—in the London air—I gathered dirt about my ankles, floating smuts and dust upon my skin. I did not know how long it would be before I should become visible from that cause also. But I saw clearly it could not be very long.'

'Not in London at any rate.'

'I went into the slums towards Great Portland Street, and found myself at the end of the street in which I had lodged. I did not go that way because of the crowd half way down it opposite to the still smoking ruins of the house I had fired. My most immediate problem was to get clothing. Then I saw in one of those little miscellaneous shops—news, sweets, toys, stationery, belated Christmas tomfoolery, and so forth—an array of masks and noses, and recalled the idea *Omnium's* toys had suggested. I turned about, no longer aimless, and went circuitously, in order to avoid the busy ways, towards the back streets north of the Strand; for I remembered, though not very distinctly where, that some theatrical costumiers had shops in that district.

'The day was cold, with a nipping wind down the northward running streets. I walked fast to avoid being overtaken. Every crossing was a danger, every passenger a thing to watch alertly. One man, as I was about to pass him at the top of Bedford Street, turned upon me abruptly and came into me, sending me into the road, and almost under the wheel of a passing hansom. The verdict of the cab-rank was that he had had some sort of stroke. I was so unnerved by this encounter that I went into Covent Garden Market and sat down for some time in a quiet corner by a stall of violets, panting and trembling. I found I had caught a fresh cold, and had to turn out after a time lest my sneezes should attract attention.

'At last I reached the object of my quest, a dirty, fly-blown little shop in a by-way near Drury Lane,* with a window full of tinsel robes, sham jewels, wigs, slippers, dominoes,* and theatrical photographs. The shop was old-fashioned and low and dark, and the house rose above it for four storeys, dark and dismal. I peered through the window, and, seeing no one within, entered. The opening of the door set a clanking bell ringing. I left it open, and walked round a bare costume stand, into a corner behind a cheval glass.* For a minute or so no one came. Then I heard heavy feet striding across a room, and a man appeared down the shop.

'My plans were now perfectly definite. I proposed to make my way into the house, secrete myself upstairs, watch my opportunity, and, when everything was quiet, rummage out a wig, mask, spectacles, and costume, and go into the world, perhaps a grotesque but still a creditable figure. And, incidentally, of course, I could rob the house of any available money.

'The man who had entered the shop was a short, slightly hunched, beetle-browed man with long arms and very short bandy legs. Apparently I had interrupted a meal. He stared about the shop with an expression of expectation. This gave way to surprise, and then anger, as he saw the shop empty. "Damn the boys!" he said. He went to stare up and down the street. He came in again in a minute, kicked the door to with his foot spitefully, and went muttering back to the house door.

'I came forward to follow him, and at the noise of my movement he stopped dead. I did so too, startled by his quickness of ear. He slammed the house door in my face.

'I stood hesitating. Suddenly I heard his quick footsteps returning, and the door re-opened. He stood looking about the shop like one who was still not satisfied. Then, murmuring to himself, he examined the back of the counter and peered behind some fixtures. Then he stood doubtful. He had left the house door open, and I slipped into the inner room.

'It was a queer little room, poorly furnished, and with a number of big masks in the corner. On the table was his belated breakfast, and it was a confoundedly exasperating thing for me, Kemp, to have to sniff his coffee and stand watching while he came in and resumed his meal. And his table manners were irritating. Three doors opened into the little room, one going upstairs and one down, but they were all shut. I could not get out of the room while he was there; I could scarcely move because of his alertness, and there was a draught down my back. Twice I strangled a sneeze just in time.

'The spectacular quality of my sensations was curious and novel, but for all that I was heartily tired and angry long before he had done his eating. But at last he made an end, and putting his beggarly crockery on the black tin tray upon which he had had his teapot, and gathering all the crumbs up on the mustard-stained cloth, he took the whole lot of things after him. His burden prevented his shutting the door behind him—as he would have done. I never saw such a man for shutting doors—and I followed him into a very dirty underground kitchen and scullery. I had the pleasure of seeing him begin to wash up, and then, finding no good in keeping down there, and the brick-floor being cold to my feet, I returned upstairs and sat in his chair by the fire. It was burning low, and scarcely thinking, I put on a little coal. The noise of this brought him up at once, and he stood aglare. He peered about the room and was within an ace of touching me. Even after that examination he scarcely seemed satisfied. He stopped in the doorway and took a final inspection before he went down.

'I waited in the little parlour for an age, and at last he came up and opened the upstairs door. I crept close after him.

'On the staircase he stopped suddenly, so that I very nearly blundered into him. He stood looking back right into my face, and listening. "I could have sworn," he said. His long, hairy hand pulled at his lower lip; his eye went up and down the staircase. Then he grunted, and went on up again.

'His hand was on the handle of a door, and there he stopped again, with the same puzzled anger on his face. He was becoming aware of the faint sound of my movements about him. The man must have had diabolically acute hearing. He suddenly flashed into rage: "If there's any one in this house——" he cried, with an oath, and left the threat unfinished. He put his hand in his pocket, failed to find what he wanted, and, rushing past me, went blundering noisily and pugnaciously downstairs. But I did not follow him; I sat on the head of the staircase until his return.

'Presently he came up again, still muttering. He opened the door of the room, and, before I could enter, slammed it in my face.

'I resolved to explore the house, and spent some time in doing so as noiselessly as possible. The house was very old and tumbledown, damp, so that the paper in the attics was peeling from the walls, and rat-infested. Most of the door handles were stiff, and I was afraid to turn them. Several rooms I did inspect were unfurnished, and others were littered with theatrical lumber, bought secondhand, I judged from its appearance. In one room next to his I found a lot of old clothes. I began routing among these, and in my eagerness forgot again the evident sharpness of his ears. I heard a stealthy footstep, and, looking up just in time, saw him peeping in at the tumbled heap and holding an old-fashioned revolver in his hand. I stood perfectly still while he stared about open-mouthed and suspicious. "It must have been her," he said slowly. "Damn her!"

'He shut the door quietly, and immediately I heard the key turn in the lock. Then his footsteps retreated. I realised abruptly that I was locked in. For a minute I did not know what to do. I walked from door to window and back, and stood perplexed. A gust of anger came upon me. But I decided to inspect the clothes before I did anything further, and my first attempt brought down a pile from an upper shelf. This brought him back, more sinister than ever. This time he actually touched me, jumped back with amazement, and stood astonished in the middle of the room.

'Presently he calmed a little. "Rats," he said in an undertone, fingers on lip. He was evidently a little scared. I edged quietly out of the room, but a plank creaked. Then the infernal little brute started going all over the house, revolver in hand, and locking door after door and pocketing the keys. When I realised what he was up to I had a fit of rage—I could hardly control myself sufficiently to watch my opportunity. By this time I knew he was alone in the house, and so I made no more ado, but knocked him on the head.'

'Knocked him on the head?' exclaimed Kemp.

'Yes—stunned him—as he was going downstairs. Hit him from behind with a stool that stood on the landing. He went downstairs like a bag of old boots.'

'But—I say! The common conventions of humanity——'

'Are all very well for common people. But the point was, Kemp, that I had to get out of that house in a disguise without his seeing me.

I couldn't think of any other way of doing it. And then I gagged him with a Louis Quatorze vest,* and tied him up in a sheet!'

'Tied him up in a sheet!'

'Made a sort of bag of it. It was rather a good idea to keep the idiot scared and quiet, and a devilish hard thing to get out of—head away from the string. My dear Kemp, it's no good your sitting and glaring as though I had done a murder. He had his revolver. If once he had seen me he would have been able to describe me——'

'But still,' said Kemp, 'in England—today! And the man was in his own house, and you were—well, robbing.'

'Robbing! Confound it! You'll call me a thief next. Surely, Kemp, you're not fool enough to dance on the old strings. Can't you see my position?'

'And his too!' said Kemp.

The Invisible Man stood up sharply. 'What do you mean to say?'

Kemp's face grew a trifle hard. He was about to speak, and checked himself. 'I suppose, after all,' he said, with a sudden change of manner, 'the thing had to be done. You were in a fix. But still——'

'Of course I was in a fix—an infernal fix! And he made me wild too—hunting me about the house, fooling about with his revolver, locking and unlocking doors. He was simply exasperating. You don't blame me, do you? You don't blame me?'

'I never blame any one,' said Kemp. 'It's quite out of fashion.* What did you do next?'

'I was hungry. Downstairs I found a loaf and some rank cheese—more than sufficient to satisfy my hunger. I took some brandy-and-water, and then went up past my impromptu bag—he was lying quite still—to the room containing the old clothes. This looked out upon the street, two lace curtains, brown with dirt, guarding the window. I went and peered out through their interstices. Outside the day was bright—by contrast with the brown shadows of the dismal house in which I found myself, dazzlingly bright. A brisk traffic was going by—fruit carts, a hansom, a four-wheeler with a pile of boxes, a fish-monger's cart. I turned with spots of colour swimming before my eyes to the shadowy fixtures behind me. My excitement was giving place to a clear apprehension of my position again. The room was full of a faint scent of benzoline,* used, I suppose, in cleaning the garments.

'I began a systematic search of the place. I should judge the hunch-back had been alone in the house for some time. He was a curious person. . . . Everything that could possibly be of service to me I collected in the clothes store-room, and then I made a deliberate selection. I found a handbag I thought a suitable possession, and some powder, rouge, and sticking-plaster.

'I had thought of painting and powdering my face and all that there was to show of me, in order to render myself visible, but the disadvantage of this lay in the fact that I should require turpentine and other appliances and a considerable amount of time before I could vanish again. Finally I chose a nose of the better type, slightly grotesque, but not more so than that of many human beings, dark glasses, greyish whiskers, and a wig. I could find no underclothing, but that I could buy subsequently, and for the time I swathed myself in calico dominoes* and some white cashmere scarves. I could find no socks, but the hunchback's boots were rather a loose fit, and sufficed. In a desk in the shop were three sovereigns and about thirty shillings-worth of silver, and in a locked cupboard I burst in the inner room were eight pounds in gold. I could go forth into the world again, equipped.

'Then came a curious hesitation. Was my appearance really creditable? I tried myself with a little bedroom looking-glass, inspecting myself from every point of view to discover any forgotten chink, but it all seemed sound. I was grotesque to the theatrical pitch—a stage miser—but I was certainly not a physical impossibility. Gathering confidence, I took my looking-glass down into the shop, pulled down the shop blinds, and surveyed myself from every point of view with the help of the cheval glass in the corner.

'I spent some minutes screwing up my courage, and then unlocked the shop door, and marched out into the street, leaving the little man to get out of his sheet again when he liked. In five minutes a dozen turnings intervened between me and the costumier's shop. No one appeared to notice me very pointedly. My last difficulty seemed overcome.'

He stopped again.

'And you troubled no more about the hunchback?' said Kemp.

'No,' said the Invisible Man. 'Nor have I heard what became of him. I suppose he untied himself or kicked himself out. The knots were pretty tight.'

He became silent, and went to the window and stared out.

'What happened when you went out into the Strand?'

'Oh! Disillusionment again. I thought my troubles were over. Practically, I thought I had impunity to do whatever I chose, everything—save to give away my secret. So I thought. Whatever I did, whatever the consequences might be, was nothing to me. I had merely to fling aside my garments and vanish. No person could hold me. I could take my money where I found it. I decided to treat myself to a sumptuous feast, and then put up at a good hotel, and accumulate a new outfit of property. I felt amazingly confident; it's not particularly pleasant to recall that I was an ass. I went into a place and was already ordering a lunch, when it occurred to me that I could not eat unless I exposed my invisible face. I finished ordering the lunch, told the man I should be back in ten minutes, and went out exasperated. I don't know if you have ever been disappointed in your appetite.'

'Not quite so badly,' said Kemp, 'but I can imagine it.'

'I could have smashed the silly devils. At last, faint with the desire for tasteful food, I went into another place and demanded a private room. "I am disfigured," I said, "badly." They looked at me curiously, but of course it was not their affair—and so at last I got my lunch. It was not particularly well served, but it sufficed, and when I had had it, I sat over a cigar, trying to plan my line of action. And outside a snowstorm was beginning.

'The more I thought it over, Kemp, the more I realised what a helpless absurdity an Invisible Man was—in a cold and dirty climate and a crowded, civilised city. Before I made this mad experiment I had dreamt of a thousand advantages. That afternoon it seemed all disappointment. I went over the heads of the things a man reckons desirable. No doubt invisibility made it possible to get them, but it made it impossible to enjoy them when they are got. Ambition—what is the good of pride of place when you cannot appear there? What is the good of the love of woman when her name must needs be Delilah?* I have no taste for politics, for the black-guardisms of fame, for philanthropy, for sport. What was I to do? And for this I had become a wrapped-up mystery, a swathed and bandaged caricature of a man.'

He paused, and his attitude suggested a roving glance at the window.

'But how did you get to Iping?' said Kemp, anxious to keep his guest busy talking.

'I went there to work. I had one hope. It was a half idea! I have it still. It is a full-blown idea now. A way of getting back! Of restoring what I have done. When I choose. When I have done all I mean to do invisibly. And that is what I chiefly want to talk to you about now——'

'You went straight to Iping?'

'Yes. I had simply to get my three volumes of memoranda and my cheque-book, my luggage and underclothing, order a quantity of chemicals to work out this idea of mine—I will show you the calculations as soon as I get my books—and then I started. Jove! I remember the snowstorm now, and the accursed bother it was to keep the snow from damping my pasteboard nose——'

'At the end,' said Kemp, 'the day before yesterday, when they found you out, you rather—to judge by the papers——'

'I did. Rather. Did I kill that fool of a constable?'

'No,' said Kemp. 'He's expected to recover.'

'That's his luck, then. I clean lost my temper, the fools! Why couldn't they leave me alone? And that grocer lout?'

'There's no death expected,' said Kemp.

'I don't know about that tramp of mine,' said the Invisible Man, with an unpleasant laugh.

'By heaven, Kemp, men of your stamp don't know what rage is! . . . To have worked for years, to have planned and plotted, and then to get some fumbling, purblind idiot messing across your course! . . . Every conceivable sort of silly creature that has ever been created has been sent to cross me. . . . If I have much more of it, I shall go wild—I shall start mowing 'em.*

'As it is, they've made things a thousand times more difficult.'

XXIV

THE PLAN THAT FAILED

'But now,' said Kemp, with a side-glance out of the window, 'what are we to do?'

He moved nearer his guest to prevent the possibility of a sudden glimpse of the three men who were advancing up the hill road—with an intolerable slowness, as it seemed to Kemp.

'What were you planning to do, when you were heading for Port Burdock? Had you any plan?'

'I was going to clear out of the country. But I have altered that plan rather since seeing you. I thought it would be wise, now the weather is hot and invisibility possible, to make for the South. Especially as my secret was known, and every one would be on the look-out for a masked and muffled man. You have a line of steamers from here to France. My idea was to get aboard one and run the risks of the passage. Thence I could go by train into Spain, or else to Algiers. It would not be difficult. There a man might always be invisible, and yet live. And do things. I was using that tramp as a money-box and luggage carrier, until I decided how to get my books and things sent over to meet me.'

'That's clear.'

'And then the filthy brute must needs try and rob me! He *has* hidden my books, Kemp. Hidden my books!

'If I can lay my hands on him! . . .'

'Best plan to get the books out of him first.'

'But where is he? Do you know?'

'He's in the town police-station, locked up, by his own request, in the strongest cell in the place.'

'Cur!' said the Invisible Man.

'But that hangs up your plans a little.'

'We must get those books; those books are vital.'

'Certainly,' said Kemp, a little nervously, wondering if he heard footsteps outside. 'Certainly we must get those books. But that won't be difficult, if he doesn't know they're for you.'

'No,' said the Invisible Man, and thought.

* * * *

Kemp tried to think of something to keep the talk going, but the Invisible Man resumed of his own accord.

'Blundering into your house, Kemp,' he said, 'changes all my plans. For you are a man that can understand. In spite of all that has happened, in spite of this publicity, of the loss of my books, of what I have suffered, there still remain great possibilities, huge possibilities——

'You have told no one I am here?' he asked abruptly.

Kemp hesitated. 'That was implied,' he said.

'No one?' insisted Griffin.

'Not a soul.'

'Ah! Now——' The Invisible Man stood up, and sticking his arms akimbo, began to pace the study.

'I made a mistake, Kemp, a huge mistake, in carrying this thing through alone. I have wasted strength, time, opportunities. Alone; it is wonderful how little a man can do alone! To rob a little, to hurt a little, and there is the end.

'What I want, Kemp, is a goal-keeper, a helper, and a hiding-place; an arrangement whereby I can sleep and eat and rest in peace and unsuspected. I must have a confederate. With a confederate, with food and rest, a thousand things are possible.

'Hitherto I have gone on vague lines. We have to consider all that invisibility means; all that it does not mean. It means little advantage for eavesdropping and so forth—one makes sounds. It's of little help— a little help, perhaps—in housebreaking and so forth. Once you've caught me you could easily imprison me. But on the other hand I am hard to catch. This invisibility, in fact, is only good in two cases. It's useful in getting away; it's useful in approaching. It's particularly useful, therefore, in killing. I can walk round a man, whatever weapon he has, choose my point, strike as I like, dodge as I like, escape as I like.'

Kemp's hand went to his moustache. Was that a movement downstairs?

'And it is killing we must do, Kemp.'

'It is killing we must do,' repeated Kemp. 'I'm listening to your plan, Griffin; but I'm not agreeing, mind. *Why* killing?'

'Not wanton killing, but a judicious slaying. The point is: They know there is an Invisible Man—as well as we know there is an Invisible Man—and that Invisible Man, Kemp, must now establish a Reign of Terror. Yes; no doubt it's startling, but I mean it. A Reign of Terror.

He must take some town, like your Burdock, and terrify and dominate it. He must issue his orders. He can do that in a thousand ways—scraps of paper thrust under doors would suffice. And all who disobey his orders he must kill, and kill all who would defend them.'

'Humph!' said Kemp, no longer listening to Griffin, but to the sound of his front door opening and closing.

'It seems to me, Griffin,' he said, to cover his wandering attention, 'that your confederate would be in a difficult position?'

'No one would know he was a confederate,' said the Invisible Man eagerly. And then suddenly, '*Hush!* What's that downstairs?'

'Nothing,' said Kemp, and suddenly began to speak loud and fast. 'I don't agree to this, Griffin,' he said. 'Understand me, I don't agree to this. Why dream of playing a game against the race? How can you hope to gain happiness? Don't be a lone wolf. Publish your results—take the world—take the nation at least into your confidence. Think what you might do with a million helpers——'

The Invisible Man interrupted—arm extended. 'There are footsteps coming upstairs,' he said.

'Nonsense,' said Kemp.

'Let me see,' said the Invisible Man, and advanced, arm extended, to the door.

And then things happened very swiftly. Kemp hesitated for a second, and then moved to intercept him. The Invisible Man started and stood still. 'Traitor!' cried the Voice, and suddenly the dressing-gown opened, and, sitting down the unseen began to disrobe. Kemp made three swift steps to the door, and forthwith the Invisible Man—his legs had vanished—sprang to his feet with a shout. Kemp flung the door open.

As it opened, there came a sound of hurrying feet downstairs and voices.

With a quick movement Kemp thrust the Invisible Man back, sprang aside, and slammed the door. The key was outside and ready. In another moment Griffin would have been alone in the belvedere study a prisoner—save for one little thing. The key had been slipped in hastily that morning. As Kemp slammed the door it fell noisily upon the carpet.

Kemp's face became white. He tried to grip the door-handle with both hands. For a moment he stood lugging. Then the door gave six inches. But he got it closed again. The second time it was jerked a foot wide, and the dressing-gown came wedging itself into the opening. His throat was gripped by invisible fingers, and he left his hold on the handle to defend himself. He was forced back, tripped, and pitched heavily into the corner of the landing. The empty dressing-gown was flung on the top of him.

Half-way up the staircase was Colonel Adye, the recipient of Kemp's letter, the chief of the Burdock police. He was staring aghast at the sudden appearance of Kemp, followed by the extraordinary sight of clothing tossing empty in the air. He saw Kemp felled and struggling to his feet. He saw Kemp reel, rush forward, and go down again, felled like an ox.

Then suddenly he was struck violently. By nothing! A vast weight, it seemed, leapt upon him, and he was hurled headlong down the stair-case, with a grip on his throat and a knee in his groin. An invisible foot trod on his back, a ghostly patter passed downstairs, he heard the two police officers in the hall shout and run, and the front door of the house slammed violently.

He rolled over and sat up staring. He saw, staggering down the staircase, Kemp, dusty and dishevelled, one side of his face white from a blow, his lip bleeding, and a pink dressing-gown and some underclothing held in his arms.

'My God!' cried Kemp, 'the game's up! He's gone!'

XXV

THE HUNTING OF THE INVISIBLE MAN

For a space Kemp was too inarticulate to make Adye understand the swift things that had just happened. They stood on the landing, Kemp speaking hurriedly, the grotesque swathings of Griffin still on his arm. But presently Adye began to grasp something of the situation.

'He is mad,' said Kemp; 'inhuman. He is pure selfishness. He thinks of nothing but his own advantage, his own safety. I have listened to such a story this morning of brutal self-seeking. . . . He has wounded men. He will kill them unless we can prevent him. He will create a panic. Nothing can stop him. He is going out now—furious!'

'He must be caught,' said Adye. 'That is certain.'

'But how?' cried Kemp, and suddenly became full of ideas. 'You must begin at once; you must set every available man to work; you must prevent his leaving this district. Once he gets away he may go through the countryside as he wills, killing and maiming. He dreams of a reign of terror! A reign of terror, I tell you. You must set a watch on trains and roads and shipping. The garrison must help. You must wire for help. The only thing that may keep him here is the thought of recovering some books of notes he counts of value. I will tell you of that! There is a man in your police-station—Marvel.'

'I know,' said Adye, 'I know. Those books—yes. But the tramp. . . .'

'Says he hasn't them. But he thinks the tramp has. And you must prevent him from eating or sleeping—day and night the country must be astir for him. Food must be locked up and secured, all food, so that he will have to break his way to it. The houses everywhere must be barred against him. Heaven send us cold nights and rain! The whole countryside must begin hunting and keep hunting. I tell you, Adye, he is a danger, a disaster—unless he is pinned down and secured, it is frightful to think of the things that may happen.'

'What else can we do?' said Adye. 'I must go down at once and begin organising. But why not come? Yes—you come too! Come, and we must hold a sort of council of war—get Hopps to help—and the railway managers. By Jove! it's urgent. Come along—tell me as we go. What else is there we can do? Put that stuff down.'

In another moment Adye was leading the way downstairs. They found the front door open and the policemen standing outside staring at empty air. 'He's got away, sir,' said one.

'We must go to the central station at once,' said Adye. 'One of you go on down and get a cab to come up and meet us—quickly. And now, Kemp, what else?'

'Dogs,' said Kemp. 'Get dogs. They don't see him, but they wind him. Get dogs.'

'Good,' said Adye. 'It's not generally known, but the prison officials over at Halstead know a man with bloodhounds. Dogs. What else?'

'Bear in mind,' said Kemp, 'his food shows. After eating, his food shows until it is assimilated. So that he has to hide after eating. You must keep on beating. Every thicket, every quiet corner. And put all weapons—all implements that might be weapons, away. He can't carry such things for long. And what he can snatch up and strike men with must be hidden away.'

'Good again,' said Adye. 'We shall have him yet!'

'And on the roads——' said Kemp, and hesitated.

'Yes?' said Adye.

'Powdered glass,' said Kemp. 'It's cruel, I know. But think of what he may do!'

Adye drew the air in sharply between his teeth. 'It's unsportsman-like. I don't know. But I'll have powdered glass got ready. If he goes too far. . . .'

'The man's become inhuman, I tell you,' said Kemp. 'I am as sure he will establish a reign of terror—so soon as he has got over the emotions of this escape—as I am sure I am talking to you. Our only chance is to be ahead. He has cut himself off from his kind. His blood be upon his own head.'*

XXVI

THE WICKSTEED MURDER

THE Invisible Man seems to have rushed out of Kemp's house in a state of blind fury. A little child playing near Kemp's gateway was violently caught up and thrown aside, so that its ankle was broken, and thereafter for some hours he passed out of human perceptions. No one knows where he went nor what he did. But one can imagine him hurrying through the hot June forenoon, up the hill and on to the open downland behind Port Burdock, raging and despairing at his intolerable fate, and sheltering at last, heated and weary, amid the thickets of Hintondean, to piece together again his shattered schemes against his species. That seems the most probable refuge for him, for there it was he reasserted himself in a grimly tragical manner about two in the afternoon.

One wonders what his state of mind may have been during that time and what plans he devised. No doubt he was almost ecstatically exasperated by Kemp's treachery, and though we may be able to understand the motives that led to that deceit, we may still imagine, and even sympathise a little with the fury the attempted surprise must have occasioned. Perhaps something of the stunned astonishment of his Oxford Street experiences may have returned to him, for he had evidently counted on Kemp's co-operation in his brutal dream of a terrorised world. At any rate, he vanished from human ken about midday, and no living witness can tell what he did until about half-past two. It was a fortunate thing, perhaps, for humanity, but for him it was a fatal inaction.

During that time a growing multitude of men scattered over the countryside were busy. In the morning he had still been simply a legend, a terror; in the afternoon, by virtue chiefly of Kemp's drily worded proclamation, he was presented as a tangible antagonist, to be wounded, captured, or overcome, and the countryside began organising itself with inconceivable rapidity. By two o'clock even, he might still have removed himself out of the district by getting aboard a train, but after two that became impossible, every passenger train along the lines on a great parallelogram between Southampton, Winchester, Brighton and Horsham, travelled with locked doors, and the goods traffic was almost entirely suspended. And in a great circle of twenty miles round Port Burdock men armed with guns and bludgeons were presently setting out in groups of three and four, with dogs, to beat roads and fields.

Mounted policemen rode along the country lanes, stopping at every cottage and warning the people to lock up their houses and keep indoors unless they were armed, and all the elementary schools had broken up by three o'clock, and the children, scared and keeping together in groups, were hurrying home. Kemp's proclamation—signed, indeed, by Adye—was posted over almost the whole district by four or five o'clock in the afternoon. It gave briefly but clearly all the conditions of the struggle, the necessity of keeping the Invisible Man from food and sleep, the necessity for incessant watchfulness, and for a prompt attention to any evidence of his movements. And so swift and decided was the action of the authorities, so prompt and universal was the belief in this strange being, that before nightfall an area of several hundred square miles was in a stringent state of siege. And before nightfall, too, a thrill of horror went through the whole watching, nervous countryside, going from whispering mouth to mouth, swift and certain over the length and breadth of the country passed the story of the murder of Mr Wicksteed.

If our supposition that the Invisible Man's refuge was the Hintondean thickets is correct, then we must suppose that in the early afternoon he sallied out again, bent upon some project that involved the use of a weapon. We cannot know what the project was, but the evidence that he had the iron rod in his hand before he met Wicksteed is to me, at least, overwhelming.

Of course we can know nothing of the details of that encounter. It occurred on the edge of a gravel pit, not two hundred yards from Lord Burdock's lodge gate. Everything points to a desperate struggle—the trampled ground, the numerous wounds Mr Wicksteed received, his splintered walking-stick—but why the attack was made, save in a murderous frenzy, it is impossible to imagine. Indeed, the theory of madness is almost unavoidable. Mr Wicksteed was a man of forty-five or forty-six, steward to Lord Burdock, of inoffensive habits and appearance, and the very last person in the world to provoke such a terrible antagonist.

Against him it would seem the Invisible Man used an iron rod, dragged from a piece of broken fence. He stopped this quiet man, going quietly home to his midday meal, attacked him, beat down his feeble defences, broke his arm, felled him, and smashed his head to a jelly.

Of course, he must have dragged this rod out of the fencing before he met his victim—he must have been carrying it ready in his hand. Only two details beyond what has already been stated seem to bear on the matter. One is the circumstance that the gravel-pit was not in Mr Wicksteed's direct path home, but nearly a couple of hundred yards out of his way. The other is the assertion of a little girl, to the effect that going to her afternoon school she saw the murdered man '*trotting*' in a peculiar manner across a field towards the gravel-pit. Her pantomime of his action suggests a man pursuing something on the ground before him and striking at it ever and again with his walking-stick. She was the last person to see him alive. He passed out of her sight to his death, the struggle being hidden from her only by a clump of beech trees and a slight depression in the ground.

Now this, to the present writer's mind at least, certainly lifts the murder out of the realm of the absolutely wanton. We may imagine that Griffin had taken the rod as a weapon indeed, but without any deliberate intention of using it in murder. Wicksteed may then have come by and noticed this rod inexplicably moving through the air. Without any thought of the Invisible Man—for Port Burdock is ten miles away—he may have pursued it. It is quite conceivable that he may not even have heard of the Invisible Man. One can, then, imagine the Invisible Man making off quietly in order to avoid discovering his presence in the neighbourhood, and Wicksteed, excited and curious, pursuing this unaccountably locomotive object, finally striking at it.

No doubt the Invisible Man could easily have distanced his middle-aged pursuer under ordinary circumstances, but the position in which Wicksteed's body was found suggests that he had the ill-luck to drive his quarry into a corner between a drift of stinging nettles and the gravel-pit. To those who appreciate the extraordinary irascibility of the Invisible Man the rest of the encounter will be easy to imagine.

But this is a pure hypothesis. The only undeniable facts—for stories of children are often unreliable—are the discovery of Wicksteed's body, done to death, and of the bloodstained iron rod flung among the nettles. The abandonment of the rod by Griffin suggests that in the emotional excitement of the affair the purpose for which he took it—if he had a purpose—was abandoned. He was certainly an intensely egotistical and unfeeling man, but the sight of his victim, his first victim, bloody and pitiful at his feet, may have released some long pent fountain of remorse which, for a time, may have flooded whatever scheme of action he had contrived.

After the murder of Mr Wicksteed, he would seem to have struck across the country towards the downland. There is a story of a voice heard about sunset by a couple of men in a field near Fern Bottom. It was wailing and laughing, sobbing and groaning, and ever and again it shouted. It must have been queer hearing. It drove up across the middle of a clover field and died away towards the hills.

In the interim the Invisible Man must have learnt something of the rapid use Kemp had made of his confidences. He must have found houses locked and secured, he may have loitered about railway stations and prowled about inns, and no doubt he read the proclamations and realised something of the nature of the campaign against him. And as the evening advanced the fields became dotted here and there with groups of three or four men, and noisy with the yelping of dogs. These men-hunters had particular instructions in the case of an encounter as to the way they should support one another. But he avoided them all. We may understand something of his exasperation, and it could have been none the less because he himself had supplied the information that was being used so remorselessly against him. For that day at least he lost heart; for nearly twenty-four hours, save when he turned on Wicksteed, he was a hunted man. In the night he must have eaten and slept, for in the morning he was himself again, active, powerful, angry and malignant, prepared for his last great struggle against the world.

XXVII

THE SIEGE OF KEMP'S HOUSE

KEMP read a strange missive, written in pencil on a greasy sheet of paper.

'You have been amazingly energetic and clever,' this letter ran, 'though what you stand to gain by it I cannot imagine. You are against me. For a whole day you have chased me—you have tried to rob me of a night's rest. But I have had food in spite of you, I have slept in spite of you, and the game is only beginning. The game is only beginning. There is nothing for it but to start the Terror. This announces the first day of the Terror. Port Burdock is no longer under the Queen, tell your Colonel of Police, and the rest of them; it is under me—the Terror! This is day one of year one of the new epoch*—the Epoch of the Invisible Man. I am Invisible Man the First. To begin with, the rule will be easy. The first day there will be one execution for the sake of example—a man named Kemp. Death starts for him to-day. He may lock himself away, hide himself away, get guards about him, put on armour if he likes—Death, the unseen Death, is coming. Let him take precautions—it will impress my people. Death starts from the pillar-box by midday. The letter will fall in as the postman comes along, then off! The game begins. Death starts. Help him not, my people, lest Death fall upon you also. To-day Kemp is to die.'

When Kemp had read this letter twice, 'It's no hoax,' he said. 'That's his voice! And he means it.'

He turned the folded sheet over and saw on the addressed side of it the postmark Hintondean, and the prosaic detail '*2d. to pay*.'

He got up slowly, leaving his lunch unfinished—the letter had come by the one o'clock post—and went into his study. He rang for his housekeeper, and told her to go round the house at once, examine all the fastenings of the windows, and close all the shutters. He closed the shutters of his study himself. From a locked drawer in his bedroom he took a little revolver, examined it carefully and put it into the pocket of his lounge jacket. He wrote a number of brief notes, one to Colonel Adye, gave them to his servant to take, with explicit instructions as to her way of leaving the house. 'There is no danger,' he said, and added a mental reservation 'to you.' He remained meditative for a space after doing this, and then returned to his cooling lunch.

He ate with gaps of thought. Finally he struck the table sharply. 'We will have him!' he said, 'and I am the bait. He will come too far.'

He went up to the belvedere, carefully shutting every door after him. 'It's a game,' he said, 'an odd game—but the chances are all for me, Mr Griffin, in spite of your invisibility. And pluck. Griffin *contra mundum** . . . with a vengeance.'

He stood at the window staring at the hot hillside. 'He must get food every day—and I don't envy him. Did he really sleep last night? Out in the open somewhere—secure from collisions. I wish we could get some good cold, wet weather instead of the heat.

'He may be watching me now.'

He went close to the window. Something rapped smartly against the brickwork over the frame, and made him start violently back.

'I'm getting nervous,' said Kemp. But it was five minutes before he went to the window again. 'It must have been a sparrow,' he said.

Presently he heard the front door bell ringing, and hurried downstairs. He unbolted and unlocked the door, examined the chain, put it up, and opened cautiously without showing himself. A familiar voice hailed him. It was Adye. 'Your servant's been assaulted, Kemp,' he said round the door.

'What!' exclaimed Kemp.

'Had that note of yours taken away from her. He's close about here. Let me in.'

Kemp released the chain, and Adye entered through as narrow an opening as possible. He stood in the hall, looking with infinite relief at Kemp refastening the door. 'Note was snatched out of her hand. Scared her horribly. She's down at the station. Hysterics. He's close here. What was it about?'

Kemp swore.

'What a fool I was!' said Kemp. 'I might have known. It's not an hour's walk from Hintondean. Already!'

'What's up?' said Adye.

'Look here!' said Kemp, and led the way into his study. He handed Adye the Invisible Man's letter. Adye read it, and whistled softly. 'And you—?' said Adye.

'Proposed a trap—like a fool,' said Kemp, 'and sent my proposal out by a maidservant. To him.'

Adye followed Kemp's profanity.

'He'll clear out,' said Adye.

'Not him,' said Kemp.

A resounding smash of glass came from upstairs. Adye had a silvery glimpse of a little revolver half out of Kemp's pocket. 'It's a window upstairs!' said Kemp, and led the way up. There came a second smash while they were still on the staircase. When they reached the study they found two of the three windows smashed, half the room littered with splintered glass, and one big flint lying on the writing-table. The two men stopped in the doorway contemplating the wreckage. Kemp swore again, and as he did so the third window went with a snap like a pistol, hung starred for a moment, and collapsed in jagged, shivering triangles into the room.

'What's this for?' said Adye.

'It's a beginning,' said Kemp.

'There's no way of climbing up here?'

'Not for a cat,' said Kemp.

'No shutters?'

'Not here. All the downstairs rooms—Hullo!'

Smash, and then the whack of boards hit hard came from downstairs. 'Confound him!' said Kemp. 'That must be—yes——it's one of the bedrooms. He's going to do all the house. But he's a fool. The shutters are up and the glass will fall outside. He'll cut his feet.'

Another window proclaimed its destruction. The two men stood on the landing perplexed.

'I have it!' said Adye. 'Let me have a stick or something, and I'll go down to the station and get the bloodhounds put on. That ought to settle him!'

Another window went the way of its fellows.

'You haven't a revolver?' asked Adye.

Kemp's hand went to his pocket. Then he hesitated. 'I haven't one—at least to spare.'

'I'll bring it back,' said Adye. 'You'll be safe here.'

Kemp, ashamed of his momentary lapse from truthfulness, handed him the weapon.

'Now for the door,' said Adye.

As they stood hesitating in the hall, they heard one of the first-floor bedroom windows crack and clash. Kemp went to the door and began to slip the bolts as silently as possible. His face was a little paler than usual.

'You must step straight out,' said Kemp.

In another moment Adye was on the doorstep and the bolts were dropping back into the staples. He hesitated for a moment, feeling more comfortable with his back against the door. Then he marched, upright and square, down the steps. He crossed the lawn and approached the gate. A little breeze seemed to ripple over the grass. Something moved near him.

'Stop a bit,' said a Voice, and Adye stopped dead, and his hand tightened on the revolver.

'Well?' said Adye, white and grim, and every nerve tense.

'Oblige me by going back to the house,' said the Voice, as tense and grim as Adye's.

'Sorry,' said Adye, a little hoarsely, and moistened his lips with his tongue. The voice was on his left front, he thought; suppose he were to take his luck with a shot.

'What are you going for?' said the Voice, and there was a quick movement of the two, and a flash of sunlight from the open lip of Adye's pocket.

Adye desisted and thought. 'Where I go,' he said slowly, 'is my own business.' The words were still on his lips, when an arm came round his neck, his back felt a knee, and he was sprawling backward. He drew clumsily and fired absurdly, and in another moment he was struck in the mouth and the revolver wrested from his grip. He made a vain clutch at a slippery limb, tried to struggle up and fell back.

'Damn!' said Adye. The Voice laughed. 'I'd kill you now if it wasn't the waste of a bullet,' it said. He saw the revolver in mid-air, six feet off, covering him.

'Well?' said Adye, sitting up.

'Get up,' said the Voice.

Adye stood up.

'Attention!' said the Voice, and then firmly, 'don't try any games. Remember I can see your face, if you can't see mine. You've got to go back to the house.'

'He won't let me in,' said Adye.

'That's a pity,' said the Invisible Man. 'I've got no quarrel with you.'

Adye moistened his lips again. He glanced away from the barrel of the revolver, and saw the sea far off, very blue and dark under the midday sun, the smooth green down, the white cliff of the head, and the multitudinous town, and suddenly he knew that life was very sweet. His eyes came back to this little metal thing hanging between heaven and earth, six yards away. 'What am I to do?' he said sullenly.

'What am *I* to do?' asked the Invisible Man. 'You will get help. The only thing is for you to go back.'

'I will try. If he lets me in will you promise not to rush the door?'

'I've got no quarrel with you,' said the Voice.

Kemp had hurried upstairs after letting Adye out, and now, crouching among the broken glass, and peering cautiously over the edge of the study window-sill, he saw Adye stand parleying with the unseen. 'Why doesn't he fire?' whispered Kemp to himself. Then the revolver moved a little, and the glint of the sunlight flashed in Kemp's eyes. He shaded his eyes and tried to see the course of the blinding beam.

'Surely!' he said. 'Adye has given up the revolver.'

'Promise not to rush the door,' Adye was saying. 'Don't push a winning game too far. Give a man a chance.'

'You go back to the house. I tell you flatly I will not promise anything.'

Adye's decision seemed suddenly made. He turned towards the house, walking slowly with his hands behind him. Kemp watched him—puzzled. The revolver vanished, flashed again into sight, vanished again, and became evident on a closer scrutiny as a little dark object following Adye. Then things happened very quickly. Adye leapt backwards, swung round, clutched at this little object, missed it, threw up his hands and fell forward on his face, leaving a little puff of blue in the air. Kemp did not hear the sound of the shot. Adye writhed, raised himself on one arm, fell forward, and lay still.

For a space Kemp remained staring at the quiet carelessness of Adye's attitude. The afternoon was very hot and still, nothing seemed stirring in all the world save a couple of yellow butterflies chasing each other through the shrubbery between the house and the road gate. Adye lay on the lawn near the gate. The blinds of all the villas down the hill road were drawn, but in one little green summer-house was a white figure, apparently an old man asleep. Kemp scrutinised the surroundings of the house for a glimpse of the revolver, but it had vanished. His eyes came back to Adye——The game was opening well.

Then came a ringing and knocking at the front door, that grew at last tumultuous, but, pursuant to Kemp's instructions, the servants had locked themselves into their rooms. This was followed by a silence.

Kemp sat listening and then began peering cautiously out of the three windows, one after another. He went to the staircase head and stood listening uneasily. He armed himself with his bedroom poker, and went to examine the interior fastenings of the ground-floor windows again. Everything was safe and quiet. He returned to the belvedere. Adye lay motionless over the edge of the gravel just as he had fallen. Coming along the road by the villas were the housemaid and two policemen.

Everything was deadly still. The three people seemed very slow in approaching. He wondered what his antagonist was doing.

He started. There was a smash from below. He hesitated and went downstairs again. Suddenly the house resounded with heavy blows and the splintering of wood. He heard a smash and the distinctive clang of the iron fastenings of shutters. He turned the key and opened the kitchen door. As he did so the shutters, split and splintering, came flying inward. He stood aghast. The window frame, save for one cross-bar, was still intact, but only little teeth of glass remained in the frame. The shutters had been driven in with an axe, and now the axe was descending in sweeping blows upon the window frame and the iron bars defending it. Then suddenly it leapt aside and vanished.

He saw the revolver lying on the path outside, and then the little weapon sprang into the air. He dodged back. The revolver cracked just too late, and a splinter from the edge of the closing door flashed over his head. He slammed and locked the door, and as he stood outside he heard Griffin shouting and laughing. Then the blows of the axe with its splitting and smashing consequences were resumed.

Kemp stood in the passage trying to think. In a moment the Invisible Man would be in the kitchen. This door would not keep him a moment, and then——

A ringing came at the front door again. It would be the policemen. He ran into the hall, put up the chain, and drew the bolts. He made the girl speak before he dropped the chain, and the three people blundered into the house in a heap, and Kemp slammed the door again.

'The Invisible Man!' said Kemp. 'He has a revolver with two shots left. He's killed Adye. Shot him anyhow. Didn't you see him on the lawn? He's lying there.'

'Who?' said one of the policemen.

'Adye,' said Kemp.

'We came in the back way,' said the girl.

'What's that smashing?' asked one of the policemen.

'He's in the kitchen—or will be. He has found an axe——'

Suddenly the house was full of the Invisible Man's resounding blows on the kitchen door. The girl stared towards the kitchen and stepped into the dining-room. Kemp tried to explain in broken sentences. They heard the kitchen door give.

'This way,' cried Kemp, bursting into activity, and bundled the policemen into the dining-room doorway.

'Poker,' said Kemp, and rushed to the fender.

He handed the poker he had carried to the policeman, and the dining-room one to the other.

He suddenly flung himself backward. 'Whup,' said one policeman, ducked, and caught the axe on his poker. The pistol snapped its penultimate shot and ripped a valuable Sidney Cooper.* The second policeman brought his poker down on the little weapon, as one might knock down a wasp, and sent it rattling to the floor.

At the first clash the girl screamed, stood screaming for a moment by the fireplace, and then ran to open the shutters—possibly with an idea of escaping by the shattered window.

The axe receded into the passage and fell to a position about two feet from the ground. They could hear the Invisible Man breathing. 'Stand away you two,' he said. 'I want that man Kemp.'

'We want you,' said the first policeman, making a quick step forward and wiping with his poker at the Voice. The Invisible Man must have started back, and he blundered into the umbrella stand.

Then, as the policeman staggered with the swing of the blow he had aimed, the Invisible Man countered with the axe, the helmet crumpled like paper, and the blow sent the man spinning to the floor at the head of the kitchen stairs.

But the second policeman, aiming behind the axe with his poker, hit something soft that snapped. There was a sharp exclamation of pain, and then the axe fell to the ground. The policeman wiped again at vacancy and hit nothing; he put his foot on the axe and struck again. Then he stood, poker clubbed, listening, intent for the slightest movement.

He heard the dining-room window open, and a quick rush of feet within. His companion rolled over and sat up, with the blood running down between his eye and ear. 'Where is he?' asked the man on the floor.

'Don't know. I've hit him. He's standing somewhere in the hall unless he's slipped past you. Dr Kemp—sir!'

'Dr Kemp,' cried the policeman again.

The second policeman began struggling to his feet. He stood up. Suddenly the faint pad of bare feet on the kitchen stairs could be heard. 'Yap!' cried the first policeman, and flung his poker. It smashed a little gas-bracket.

He made as if he would pursue the Invisible Man downstairs. Then he thought better of it, and stepped into the dining-room.

'Dr Kemp——' he began, and stopped short.

'Dr Kemp's a hero,' he said, as his companion looked over his shoulder.

The dining-room window was wide open, and neither housemaid nor Kemp was to be seen.

The second policeman's opinion of Kemp was terse and vivid.

XXVIII

THE HUNTER HUNTED

MR HEELAS, Mr Kemp's nearest neighbour among the villa holders, was asleep in his summer-house when the siege of Kemp's house began. Mr Heelas was one of the sturdy majority who refused to believe in 'all this nonsense' about an Invisible Man. His wife, however, as he was subsequently to be reminded, did. He insisted upon walking about his garden just as if nothing was the matter, and he went to sleep in the afternoon, in accordance with the custom of years. He slept through the smashing of the windows, and then woke up suddenly, with a curious persuasion of something wrong. He looked across at Kemp's house; rubbed his eyes, and looked again. Then he put his feet to the ground and sat listening. He said he was damned, but still the strange thing was visible. The house looked as though it had been deserted for weeks—after a violent riot. Every window was broken, and every window, save those of the belvedere study, was blinded by internal shutters.

'I could have sworn it was all right'—he looked at his watch—'twenty minutes ago.'

He became aware of a measured concussion, and the clash of glass far away in the distance. And then, as he sat open-mouthed, came a still more wonderful thing. The shutters of the dining-room window were flung open violently, and the housemaid, in her outdoor hat and garments, appeared struggling in a frantic manner to throw up the sash. Suddenly a man appeared beside her, helping her—Dr Kemp! In another moment the window was open and the housemaid was struggling out; she pitched forward and vanished among the shrubs. Mr Heelas stood up, exclaiming vaguely and vehemently at all these wonderful things. He saw Kemp stand on the sill, spring from the window, and reappear almost instantaneously running along a path in the shrubbery and stooping as he ran, like a man who evades observation. He vanished behind a laburnum, and appeared again clambering a fence that abutted on the open down. In a second he had tumbled over, and was running at a tremendous pace down the slope towards Mr Heelas.

'Lord!' cried Mr Heelas, struck with an idea, 'it's that Invisible Man brute! It's all right after all!'

With Mr Heelas to think things like that was to act, and his cook, watching him from the top window, was amazed to see him come pelting towards the house at a good nine miles an hour. There was a slamming of doors, a ringing of bells, and the voice of Mr Heelas bellowing like a bull. 'Shut the doors, shut the windows, shut everything—the Invisible Man is coming!' Instantly the house was full of screams and directions and scurrying feet. He ran himself to shut the French windows that opened on the veranda, and as he did so Kemp's head and shoulders and knee appeared over the edge of the garden fence. In another moment Kemp had ploughed through the asparagus, and was running across the tennis-lawn to the house.

'You can't come in,' said Mr Heelas, shooting the bolts. 'I'm very sorry if he's after you—but you can't come in!'

Kemp appeared with a face of terror close to the glass, rapping and then shaking frantically at the French window. Then, seeing his efforts were useless, he ran along the veranda, vaulted the end, and went to hammer at the side door. Then he ran round by the side gate to the front of the house, and so into the hill road. And Mr Heelas staring from his window—a face of horror—had scarcely witnessed Kemp vanish ere the asparagus was being trampled this way and that by feet unseen. At that Mr Heelas fled precipitately upstairs, and the rest of the chase is beyond his purview. But as he passed the staircase window he heard the side gate slam.

Emerging into the hill road, Kemp naturally took the downward direction, and so it was that he came to run in his own person the very race he had watched with such a critical eye from the belvedere study only four days ago.* He ran it well for a man out of training, and though his face was white and wet his wits were cool to the last. He ran with wide strides, and wherever a patch of rough ground intervened, wherever there came a patch of raw flints, or a bit of broken glass shone dazzling, he crossed it, and left the bare invisible feet that followed to take what line they would.

For the first time in his life Kemp discovered that the hill road was indescribably vast and desolate, and that the beginnings of the town far below at the hill foot were strangely remote. Never had there been a slower or more painful method of progression than running. All the gaunt villas, sleeping in the afternoon sun, looked locked and barred; no doubt they were locked and barred by his own orders. But at any rate they might have kept a look-out for an eventuality like this! The town was rising up now, the sea had dropped out of sight behind it, and people below were stirring. A tram was just arriving at the hill foot. Beyond that was the police-station. Were those footsteps he heard behind him? Spurt.

The people below were staring at him, one or two were running, and his breath was beginning to saw in his throat. The tram was quite near now, and the 'Jolly Cricketers' was noisily barring its doors. Beyond the tram were posts and heaps of gravel—the drainage works. He had a transitory idea of jumping into the tram and slamming the doors, and then he resolved to go for the police-station. In another moment he had passed the door of the 'Jolly Cricketers,' and was in the blistering fag end of the street, with human beings about him. The tram driver and his helper—astounded by the sight of his furious haste—stood staring with the tram horses unhitched. Further on the astonished features of navvies appeared above the mounds of gravel.

His pace broke a little, and then he heard the swift pad of his pursuer, and leapt forward again. 'The Invisible Man!' he cried to the navvies, with a vague indicative gesture, and by an inspiration leapt the excavation, and placed a burly group between him and the chase. Then, abandoning the idea of the police-station, he turned into a little side street, rushed by a greengrocer's cart, hesitated for the tenth of a second at the door of a sweetstuff shop, and then made for the mouth of an alley that ran back into the main Hill Street again. Two or three little children were playing here, and shrieked and scattered running at his apparition, and forthwith doors and windows opened, and excited mothers revealed their hearts. Out he shot into Hill Street once more, three hundred yards from the tram-line end, and immediately he became aware of a tumultuous vociferation and running people.

He glanced up the street towards the hill. Hardly a dozen yards off ran a huge navvy, cursing in fragments and slashing viciously with a spade, and hard behind him came the tram conductor with his fists clenched. Up the street others followed these two, striking and shouting. Down towards the town men and women were running, and he noticed clearly one man coming out of a shop door with a stick in his hand. 'Spread out! Spread out!' cried some one. Kemp suddenly grasped the altered condition of the chase. He stopped and looked round panting. 'He's close here!' he cried. 'Form a line across——'

He was hit hard under the ear, and went reeling, trying to face round towards his unseen antagonist. He just managed to keep his feet, and he struck a vain counter in the air. Then he was hit again under the jaw, and sprawled headlong on the ground. In another moment a knee compressed his diaphragm, and a couple of eager hands gripped his throat, but the grip of one was weaker than the other; he grasped the wrists, heard a cry of pain from his assailant, and then the spade of the navvy came whirling through the air above him, and struck something with a dull thud. He felt a drop of moisture on his face. The grip at his throat suddenly relaxed, and with a convulsive effort Kemp loosed himself, grasped a limp shoulder, and rolled uppermost. He gripped the unseen elbows near the ground. 'I've got him!' screamed Kemp. 'Help! help—hold! He's down! Hold his feet!'

In another second there was a simultaneous rush upon the struggle, and a stranger coming into the road suddenly might have thought an exceptionally savage game of Rugby football was in progress. And there was no shouting after Kemp's cry—only a sound of blows and feet and a heavy breathing.

Then came a mighty effort, and the Invisible Man staggered to his feet. Kemp clung to him in front like a hound to a stag, and a dozen hands clutched and tore at the unseen. The tram conductor got the neck, and lugged him back.

Down went the heap of struggling men again. There was, I am afraid, some savage kicking. Then suddenly a wild scream of 'Mercy, mercy!' that died down swiftly to a sound like choking.

'Get back, you fools!' cried the muffled voice of Kemp, and there was a vigorous shoving back of stalwart forms. 'He's hurt, I tell you. Stand back.'

There was a brief struggle to clear a space, and then the circle of eager faces saw the doctor kneeling, as it seemed, fifteen inches in the air, and holding invisible arms to the ground. Behind him a constable gripped invisible ankles.

'Don't you leave go of en!' cried the big navvy, holding a blood-stained spade; 'he's shamming.'

'He's not shamming,' said the doctor, cautiously raising his knee, 'and I'll hold him.' His face was bruised, and already going red; he spoke thickly, because of a bleeding lip. He released one hand, and seemed to be feeling at the face. 'The mouth's all wet,' he said. And then, 'Good Lord!'

He stood up abruptly, and then knelt down on the ground by the side of the thing unseen. There was a pushing and shuffling, a sound of heavy feet as fresh people turned up to increase the pressure of the crowd. People now were coming out of the houses. The doors of the 'Jolly Cricketers' were suddenly wide open. Very little was said. Kemp felt about, his hand seeming to pass through empty air. 'He's not breathing,' he said, and then, 'I can't feel his heart. His side—ugh!'

Suddenly an old woman, pushing under the arm of the big navvy, screamed sharply. 'Looky there!' she said, and thrust out a wrinkled finger. And looking where she pointed, every one saw, faint and transparent, as though made of glass, so that veins and arteries, and bones and nerves could be distinguished, the outline of a hand—a hand limp and prone. It grew clouded and opaque even as they stared.

'Hullo!' cried the constable. 'Here's his feet a-showing!'

And so, slowly, beginning at his hands and feet, and creeping slowly along his limbs to the vital centres of his body, that strange change continued. It was like the slow spreading of a poison. First came the little white veins, a hazy grey sketch of a limb, then the glassy bones and intricate arteries, then the flesh and skin, first a faint fogginess and then growing rapidly dense and opaque. Presently they could see his crushed chest and his shoulders, and the dim outline of his drawn and battered features.

When at last the crowd made way for Kemp to stand erect, there lay, naked and pitiful on the ground, the bruised and broken body of a young man about thirty. His hair and brow were white—not grey with age, but white with the whiteness of albinism—and his eyes were like garnets. His hands were clenched,* his eyes wide open, and his expression was one of anger and dismay. The people shivered at the sight of him, and three little children, pushing forward through the crowd, were suddenly twisted round and sent packing off again.

Some one brought a sheet from the 'Jolly Cricketers,' and having covered him, they carried him into that house. And there, on a shabby bed in a tawdry, ill-lighted bedroom, ended the strange experiment of the Invisible Man.

APPENDIX I

THE EPILOGUE

[*From the second English edition, November 1897.*]

So ends the story of the strange and evil experiment of the Invisible Man. And if you would learn more of him you must go to a little inn near Port Stowe and talk to the landlord. The sign of the inn is an empty board save for a hat and boots, and the name is the title of this story. The landlord is a short and corpulent little man with a nose of cylindrical protrusion, wiry hair, and a sporadic rosiness of visage. Drink generously, and he will tell you generously of all the things that happened to him after that time, and of how the lawyers tried to do him out of the treasure found upon him.

'When they found they couldn't prove who's money was which, I'm blessed', he says, 'if they didn't try to make me out a blooming treasure trove! Do I *look* like a Treasure Trove? And then a gentleman gave me a guinea a night to tell the story at the Empire Music 'all—just tell 'em in my own words—barring one.'

And if you want to cut off the flow of his reminiscences abruptly, you can always do so by asking if there weren't three manuscript books in the story. He admits there were and proceeds to explain with asseverations that everybody thinks *he* has 'em! But bless you! he hasn't. 'The Invisible Man it was took 'em off to hide 'em when I cut and ran for Port Stowe. It's that Mr Kemp put people on with the idea of *my* having 'em.'

And then he subsides into a pensive state, watches you furtively, bustles nervously with glasses, and presently leaves the bar.

He is a bachelor man—his tastes were ever bachelor, and there are no women folk in the house. Outwardly he buttons—it is expected of him—but in his more vital privacies, in the matter of braces for example, he still turns to string. He conducts his house with enterprise, but with eminent decorum. His movements are slow, and he is a great thinker. But he has a reputation for wisdom and for a respectable parsimony in the village, and his knowledge of the roads of the South of England would beat Cobbett.*

And on Sunday mornings, every Sunday morning all the year round, while he is closed to the outer world, and every night after ten, he goes into his bar-parlour bearing a glass of gin faintly tinged with water; and having placed this down, he locks the door and examines the blinds, and even looks under the table. And then, being satisfied of his solitude, he unlocks the cupboard and a box in the cupboard and a drawer in that box, and produces three volumes bound in brown leather, and places them solemnly in the middle of the table. The covers are weather-worn and tinged with algal green—for once they sojourned in a ditch and some of the pages have been washed blank by dirty water. The landlord sits down in an armchair, fills a long clay pipe slowly—gloating over the books the while. Then he pulls one towards him and opens it, and begins to study it—turning over the leaves backwards and forwards.

His brows are knit and his lips move painfully: 'Hex, little two up in the air, cross and fiddle-de-dee. Lord! what a one he was for intellect!'

Presently he relaxes and leans back, and blinks through his smoke across the room at things invisible to other eyes. 'Full of secrets,' he says. 'Wonderful secrets!

'Once I get the haul of them—*Lord!*

'I wouldn't do what *he* did; I'd just—well!' He pulls at his pipe.

So he lapses into a dream, the undying wonderful dream of his life. And though Kemp has fished unceasingly, no human being save the landlord knows those books are there, with the subtle secret of invisibility and a dozen other strange secrets written therein. And none other will know of them until he dies.

APPENDIX II

VARIANT ENDINGS TO CHAPTER XXVIII

[*These follow the sentence ending 'anger and dismay' in the penultimate paragraph of the book.*]

Serial Version: Pearson's Weekly, *7 August 1897*

The people shivered at the sight of him.

Someone brought a sheet from the 'Jolly Cricketers', and having covered him, they carried him into that house. And there on a shabby bed in a tawdry, ill-lighted bedroom, ended the career of the Invisible Man, ended the strangest and most wonderful experiment that man has ever made.

Second English Edition: Pearson, 1897

'Cover his face!' cried a man. 'For Gawd's sake cover that face!'

Some one brought a sheet from the 'Jolly Cricketers', and having covered him, they carried him into that house. And there it was, on a shabby bed in a tawdry, ill-lighted bedroom, surrounded by a crowd of ignorant and excited people, broken and wounded, betrayed and unpitied, that Griffin, the first of all men to make himself invisible, Griffin, the most gifted physicist the world has ever seen, ended in infinite disaster his strange and terrible career.

First American Edition: Edward Arnold, 1897

'Cover his face!' said a man. 'For Gawd's sake, cover that face!' and three little children, pushing forward through the crowd, were suddenly twisted round and sent packing off again.

Someone brought a sheet from the Jolly Cricketers, and having covered him, they carried him into that house.

EXPLANATORY NOTES

References to David Lake are to his edition of *The Invisible Man*, introduction by John Sutherland (New York: Oxford University Press, 1996). The *OED* is the *Oxford English Dictionary*. Quotations from the Bible are from the King James Version.

THE INVISIBLE MAN

5 *Bramblehurst*: an invented location, though there is a cluster of houses in East Grinstead, Sussex—mentioned in the 1881 Census—that go by this name.

sovereigns: gold coins each worth £1.

Iping: a village in West Sussex, 2 miles from Midhurst (where Wells had lived and worked in the 1880s).

6 *blue spectacles*: the Victorians used blue-tinted lenses to shield their wearers from the sun's rays, and these were often used outdoors by those with sensitive eyes. John Ruskin, for example, wore spectacles of this kind as an undergraduate, and was consequently known as 'Giglamps'.

10 *clock-jobber*: a clock mender (the word 'jobber', derived from the verb 'to job', meaning to penetrate or prod, is an onomatopoeic term supposedly imitative of a bird's pecking).

16 *chiffonnier*: a piece of furniture containing drawers or a small cupboard.

19 *artisks*: in Wells's short story 'The Hammerpond Park Burglary' (1894)—which opens, like *The Invisible Man*, with a scene in a public house in Sussex called the Coach and Horses—the burglar disguises himself as a 'landscape painter' in order not to seem conspicuous. Wells, whose ear for regional accents such as the one exhibited by Mrs Hall was extremely fine, used to refer to his own satirical cartoons as 'picshuas'.

20 *middle or end of February*: this detail is inconsistent with the first sentence of the novel, which states that 'the stranger came early in February'.

National School: a school set up by the National Society for Promoting Religious Education in Accordance with the Principles of the Church of England, an institution founded in 1811 to provide elementary education for working-class children.

anarchist: in 1894 the French anarchist Martial Boudin accidentally detonated a bomb apparently intended to destroy the Royal Observatory at Greenwich in London—an incident fictionalized by Joseph Conrad in *The Secret Agent* (1907).

man with the one talent: see Matthew 25:14–30, the Parable of the Talents, which is centred on a servant who buries the money given to him by his master and therefore fails to profit from it. Wells hints in satirical tones that Silas Durgan, who thinks himself 'a bit of a theologian', misconstrues the word 'talent', taking it to mean a natural aptitude or skill rather than an ancient unit of currency (the former definition is, however, derived from the latter).

21 *urban brain-worker*: in *American Nervousness: Its Causes and Consequences* (1881), the influential North American neurologist George Miller Beard, who diagnosed 'neurasthenia' as a psychopathological condition characteristic of modern, metropolitan life, wrote that 'one of the first signs of real nervousness, is mental irritability, a disposition to become fretted over trifles'.

'The Bogey Man!': the song 'Hush, Hush, Hush, Here Comes the Bogey Man' was popular in music halls in the 1890s (the term 'bogey' is probably derived from the Scottish term 'bogle', common in print from the sixteenth century, which refers to a goblin or phantom).

22 *ammonite*: a fossil 'consisting of whorled chambered shells' (*OED*)—here used as a paperweight.

cork arm: a 'cork arm' (or, more commonly, 'cork leg') was so named not because it was made from cork but because it was likely to have been manufactured in Cork Street, Piccadilly. In contrast to a wooden limb, this was a relatively sophisticated and indeed expensive form of prosthesis, composed of materials such as ivory, leather, steel, and vulcanized rubber, which provided articulated movement.

25 *Club festivities*: David Lake notes that 'such festivities, which might include a church service followed by a feast and a fair on the village green, were common throughout the villages of West Sussex'.

two pounds ten in half sovereigns: £2 and 10 shillings (or £2.50); a 'half-sovereign' was a gold coin worth 10 shillings (or 50 pence).

27 *sarsaparilla*: a non-alcoholic drink, not unlike root beer, flavoured with sarsaparilla, the dried roots of a climbing plant found in Latin America. Lake observes that 'Mr and Mrs Hall are watering their beer, and adding sarsaparilla, the strong taste of which may disguise the weakness of what they supply to their customers'.

slouch hat: 'a hat of soft or unstiffened felt or other material, esp. one having a broad brim which hangs or lops down over the face' (*OED*).

29 *horseshoes*: according to English folklore, a horseshoe acts as a charm against the Devil and brings good luck. Its talismanic origins lie in the legend of the tenth-century abbot St Dunstan, who supposedly nailed a horseshoe to the Devil's hoof and then refused to remove it until the latter had promised never to enter a house surmounted by one. See Edward G. Flight, *The Horse Shoe: The True Legend of St Dunstan and the Devil* (1852), illustrated by George Cruikshank.

31 *piqué paper ties*: ties characterized by a ribbed or raised pattern, made to look as if they have been quilted by hand.

31 *Whit Monday*: the holiday celebrated the day after Pentecost (which is
the seventh Sunday after Easter), commemorating the descent of the Holy
Spirit to the disciples during the Jewish festival of Pentecost.

ordinary bicycles: these were popularly known as penny-farthings because
of their large front wheels and small back ones (by the time Wells was
writing they had been superseded by so-called 'safety bicycles', which
have remained the dominant design ever since).

first Victorian Jubilee: 20 June 1887—the fiftieth anniversary of Queen
Victoria's accession to the throne.

35 *sounding*: 'causing, emitting, producing, a sound or sounds, esp. of a loud
character; resonant, sonorous; reverberant' (*OED*).

39 *embonpoint*: plumpness.

agrimony: perennial herbaceous plants of the genus *agrimonia*.

42 *Vox et*: in full, this classical dictum reads *Vox et praeterea nihil* ('A voice
and nothing more').

dooce: i.e. 'deuce', literally meaning bad luck or mischief—a common
exclamation or imprecation.

43 *A voice out of heaven!*: see Revelation 21:3: 'And I heard a great voice out
of heaven saying, Behold, the tabernacle of God *is* with men, and he will
dwell with them, and they shall be his people, and God himself shall be
with them, *and be* their God.'

45 *canister*: 'a small case or box, usually of metal, for holding tea, coffee, etc.'
(*OED*).

46 *'subsequent proceedings interested him no more'*: a quotation from 'The
Society upon the Stanislaus' (1868), by the American poet Bret Harte.

48 *Tap*: the Tap-Room or public bar.

49 *vamp*: to vamp is to improvise or make up (the verb is derived from the
noun 'vamp', meaning the part of a stocking that covers the foot and ankle,
which was proverbially in need of frequent patching up).

57 *saving his regard*: this phrase is equivalent to 'save-reverence' or 'sirrever-
ence', corruptions of the Latin *salva reverentia*, an expression of apology
meaning, literally, 'saving [your] reverence', or 'with all respect'.

58 *Alteration*: i.e. altercation (though perhaps this malapropism deliberately
evokes the idea of an Ovidian metamorphosis too).

61 *London and County Banking Company*: established in 1836 as the Surrey,
Kent, and Sussex Banking Company, this joint stock bank was renamed
the London and County Banking Company in 1839. Based at 21 Lombard
Street, London, it had country branches in a number of Sussex towns,
including Midhurst. By the final quarter of the nineteenth century it was
the largest bank in Britain.

rouleaux: stacks of coins.

62 *solar lamp*: a descendant of the so-called Argand lamp, an oil lamp with a circular wick and cylindrical glass chimney invented by Aimé Argand in 1780.

Royal Society: the Royal Society of London for Improving Natural Knowledge, the first and most eminent British learned society for the promotion of science, founded in 1660.

64 *Burton*: beer brewed in Burton upon Trent, Staffordshire.

66 *'I'm out o' frocks'*: i.e. 'I'm no longer a child'—'frocks' were cotton or linen dresses worn by boys before they were ritually 'breeched', sometime between the ages of 2 and 8, and thenceforth dressed in breeches or trousers.

leveret: a young hare.

68 *remote speculation of social conditions of the future*: Kemp, who here resembles Wells himself, is very much an individual of his time, for utopian speculation was rife at the *fin de siècle*. (In 1898, in an article in the *Academy* on 'What the People Read', 'a Wife' is interviewed and asked whether she likes 'novels about the future' of the kind Wells was publishing from *The Time Machine* (1895) on—'She pondered a moment, wrinkling her brows. "Well, I can't say that I exactly *like* them", she said; "but one has to read them, because everyone talks about them".')

runaway ring: a mischievous game, sometimes known as 'Knockdown Ginger', in which children ring a doorbell and run away before it is answered. It is possible that Wells is also making a playful reference to the mythical Ring of Gyges, discussed in Plato's *Republic*, which magically rendered its wearer invisible.

69 *vest*: waistcoat.

'eerie': fear-inspiring, strange, weird—presumably Wells places it in inverted commas because it is associated with Scottish dialect.

71 *University College*: University College London, founded in 1826. In 1890 Wells had completed a science degree by correspondence with the University of London, before becoming a tutor for the University Tutorial College.

the seat was depressed: see 'No. 11, Welham Square' by Herbert Stephens, published under the pseudonym 'Edward Masey' in the *Cornhill Magazine* of May 1885, in which the narrator is haunted by a ghostly being with the substance of an invisible body: 'As I looked at this chair it struck me that the seat was considerably depressed, as though some one had recently sat down upon it, and the seat had failed to resume its ordinary level. This surprised me, for I had sat in the chair that morning and felt sure the springs had then been in good order . . . It looked for all the world as if an invisible but substantial human frame was then actually sitting in the chair. When this notion occurred to me, I sat dazed with an indescribable horror, staring stupidly at the chair, which did not move.'

73 *nares*: nostrils.

75 *new moon*: a new moon sets before midnight, whereas this scene takes place after 2 a.m., so this is an impossibility.

76 *nauplii...tornarias*: *nauplius* is 'the free-swimming larval stage in many crustaceans', a *tornaria* is 'the larval form of species of the Sea-acorn, *Balanoglossus*' (*OED*).

St James's Gazette: an evening newspaper published in London from 1880 to 1905, when it merged with the *Evening Standard*.

77 *cum grano*: an abbreviated form of the Latin phrase *cum grano salis*, meaning 'with a grain of salt'.

80 *refractive index*: David Lake provides this exemplary explanation: 'for any transparent or semi-transparent substance, this index shows how much a ray of light is bent on entering. The index for air is near 1 (= very little bending); for water about 1.34; and for glass about 1.5. As Griffin explains, glass is nearly invisible in water because the indices of the two substances are so similar. Griffin's task was to reduce the index of the human body to nearly 1—after making it transparent in the first place.'

82 *the knavish system of the scientific world*: again, David Lake is an excellent guide: 'the practice of professors signing the work of their juniors as co-authors'.

albino: someone who, for congenital reasons, lacks the pigment melanin, and therefore has abnormally pale skin, hair, and eyes. The lack of this pigment means, according to Griffin's scientific theory, that an albino such as him is more susceptible to being made invisible.

84 *Great Portland Street*: a road in London's West End running from Oxford Street in the south to the Euston Road in the north. In *Life and Labour of the People in London* (1889), Charles Booth underlines its social diversity in the late nineteenth century, and describes it as a 'mixed st., [with] shops, restaurants, many curio and antique shops, many doubtful massage establishments'. Griffin refers to it as 'a disreputable neighbourhood' on p. 88.

jerry builders: unprofessional, cynically profiteering builders who use inferior materials and methods for construction (the term had probably been in use only for about thirty years before Wells employed it).

85 *Röntgen vibrations*: X-rays. The German physicist Wilhelm Röntgen discovered X-rays and their photographic application in 1895. At this time, visible light was thought to consist of transverse vibrations in the so-called ether; Röntgen's theory was that X-rays consisted of longitudinal vibrations of the ether.

white cat: in February 1897, the *Black Cat: A Monthly Magazine of Original Short Stories*, which was published in Boston, printed Katherine Kip's 'My Invisible Friend'. It featured a scientist, living in a boarding house, who successfully makes a cat invisible before conducting the same experiment on his own person, with consequences that ultimately prove fatal.

truckle-bed: 'a low bed running on truckles or castors, usually pushed beneath a high or "standing" bed when not in use' (*OED*). It implies indigence.

butter: the idea is that, if it is lightly smeared with butter, the cat will lick its coat and so settle.

processed: to process, in this context, means 'to subject to or treat by a special process; to operate on mechanically or chemically'—a meaning that the *OED* dates to the late 1870s.

86 *Tapetum*: the choroid membrane of a cat's eye, which shines because of the absence of black pigment.

miawled: 'of a cat: to mew, miaow, yowl' (*OED*).

vivisecting: the National Anti-Vivisection Society was founded in 1875; and in 1876 the government introduced the Cruelty to Animals Act. In the 1890s, vivisection was central to debates about the politics of professional science. Wells's *The Island of Dr Moreau* (1896), published the year before *The Invisible Man*, comprises a critique of this practice.

87 *barracks in Albany Street*: also known as Regent's Park Barracks, they were the base from 1896 of the Royal Horse Guards.

88 *Strychnine*: in non-lethal doses, this poison causes uncontrollable convulsions.

89 *racking anguish*: compare Jekyll's account of taking the potion that transforms him into Mr Hyde in Robert Louis Stevenson's *Dr Jekyll and Mr Hyde* (1886): 'The most racking pains succeeded: a grinding in the bones, deadly nausea, and a horror of the spirit that cannot be exceeded at the hour of birth or death.'

91 *costermonger*: someone who sells fruit, vegetables, or fish from a barrow in the street (the name is derived from a variety of apple, the costard).

"horrors": Wells might have placed this term in inverted commas in order momentarily to associate Griffin's apartment with the popular room in Madame Tussaud's known since the 1840s as 'the Chamber of Horrors' (this famous wax museum was, and still is, located a few minutes' walk from Great Portland Street on Baker Street).

92 *city of the blind*: 'The Country of the Blind', one of Wells's most celebrated short stories, which centres on the adventures of a sighted man who inadvertently discovers an entire community of the blind in an isolated valley in Ecuador, was published in the *Strand Magazine* in 1904.

93 *Mudie's*: originally a stationery shop, one from which Charles Edward Mudie started lending books in 1842, Mudie's Circulating Library moved to 30–4 New Oxford Street in 1852. From there it came to dominate the nineteenth-century fiction industry, both in commercial and aesthetic terms. Its fortunes as a subscription library declined with the demise of the three-decker novel, whose rise it had sponsored, in the mid-1890s.

yellow-labelled books: the front boards of books belonging to Mudie's Select Library bore distinctive yellow labels on which Mudie's address and the relevant subscription details were printed.

93 *Museum*: the British Museum, founded in 1753, located on Great Russell Street.

   Pharmaceutical Society's offices: the Pharmaceutical Society of Great Britain, founded in 1841, located at 17 Bloomsbury Square.

   Salvation Army: a Christian denomination run on military lines, founded in London's East End in 1865 by the former Methodists William and Catherine Booth. William Booth's work of social investigation, *In Darkest England, and the Way Out* (1890), which compared levels of poverty and exploitation at home to those in 'the Equatorial Forest traversed by Stanley', sold more than 300,000 copies in its first year.

94 *"When shall we see His face?"*: perhaps he is thinking of a popular hymn composed by Horatius Bonar in 1855, which opens, 'Here, O my Lord, I see Thee face to face; | Here would I touch and handle things unseen.'

   detectives: these 'urchins' recall the Baker Street Irregulars, the street children employed by Sherlock Holmes in Arthur Conan Doyle's novels and short stories, who made their first appearance, like the famous detective, in *A Study in Scarlet* (1887).

95 *Crusoe's solitary discovery*: the eponymous character's discovery of a single footprint on the island where he is shipwrecked in Daniel Defoe's *Robinson Crusoe* (1719).

96 *Omniums*: an imaginary department store, perhaps a near neighbour of Heal's, the furniture supplier, which had operated from premises in Tottenham Court Road since 1818.

98 *wrinked*: wrinkled.

102 *Drury Lane*: a street famous in the nineteenth century for its theatres and its low life, which runs south-east from High Holborn to Aldwych. It is not perhaps irrelevant that the Theatre Royal Drury Lane is reputedly haunted by at least one ghost.

   dominoes: loose hooded cloaks, traditionally worn at masquerades, which conceal the upper part of the face with a small mask.

   cheval glass: a full-length mirror swung on a frame.

105 *Louis Quatorze vest*: according to David Lake, this is 'a long waistcoat imitating a fashion of c.1670–1715'. He adds drily that 'it seems a very large article for a gag'.

   out of fashion: moral relativism of the kind implicitly mocked here by Kemp was commonly seen as characteristic of those criticized as decadent at the *fin de siècle*. See for example this statement from Lord Henry in Oscar Wilde's *The Picture of Dorian Gray* (1891): 'I never approve, or disapprove, of anything now. It is an absurd attitude to take towards life. We are not sent into the world to air our moral prejudices.'

   benzoline: the commercial name for a liquid containing the chemical benzene, popularly used in the late nineteenth century to dissolve or remove spots of grease.

106 *calico dominoes*: see note to p. 102; in this case the cloaks are made of plain white cotton.

107 *Delilah*: in Judges 16 Delilah betrays Samson to the Philistines for eleven hundred pieces of silver from each of them.

108 *mowing 'em*: in this transitive sense, current from the sixteenth century on, 'to mow' means 'to destroy or kill indiscriminately or in great numbers' (*OED*).

114 *His blood be upon his own head*: see Ezekiel 33:4: 'Then whosoever heareth the sound of the trumpet, and taketh not warning; if the sword come, and take him away, his blood shall be upon his own head.'

119 *day one of year one of the new epoch*: an allusion to the first day of the first year of the Republican era, 22 September 1792 (the day after the official abolition of the monarchy), when the French National Convention introduced the Revolutionary Calendar.

120 *contra mundum*: Latin for 'against the world'.

125 *Sidney Cooper*: a canvas by Thomas Sidney Cooper (1803–1902), sometimes called 'Cow' Cooper, a popular and highly successful Victorian painter who specialized in pictures of unspoilt landscape featuring cattle and sheep.

128 *four days ago*: David Lake points out that it is in fact 'only two days since Marvel was running'.

131 *clenched*: there is a contradiction here, as David Lake notices, for only a few lines earlier Wells has referred to one of Griffin's hands, only moments before, as 'limp and prone' (p. 131).

APPENDIX I

133 *Cobbett*: William Cobbett (1763–1835), a native of Farnham, Surrey, in south-east England, was a celebrated farmer, journalist, pamphleteer, and political reformer. His most famous publication, *Rural Rides* (1830), documented his travels through south-east England on horseback in the interest of compiling a detailed empirical account of early nineteenth-century agricultural life.

The Oxford World's Classics Website

www.worldsclassics.co.uk

- Browse the full range of Oxford World's Classics online

- Sign up for our monthly e-alert to receive information on new titles

- Read extracts from the Introductions

- Listen to our editors and translators talk about the world's greatest literature with our Oxford World's Classics audio guides

- Join the conversation, follow us on Twitter at OWC_Oxford

- Teachers and lecturers can order inspection copies quickly and simply via our website

www.worldsclassics.co.uk

American Literature

British and Irish Literature

Children's Literature

Classics and Ancient Literature

Colonial Literature

Eastern Literature

European Literature

Gothic Literature

History

Medieval Literature

Oxford English Drama

Philosophy

Poetry

Politics

Religion

The Oxford Shakespeare

A complete list of Oxford World's Classics, including Authors in Context, Oxford English Drama, and the Oxford Shakespeare, is available in the UK from the Marketing Services Department, Oxford University Press, Great Clarendon Street, Oxford OX2 6DP, or visit the website at www.oup.com/uk/worldsclassics.

In the USA, visit www.oup.com/us/owc for a complete title list.

Oxford World's Classics are available from all good bookshops. In case of difficulty, customers in the UK should contact Oxford University Press Bookshop, 116 High Street, Oxford OX1 4BR.

	Late Victorian Gothic Tales
	Literature and Science in the Nineteenth Century
JANE AUSTEN	**Emma**
	Mansfield Park
	Persuasion
	Pride and Prejudice
	Selected Letters
	Sense and Sensibility
MRS BEETON	**Book of Household Management**
MARY ELIZABETH BRADDON	**Lady Audley's Secret**
ANNE BRONTË	**The Tenant of Wildfell Hall**
CHARLOTTE BRONTË	**Jane Eyre**
	Shirley
	Villette
EMILY BRONTË	**Wuthering Heights**
ROBERT BROWNING	**The Major Works**
JOHN CLARE	**The Major Works**
SAMUEL TAYLOR COLERIDGE	**The Major Works**
WILKIE COLLINS	**The Moonstone**
	No Name
	The Woman in White
CHARLES DARWIN	**The Origin of Species**
THOMAS DE QUINCEY	**The Confessions of an English Opium-Eater**
	On Murder
CHARLES DICKENS	**The Adventures of Oliver Twist**
	Barnaby Rudge
	Bleak House
	David Copperfield
	Great Expectations
	Nicholas Nickleby

Anthony Trollope

The American Senator
An Autobiography
Barchester Towers
Can You Forgive Her?
Cousin Henry
Doctor Thorne
The Duke's Children
The Eustace Diamonds
Framley Parsonage
He Knew He Was Right
Lady Anna
The Last Chronicle of Barset
Orley Farm
Phineas Finn
Phineas Redux
The Prime Minister
Rachel Ray
The Small House at Allington
The Warden
The Way We Live Now